MIDNIGHT EMBRACE

LISA MARIE RICE

OLIVERHEBERBOOKS

Published by Oliver-Heber Books

Midnight Embrace © by Lisa Marie Rice

Cover Design by Sweet 'N Spicy Designs

0 9 8 7 6 5 4 3 2 1

 Created with Vellum

1

ALPHA SECURITY INTERNATIONAL
HEADQUARTERS, PORTLAND, OREGON

"Hello, ladies."

Raul Martinez smiled smugly as he closed the door behind him. He knew he was bringing the nuclear bomb of treats to the Queens of IT. Felicity O'Brien and Hope Ellis weren't actual, real-life queens, but you wouldn't know that from the way the guys at his company, ASI, treated them.

He entered the large, cool room. Someone once calculated they had the computing chops of a small country, given the size of the servers, both in house and in a remote location. The big room was cooled, year-round, approximately to the temperature of Antarctica. Hope and Felicity, not being dummies, wore sweaters and fingerless gloves while working. The guys of ASI, being macho, refused to put on a jacket when entering the room and winced when they crossed the threshold.

First Hope, then Felicity, turned in their super ergonomic space-age chairs and smiled at him as he entered. His best friend, Pierce Jordan, turned and scowled. Having the Queens all to yourself was a treat and Pierce was enjoying it. Having the two super smart and beautiful women pay you attention was like basking in sunshine, even in the cold. Not to mention the fabulous tips on gaming.

It wasn't flirtation. No, sir. Not not not. Raul and Pierce knew better than that. Felicity was married to Metal who didn't look kindly on men flirting with his wife. Who happened to be hugely pregnant with twins.

Hope had only recently arrived, and her fiancé, Luke Reynolds, parked himself right next to her that first week to make sure everyone understood it was a hands-off situation. He all but had a big red arrow in the air pointing down at her saying FUCK OFF SHE'S MINE!

ASI guys didn't poach. But boy, Hope and Felicity were fun to be with, and if you had any tech issues at all, they could and would help. Not to mention Hope's lessons on surviving and thriving at *Dark Souls*.

"Hey, Raul," Felicity said, nodding at the box in his hands. "Are you bearing

gifts?"

"Indeed I am." Smiling slyly at Pierce, whose own greasy box of supermarket pastries sat, untouched, Raul put down the elegantly wrapped container, some sort of magic origami shaped like a swan, and carefully opened it up. "Behold."

He waved his hand over the pastries inside, just as magical as the container. Hotcakes with tiny nerikiri cats on top. Small bitter chocolate disks with thinly sliced fruit on top. Bite-sized lemon blueberry cheesecakes. Apple roses.

Hope and Felicity oohed and ahhed as they bent over the package. Raul shot Pierce a triumphant glance. Pierce scowled as he looked down at the greasy cardboard container of four Danish and four bear claws that sat there, unloved and uneaten.

Raul had saved the best for last.

"There's more, ladies."

Two pretty faces looked up at him. "More?" Hope asked.

He pulled out the box he'd set aside, hoping what was inside hadn't broken down. Setting it gently on Hope's desk, he gingerly opened the top, then stood back so they could admire it. Felicity's blue eyes and Hope's green eyes widened.

Yeah. This was the pastry equivalent of shooting 100 on the range.

"What is it?" Pierce asked suspiciously.

It looked like a fist-sized drop of water, a physical impossibility. "Japanese raindrop cake." Raul shot another triumphant smirk at Pierce. "Vegan."

Pierce shook his head, rolling his eyes as he acknowledged defeat. "You win, bro."

"Win what?" Felicity had just popped an apple rose in her mouth, humming with delight, when something signaled on her monitor. An angry monstrous blubbery thing, stomping in rage. The Goblin King. It appeared on Hope's monitor, too. It was their symbol for a loathsome boss they'd had at the NSA, who had harassed them. Every single operator at ASI hated that man with a passion when they heard the stories.

The two women looked at each other, startled. "The HER room," Hope said and Felicity nodded.

It was a place in the dark web the women had set up to be able to talk about the Boss from Hell and warn each other he was coming. The HER room was named after Hope, Emma and Riley, having been set up before Felicity joined the NSA for a brief time. It was now a place where they asked each other for help. Sort of like the bat signal, only cooler.

Raul stiffened. The HER room had four members and two were here. The other two were Emma Holland and Riley Robinson. If someone needed help, there was a 50-50 chance it could be Emma. Emma was the reason he stopped by the IT office so often. True, he liked the company of Hope and Felicity, and, true, every time he talked to them, he learned something.

But the big attraction was the large photograph pinned to a corkboard on the wall.

Four beautiful women, arms around each other's shoulders, smiling at the camera. Felicity, Hope, Emma, Riley. Two blondes, a brunette and a red-head. Each woman was a magnet for male eyes but Raul had eyes only for the red-head, Emma. She just seemed to glow in that photo and in the other photos Raul had seen of her on Hope's phone.

She looked like a curvy porcelain doll, with creamy ivory skin, shockingly bright red hair, wide sky-blue eyes. Looks were deceiving, though. That china doll look hid a steel trap mind. Raul could think of absolutely nothing more enticing than a sharp mind encased in that uber female body that made him salivate just looking at her.

But something was wrong. Pierce felt it, too. The two women were silent as they absorbed what was on their monitors. Both their monitors had had some kind of magic spell woven around them that made the monitors legible only if you were squarely facing it. If you were to the side, like he was with Hope's monitor and Pierce was with Felicity's, all you saw was a blank screen.

Their body language wasn't blank, though. Both looked pale and tense, worried.

Uh, oh. "Is something happening with Emma?" Raul asked, without thinking.

"Something wrong with Riley?" Pierce asked.

"Emma," Hope and Felicity said at the same time. Raul went behind Hope to look at the monitor full on. All he saw were streaming numbers, rippling by so fast there was no hope of catching on to even one of them. Like the Matrix only horizontal.

"What am I looking at?" he asked the air. God knows the monitor wasn't helping.

"Trouble," Felicity said, looking somber. Felicity knew trouble. Her father, a Russian Nobel Prize-winning nuclear physicist who defected with his pregnant wife, had had his family placed in the Witness Protection Program. Felicity had been brought up knowing her story was a lie without knowing what the truth was. By the time she came of age, she'd had three names. Felicity twisted her head to look at Raul. "Bad trouble."

Raul knew trouble, too. Something crackled at the nape of his neck, his own personal and infallible trouble detector. It had never failed him yet.

The back of his neck had nearly exploded the day the new commander had been introduced to his team. Commander Morris Buchanan had come highly recommended, with medals up his ass, but Raul had looked into those bright blue eyes and seen a stone-cold killer and that feeling of bad juju just crackled along his neck.

He kept his voice even with effort. "What kind of trouble?" he asked.

Felicity's blonde eyebrows drew together. She dropped her hand to caress her belly where two Metal mini-mes were growing. "I ... I don't really know. Hope?"

This was not good. Felicity was super smart. If there was something bad happening that she couldn't figure out, Emma was in deep shit.

Hope shook her head, frowning. She knew trouble, too. She'd only found out not too long ago that her whole life had been a lie and that her grandfather had had her mother killed. Like Felicity, Hope didn't have many illusions about the world.

"Emma caught something, but we can't tell what it is, exactly. Sort of like looking at a black hole and not seeing it, even though you can tell its presence by the gravitational pull."

"Like that." Felicity nodded, narrowed her eyes and moved her head closer to her monitor. "Only weirder."

"What's weird?" The two women jumped at the deep voice behind them. Felicity's husband, Metal. He lay a gentle hand on his wife's shoulder. Felicity had had a very rough start to her pregnancy, spending more time barfing than eating, and Metal had been very, very worried. Had aged about ten years, in fact. Felicity was better now and hadn't barfed for a couple of days. Metal checked her work schedule and didn't let her work more than four hours, all in the morning, which is what the ob gyn had said. Metal followed the doctor's instructions closely and hid her laptop at home during what he called her downtime.

Felicity could whine that she only had 'one thing' to finish, but he didn't care. He loved Felicity and was putty in her hands, but this was the one thing he was being a hardass about. Her safety.

Felicity smiled at the screen without moving her head. "Hi, darling. We're trying to solve a puzzle that Emma threw our way."

Metal bent to kiss the top of her head, took her gently by the shoulders and lifted her out of her chair.

"But Metal –"

"Nope," he said. "The doctor said you can work four hours in the morning. And if everything goes well, next week you can work a few hours in the afternoon. It's not next week yet."

"But Emma needs –"

"Hope can take care of it. Hope's really good." Huh. That was crafty. Everyone knew Hope was good. Now, if Felicity insisted on staying, it would look like she thought Hope couldn't deal with the issue on her own. "She can take care of it."

Hope gave him a two fingered salute off her forehead. "Hope will indeed take care of it," she confirmed.

Felicity touched her husband's chest. "Metal, darling," she said softly. "Emma might be in trouble. We have to help."

That stopped him, but only for a minute. "Raul," he barked. "Felicity's friend might be in trouble in San Francisco."

Raul turned his head sharply from studying the impenetrable figures on Felicity's screen. Trouble. He wasn't good at dealing with math. But by God he was good at dealing with trouble. Dealing with trouble was his superpower.

"On it." He started moving toward the door, making a mental check list of what he'd need to pack to deal with trouble. Weapons first. "Brief me while I'm in the air. Tell Emma I'm on my way."

*.**

WHITAKER HAMILTON III, CEO OF PACIFIC INVESTMENT BANK, stood at his window on the corner office of the 34th floor of the Merritt Building in the heart of the Financial District of downtown San Francisco. It was a beautiful day and he had a glorious view, both east across the bay to Oakland and north to Marin. The view of a god.

He stood, hands in his pockets, rocking back and forth in his Gucci loafers, watching the sun paint Oakland gold and wash the Bay Bridge with blinding light. Sometimes he put his forehead against the glass to look down and watch people walking along the sidewalks. They looked like ants, scurrying here and there.

Not today, though. He wasn't looking down. Today the ants were even less relevant to his existence. They didn't even register as life forms. A new life had started. An almost unimaginable life.

On his desk were reports of PIB's activities worldwide over the last 24 hours. He had the files but the members of the Board, tech-Neanderthals all, insisted on hard copies of the daily reports so he had several dossiers on his desk, ready for distribution.

He never read the paper files but he read the computer files, oh yeah. Something the other board members rarely did. Unlike them, he understood the files, the trends. What money did and what money could do.

People got it wrong. Money didn't make the world go round. Money was *gravity*, pulling people and things toward it. The strongest force in the universe. He could see that in the reports.

The data guys down on the 20th floor were able to observe that gravity in action, without being able to see the celestial body that exerted all that gravity. That celestial body was his to command and no one else could see it. The quants could speculate all they wanted about market 'anomalies'. He, Whittaker Hamilton III, was managing a river of money as wide as the Mississippi, and no one knew. From the day that Brandon Rutherford walked into his office, his real life began. He'd unlocked the key and the world would be his, soon.

Rutherford was a man of mystery, old California money. Patrician, regal even. With an extraordinary offer. Hamilton was to short a broad range of stocks, due date June 10, and for a week thereafter, and he was to do so in secret. He could place some of the shorts as PIB, but just a fraction. The amount involved was ... and here Hamilton held his breath ... a billion dollars. And Hamilton could keep ten percent himself. Personally.

There was literally no downside, but Hamilton realized how much money Rutherford was going to make if he had insider knowledge of some big catastrophe that was due on June 10.

Which clearly, he did.

So, Hamilton started making bets of his own. He liquidated all his holdings and then bet big in secret with the bank's assets. They'd forgive him when the torrent of money started flowing.

Such power. Such amazing power. He was investing so much money he was essentially reconfiguring the stock market.

But who was to know if they couldn't see? Up until now, his job had been investing large sums of money in well-run companies with a future on behalf of a known entity, the Pacific Investment Bank. Safe, solid investments, with low margins, but the profit came with the amounts invested.

But a couple of times, he invested a lot of money in cheap stock. Ailing companies, companies with bad management or outdated tech. He could almost feel the market startling awake, the rumbles of astonishment, the first tentative moves to invest in a stock which was inexplicably going up. He'd wait until it reached its highest point, then sold.

All of it made money, all of it. Like a printing press going brrrrr.

And then – the quantum leap, thanks to Rutherford. To the top of the heap. He had money to throw around, so much money it created its own reality. He was short-selling, yes, but also investing so much he could pretty much operate at random. Stick a pin in the Dow Jones Index. Throw darts at stocks and pick those. The very fact that so much money was being thrown at them created its own weather and the stocks went up.

He was making money. All the money in the world. Outrageous sums of it. Money that went straight abroad in numbered accounts. Hamilton was careful, didn't change his spending, but the fact that he knew he could afford anything, anything at all, changed him.

It was like a magic wand that made everything easier. Nothing could touch him because he could buy his way out of anything. When he got a little too rambunctious with his mistress – nothing that serious, just a broken wrist and contusions – he called an old friend, a cop on the brink of retirement, and good old Detective Chris Ricks took care of it.

Only cost him $200K. Nothing.

He saw that having a cop on his payroll was useful and paid

for him to retire early. He kept Ricks on a generous retainer because there were going to be incidents in his future. He also engaged the services of an LA-based security company that wasn't too picky as long as the money was right. Hamilton could throw buckets of money at them. Sierra Security Services. It was like having an army at his beck and call.

Hamilton felt his powers swell, grow to gigantic proportions. He couldn't be constrained by normal rules. When he broke them, Ricks would be there.

He could do whatever he wanted from now on.

He was a god.

OH MY, EMMA HOLLAND THOUGHT AS SHE SAW THE MAN COMING toward her, and had to stop herself from patting her chest over her heart. Wow.

We're sending you someone from the company, Raul Martinez, Hope had emailed. Hope and Felicity worked for a security company, so Emma was thinking muscle bound guy who could shoot and maybe had some smarts. Maybe. She wasn't thinking at all in terms of a hotness quotient, which in this case was off the charts.

Emma wasn't really that susceptible to beefcake. She'd dated a couple of hardbodies in college, and over dinner she'd been bored by dessert.

But, man ...

Raul Martinez. So – Hispanic origin, obviously. Tall but not too tall, because she was definitely on the short side and very tall men gave her the creeps. He was a complete package. Broad, broad shoulders tapering down to a lean waist. Sharp, handsome features, olive skin, blue-black hair. Casually elegant clothes. Moving like an athlete. That alpha vibe. Whew.

He met her eyes and electricity crackled. Her breath

stopped for a moment. She knew he recognized her because she was the only redhead in the upscale coffee shop and anyone describing her would start with the color of her hair. He was making a beeline for her table next to the floor to ceiling windows looking out over the Bay.

After that first electric glance, though, his attention was totally taken with his surroundings, scrutinizing the other patrons. What a security-conscious guy would do, she supposed. Though not too many terrorists or serial killers in On the Bay, the fancy coffee shop right on the waterfront, a ten-minute walk from her office in the Financial District. Nobody dangerous in the place. Just jerkwad finance people, intent on making more money, when most of them had enough for several lifetimes.

The man had given an x-ray sweep of the sunny, pleasant premises of On the Bay and was again focused like a laser beam on her as he stopped at her table. "Emma? Emma Holland?"

His voice was deep but quiet. No one else would have heard him.

"Yes," she said and held out her hand. He took her hand in his large one, squeezed briefly and released it. She liked that, hated those guys who took your hand and held it forever. Trying to gaze soulfully into your eyes. Making a big deal of the physical contact. "Raul Martinez, I presume?"

"Yes." He nodded, flashed a brief grin, and pointed at an empty chair. "May I?"

"Please." He sat down but didn't sit back and relax. Just folded his big hands as he looked at her, waiting. Getting right down to it.

Damn, this was going to be hard. Emma dealt in cold hard facts – since her business was cold hard cash – but this was all so nebulous and uncertain.

But first, manners.

"Would you like something?" From what she understood,

Raul Martinez was here to help her, as a favor to both Felicity and Hope. Against her wishes, there was no question of her paying for his services. She'd argued, but lost. He was going out of his way to provide free advice and counsel in what could be – probably wasn't but still *could* be – a nasty situation. The least she could do was offer him a drink.

"Thanks." He nodded. "What you're having."

She had ordered an espresso, realizing that she wanted caffeine this late in the day because on some level she was scared, and wanted to be alert. She lifted a finger and caught the attention of André, the waiter. Added a second finger to signal two. He nodded. André was smart and she knew he got it.

Emma lifted her eyes and met his. Oh God. A real punch to the stomach. She worked with money and money men and was used to presenting a poker face so she knew she wasn't showing anything of what she felt. But man, this guy was walking sex.

It was dangerous for her to be so distracted right now. Unfair, too. This past year and a half that she'd been working this job in San Francisco she hadn't met one man who attracted her. Not *one*. Out of principle, she'd dated, but it never went beyond drinks or, at most, dinner. No one had even faintly enticed her enough to go to bed with them. Not even close.

Pity because she'd been completely free. No big work issues, no problems, she earned very well so no money issues and she'd been free as a bird. An affair would have been a welcome addition. Something fun to occupy her time.

But no.

And now her dormant hormones woke up and were sand-bagging her when she needed her wits about her.

The man exuded pheromones, like a cloud. Damn, it was like the air around his head shimmered with them.

She blinked and realized that she'd been caught up in her head. Emma tried not to do that. Hope and Felicity could, because they dealt with raw data, but Emma dealt with money and you don't lose yourself in your thoughts with people's livelihoods.

She looked at him, full face. Trying very hard not to notice the high cheekbones, blade of a nose, sharp jaw, beautiful dark skin. He was sitting very still, big hands clasped on the table in front of him. Professional expert waiting to hear from the client what her problem was. The only sign that he was not a robot was the gleam in his chocolate brown eyes.

That was male interest. She recognized it because she got it a lot. But that gleam of intense male interest usually went with a smarmy smile and body language that said – *baby, come and get it.*

Raul Martinez's body language showed patience and nothing else. A pro.

Okay.

She was a pro, too.

Emma stifled a sigh and leaned forward slightly. There was no one around, not at nearby tables or even walking by. She knew the place and had chosen the table that would give them maximum discretion. But still, what she had to say was for his ears alone.

"I might or might not have a problem."

He didn't even blink. "In my world, given the two options, it's probably door number one. You have a problem. Let's take that as an assumption."

She nodded. "Okay, let's."

She stopped because André was coming up behind Raul. He discreetly set

an espresso in front of Raul and left. Raul drank the espresso in one gulp, black and hot, and set the small cup back in its saucer. Then waited, with no signs of impatience.

"I have facts and then I have conjecture," she warned.

He nodded. "Let's start with the facts. But conjecture is

important, too. We often notice things subliminally that are important but they don't fit the narrative. One of my teammates stopped his team from walking into an ambush because it was too quiet."

That made sense. "Facts. Okay. I have them but not that many."

He just looked at her, expression unchanged. "I'm used to briefings. Sometimes there are a lot of unknowns."

"Lot of unknowns." She looked him straight in the eyes and tried not to notice how beautiful they were. Deep brown with tiny flecks of yellow. Highly intelligent. "Do you know what I do?"

The merest flicker of a smile. "Something hard and abstruse. Involving math and money. Honestly? Two things I don't know much about. But you have trouble and I do know about trouble."

I'll just bet you do, Emma thought. She didn't know much about him but she did know he'd seen trouble. Hope told her the story in a video conference while Raul was flying down to her. He and another new recruit at Hope and Felicity's company, ASI, had been Navy SEALs on patrol in Afghanistan, gathering intel and trying to do whatever it was that Special Forces did in war zones. Their commander was badly wounded and they were assigned a new commanding officer who turned out to be batshit crazy. A psychopath who enjoyed shooting civilians. They'd reported him but the psychopath apparently also enjoyed powerful political protection and the two of them were jailed and threatened with a court martial.

Hope said there'd been a fierce uproar because both men were highly decorated officers. In the end, charges were dropped but they were released from military duty with an other-than-honorable discharge. All from reporting a murderer.

Yeah, he knew trouble.

"Okay. Here." Emma drew her business card from a suitcoat pocket and lay it down on the table. She watched him and didn't look down. It was an amazing card, on heavy ganpi paper, and in the center was a hologram of her in profile. She nudged it with her finger and her portrait moved its head full-face toward the viewer and smiled.

"Neat trick," he said.

Yes, it was. Toby had designed it for her. "Do you see what it says under my name?"

"Emma Holland," he read aloud. "Risk Management Analyst." He looked back up at her. "Sounds fancy. Not too sure what it means."

"It means I study money. I study its flows the way a geologist studies a river in its riverbed. The river might meander, and it might go underground and it might overflow, but it follows the laws of physics. Money is the same. It follows the laws of human greed which are knowable. Like geology, economics makes sense. At least in the aggregate and over time. If it doesn't, something is deeply wrong. Water doesn't flow uphill."

"Okay." He was watching her carefully.

"Some water has been flowing uphill lately."

"Okay," he said again.

"I work in the analysis department of a big investment bank, PIB. Pacific Investment Bank. We're the fourth-largest investment bank in the world. We have forty analysts producing policy studies. We review companies and write reports but we also keep an eye on markets. We have sell-side analysts and buy-side analysts and quantitative analysts, known as quants. I run the quant department together with a colleague, Toby Jackson. I'm foreign markets, he's domestic markets. We're the ones with the biggest picture. We're well remunerated to pay attention to the overall situation and crunch numbers. And, as of a couple of months ago, the overall situation in the money markets has been ... well, unstable." She frowned. "No, not unstable, more like irrational. The market can be skittish and volatile but we are always aware of *why* a market is behaving erratically. Even when the market is wrong, we can understand the reasons why. But recently, the market has been behaving like someone with a psychiatric disorder. We've been pulling in data from a lot of different places to see if we can find an explanation. But we can't." She stared in frustration at the tabletop, trying to find the words to explain her and Toby's unease.

"Okay," Raul said again. "Gotcha. You're watching the effects of something big and maybe dangerous, but you can't see the cause yet."

She lifted her head, met his eyes. He got it. "Exactly. There's something big going on and Toby and I can feel it and almost taste and smell it but we can't *see* it.

Even though it's centered in San Francisco."

Raul's eyes opened slightly, which in soldier-speak was probably stunning astonishment. "This is a stock market or investment market or whatever you want to call it thing, and it's centered *here*?" His long forefinger pointed down at their table.

"More like there." Emma smiled faintly, pointing her thumb to where the Financial District skyscrapers stood tall and proud. "But yes. Our city is responsible for the market going haywire."

"And other people haven't noticed?"

"Well, journalists and some hedge funds have noticed that the market is not behaving rationally, yes. The explanations have ranged from geopolitics to solar flares to Neptune in retrograde. But Toby and I have been following the dark pools."

His brows drew together. "Dark pools? Don't know what those are, but it sounds ominous."

"Dark pools originated about fifteen years ago. They are basically an alternative trading system, created as private exchanges. No private individual investors have access. They're used by large institutional investors to place large orders without unduly rocking the market."

Raul sat back. The skin around his eyes tightened. "Let me get this straight. There's like an underground stock market where the rich get to place their bets? Without ordinary people knowing?"

"That's about it." Emma nodded. "It's disgusting, I agree."

"I'm really glad I don't have that much money and what I have, I invest in local businesses. And my cousins' businesses. I have about sixty first and second cousins. Keeps me busy."

Emma's jaw dropped, her problems temporarily forgotten. "What? Sixty cousins? You're joking!"

She couldn't even begin to imagine a family of sixty people. She had no siblings, her parents had been only children. She had no cousins. Her mother died when she was twelve. Her father slept around a lot and had had an endless succession of mistresses but had never remarried. She heard from him twice a year – at Christmas and on her birthday. At the moment, she didn't even know where he was.

"Nope. My cousin count is sixty-two and rising." That firm mouth tilted up slightly as he watched her reaction. "That's not all. I have three brothers and two sisters, who have all married and produced offspring, and as of now, I have twelve nieces and nephews. Thirteen in November. Rosario's expecting again."

"And a partridge in a pear tree?"

That earned her a dazzling smile. "Yep. That's about the size of it. So, as you can see, I have plenty of investment opportunities." He spread his hands. "I am the happy part owner of two cleaning companies, a landscaping service, two construction companies, an art restoration company, a boutique publishing house, three restaurants, two coffee shops, a bakery, a travel agency, a lingerie shop and a translation agency. They do me proud."

Oh God. To do that. To actually help people achieve their

dreams. To take a seed and watch it grow. Nourish and encourage it. To help *family*. It was so far from what Emma did, which was to help investment banks suck the markets dry, that it made her dizzy.

Focus. She took a deep breath. "Well, no one is helping anyone right now. The opposite is happening. Stocks are being driven to insane highs and being sold massively at the top of the curve. Markets are often manipulated – by the daily news, by a company preparing for an IPO, by a lot of things. But markets also mostly reflect ... reality, for lack of another term.

"Right now, the market isn't reflecting reality. It isn't reflecting anything that I can see. But someone is earning a lot of money and hollowing the market out."

Raul frowned, tilted his head. "How much money are we talking about?"

She sighed, adding up today's numbers. "I'd say that just today, about two billion dollars has been made in a way that is puzzling and probably illegal."

"Whoa." He straightened in his chair. "That's a hell of a lot of money."

She bowed her head. "It is. In just a day. Multiply that by 365 days and by twelve months, by the years to come. It has the potential to completely distort the market. It is siphoning off money the market needs to function, to invest in new businesses."

"Why haven't I heard of this? I mean I don't follow the markets but this sounds like something that would hit the papers."

"Because it's invisible. Toby and I both noticed it, but we're deep in the weeds and have access to data most analysts don't. As a matter of fact –" Emma stopped.

Raul waited. This next part was hard to put in words. He wasn't putting any pressure on her to talk.

"As a matter of fact," she continued slowly, "we suspect we might be involved."

Raul tilted his head to the side, the only sign of surprise. "You and your colleague, Toby, might be distorting the market to the tune of billions and billions of dollars?"

Emma huffed out a little laugh. "No. Hardly. I was using 'we' to mean our company, Pacific Investment Bank. It's ... it's all pretty nebulous though. It was Toby who first wondered if we were involved."

"Any chance of talking to this Toby?"

Emma shifted in her chair, rearranging the sugar packets. "Ordinarily, of course. But apparently Toby quit and accepted a job in Taiwan that gets a lot of money from mainland China to invest."

Raul's gaze intensified. "You don't believe that."

"I don't?" Emma met his gaze. He gazed back steadily. He'd nailed it. "Yeah, you're right. I don't. That's just a rumor making the rounds in the office. Toby never even said goodbye. Not to me nor to anyone else in the office. It's true that we quants are a transient lot. We go from job to job. I'm thinking of changing jobs, too. But – he didn't say goodbye. That's really weird because he's the kind of guy who'd want to go out for a glass of champagne and oysters to celebrate a new job. We are good friends and have a good working relationship. We both like our immediate boss and hate our CEO, Whittaker Hamilton. The third." Emma found it hard to keep the sarcasm out of her voice. Bad mouthing your CEO was never a good idea, but Raul wouldn't talk. "So, Toby just disappeared. He didn't even stop by to clear out his desk. He's actually still on the company payroll. And then I got this email ..."

"What kind of email? Threatening?" Raul's voice was sharp.

She shook her head. "No, nothing like that. I'm not even sure who it was from. It was an email address I wasn't familiar with. It was signed Bebop."

"Bebop, huh. Anyone you know?"

"Nope. I don't know anyone called Bebop. But once … once Toby came into the office and he was sort of dancing, like in celebration. He'd met this guy at a club the night before. It didn't last but, man, Toby was hooked. And I said he was bebopping when he came in. That's the only thing I can think of. The g-mail address was Stevemartin1234. I don't know anyone by that name. But both of us are big fans of the actor. So – it might be a spoofed email he set up. I tried to trace it back but couldn't, it's gone. A one-time email address. Responding to it, the email just bounces."

"And what did it say?"

Her heart set up a dull thudding. She'd sort of laughed it off but with Raul here, a serious man who took things seriously, she realized how worried she'd been. And still was.

She sighed. "It said – *Run.*"

2

_____

The back of Raul's neck crackled like crazy.

But his hormones were crackling, too, interfering with everything.

This never happened. Raul liked women – a lot – and was, um, susceptible to their charms. But not on the job. Never on the job. He switched that part of himself off entirely when working. Thought only with his big head and never with his little head. So ... fuck. What was happening to him was all *wrong*.

He had good instincts for danger and they were firing up like crazy. Just what he'd heard so far – insane amounts of money floating around that no one could account for, a missing person, a warning to Emma – was enough to sound the alarms. Everything in him wanted to wrap his arms around her and cart her off somewhere safe.

But then other parts of him wanted to cart her off, yeah, but not to make her safe. Nope. What he really wanted was to rip her clothes off and touch every inch of that creamy skin and then bury himself deep inside her.

I mean, who could blame him? Just *look* at her! He had been wildly attracted just seeing her in a couple of snapshots but in person ... whoa. Walking into the coffee house he'd lost situational awareness there for a minute. If he'd been on active duty that would have been fucking dangerous, but luckily he wasn't in a dusty street in a dusty hamlet in a Stan, he was on the Bay in downtown San Francisco. But still, Raul never lost situational awareness. And yet when he'd seen Emma Holland, everyone else in the big room disappeared. The upscale patrons, the soft jazz playing in the background, the clinking of silverware on plates, the murmur of conversation – gone.

There was only her. Absolutely glowing, a magnet for the eyes. And the colors -- bright red hair, like flames. Turquoise-blue eyes. Creamy pale skin. Not that awful deathly skim-milk color Raul hated but creamy with a rosy undertone. Small and slender and curvy. He'd never seen anyone like her. He had to stop himself from leaning nearer to her, something he really wanted to do. If he got closer he'd get a better sniff of that warm flowery scent filling the air. He wanted to just stick his nose against her neck and sniff like a dog. And while he was at it, he wanted to touch her neck, slender and delicate. Run his hand along it, over the shoulders, down to her breast. It looked small and plump, it looked like it would fit perfectly in the palm of his hand, her nipple right in the center of his palm ...

Fuck. Just what he needed in the middle of a fancy coffee shop, talking to a woman he was here to protect. A semi woodie.

Fuck. He was aroused and she was looking at him oddly. Lucky his skin was dark so she couldn't see the red flush of arousal because right now, he was more excited just talking to Emma than he'd been fucking his last date. Whose name he couldn't remember.

He breathed himself down. This was serious shit, and he needed to be at the top of his game. She might or might not be in danger but in his experience, where there was a lot of money, there were dangerous people. Plus, this was a very smart woman and dangerous people didn't like smart people. Smart people saw right through greed and bullshit.

Raul had no idea what was going on. Money wasn't in his wheelhouse, but bad people *were* and there was a real possibility of bad people targeting this beautiful woman, whose only crime was being too bright.

Raul had had a decade-long exposure to the bad shit bad people could do. He had images that would stay with him the rest of his life, of torn limbs, shredded flesh and lakes of blood. No matter how attracted he was, his first imperative was keeping her safe from the bad guys and he needed to start doing that *now*. He needed for his dick to stand down.

And it did.

He leaned forward. "Tell me more about Toby."

That lost expression she'd had while he'd been basically talking to his dick disappeared. He wanted data from her and she lived data.

Emma met his gaze and he was swept away by the beauty of those bright blue eyes and by the blazing intelligence in them.

"Toby. Okay. He's young. Most quants are, it's the nature of the game. I'm at the upper end of it and someday will age out of it. The job is intense and no matter how much you love the challenge, the job tends to get you down after a number of years. Which is why I wasn't surprised that Toby left, I was just surprised that he hadn't said goodbye. And surprised that he hadn't told me he was job hunting. It's the kind of thing we'd have talked about. For him to just disappear ..." Pretty dark red eyebrows drew together. "It's not like him at all."

"Give me the stats," Raul said.

Goddamn. He couldn't look at her for too long without getting lost in those eyes. So, he broke eye contact frequently to look away. He tried to make it look deliberate so she'd take it as him checking their environment.

And then he realized he *should* be checking the environment. He took the big, airy room in quadrants. One quarter, blink to black, another quarter ... it didn't take long. There were no discernable sources of danger, unless it was to your liver or your arteries.

She nodded. "Toby Jackson. Twenty-six. Originally from Iowa. Blasted through high school, graduated at fifteen. Undergraduate degree from MIT, full scholarship. Masters and doctorate from Stanford. His dissertation on Topology of Dynamic Data is used by the National Oceanic and Atmospheric Administration to study ocean currents and they offered him a job right out of school."

"He didn't take it?"

"No. Absolutely not. They wanted him at Silver Spring, at headquarters. Dullsville. Toby's very smart, but he is more than just brains. He's lively, social. Likes the good life. Likes having good money to go out to fancy restaurants, to buy nice clothes. He had one of those harsh religious upbringings that stifled him and he is estranged from his family. Which is why I didn't try contacting them, they wouldn't know where he is and –" She swallowed. "From what I understand, they wouldn't care."

"That's hard." Raul himself didn't understand family estrangement. He had a huge family and when they had fights, they got down to it, shouted at each other, and then made up. He couldn't even imagine not talking to his parents.

"Yeah. I think it was hard. At any rate, he wanted bright lights, big city and after Stanford, he wanted to work in San Francisco. With his credentials, he found work immediately. Toby often said he felt like he started his life here. He made a lot of friends. Including me." Her eyes turned shiny. She sniffed. "Sorry. I didn't realize how much I miss him until now."

"A lot," Raul said.

"A lot," she agreed.

He didn't have the heart to tell her he suspected her friend might be gone. This Toby might have severed his ties with her abruptly, out of fear. But he also might be lying at the bottom of the Bay.

Either way, she was hurting.

Raul couldn't help it. He put his hand over hers and squeezed gently. The human gesture of someone expressing sympathy. *I'm here for you.* Raul had done it hundreds of times. This time was different. Her hand felt like warm silk and gave him a mild electric shock he felt all along his arm.

Fuck.

She felt it too. Those china-doll blue eyes widened.

He squeezed again and withdrew his hand, sliding it away. Damn, she felt so good. And the sight of his dark hand on her pretty pale one ...

Raul sat back. However attracted he was, there was a problem here that felt serious and he had to have a better understanding of it. Because the world wasn't always kind to beautiful women, especially the smart ones.

"So, the two of you had a good relationship?"

She tilted her head, considering. "Yeah. I never really analyzed it. I generally keep work relationships separate from the rest of my life, but Toby's a lot of fun. Easy to talk to. And wicked good at his job. And though we didn't complain out loud at work – the NSA broke me of any semblance of honesty on the job – we understood at a glance when something was wrong. Which has been all the time recently."

There it was. Most problems begin with something being wrong. "Wrong? Wrong how? Walk me through it."

She shrugged, frowned. "It's a bank. An investment bank. It plays with other people's money. Markets go up and they go down. Toby and I just track it, analyze the movements, but the others in the bank, the investment department, customer relations, asset management, they can get jittery when stocks fall. But jittery isn't a good look for an investment banker so it usually translates into aggression. Toby and I knew to avoid absolutely everyone when there were losses. We'd keep our heads down, give each other the side-eye when people walked by, and we went out for cocktails afterward. And then sometimes things went really well. When things were going well, we had totally separate lives. He'd take off for the clubs. In a way, we were sort of bad-weather buddies."

Raul could relate to that. There were a couple of teammates who'd transitioned through the teams that weren't fun to know as people. But when the bullets started flying, they all instantly became best buds and had each other's backs.

Bullets weren't flying here, but something was happening.

"Tell me about the last month."

"More like the last three months."

He nodded. "The last three months, then."

Emma pursed that pretty mouth and Raul concentrated on what she was saying and not how her mouth looked saying it.

"Well, the market was its normal schizophrenic self a couple of months ago, but then something happened. It was like PIB got some kind of dispensation. We never lost money. Not once. That just doesn't happen." She leaned forward a little and looked him right in the eyes.

She really shouldn't do that, he thought in alarm and almost drew back before he stopped himself. Her gaze was mesmerizing. He'd never seen eyes that intense before, like they could light up a room. It messed with his head, made him feel like he was falling into her. He had to wrench his gaze from hers and ostentatiously checked the door, the tables, the open kitchen. No crazed killers had entered in the five minutes since he'd last checked. Finally, he brought his gaze back to hers and fell right back into her eyes.

Had to focus hard on what she was saying.

"Remember we're talking about the market. The *world* market. Something bad is happening somewhere, every second of every day. Never losing is nearly impossible. No, scratch that. It *is* impossible. A really good day is when you lose five million dollars and make nine. It was like PIB was receiving memos from God. All our investments were golden, but there wasn't a good feel to it. Toby and I met a couple of times after work and compared notes and never understood what was going on. And remember, understanding what's going on is the very heart of what Toby and I do. That's what the quant department does. I mean, there could well be outside forces conspiring to make something like PIB lose a lot of money. But neither of us could figure out what could conspire to make PIB a lot of money with no losses."

"No losses at all?"

She stopped and watched him. "I think a suitable analogy would be during a firefight where a million bullets are shot, but no one is hit."

"Yeah. That doesn't happen outside the movies. So, what did you and Toby do?"

She shrugged. "Nothing. What could we do? The company was making money – a lot of it – which is why we were there. The other quants were clueless, and basically didn't care. One of them is actively looking for another job in New York and isn't paying any attention at all. Another is getting married this month. I wrote a memo to our immediate boss that something was off, but got no answer. I got an acknowledgement and that's it. He's a nice guy but really, his job isn't to question making too much money. Last month we made a bigger profit than in Q3 and Q4 of last year combined. And the trend is rising."

She sighed. "It's a problem, but a problem a lot of hedge funds and banks would kill to have."

Silence. Emma drew a pattern in the white tablecloth with a pink-tipped fingernail. She hadn't heard what she'd said but he had. A situation people would *kill* to have.

"There's more, isn't there?" Raul asked. "You're *really*

worried about Toby. And –" Emma's head was bowed and she was staring at the tabletop. Raul bent to look her in the eyes. "I think there might be something else, too."

She blinked as she thought. He could almost see things whizzing around in the beautiful red-haired head. "Mmm," she murmured.

Yeah. Something else. Raul was good at interrogating. He was a human lie detector and could read people very well. Emma wasn't lying but she wasn't telling the entire truth.

However – this was a smart woman. And she was a good friend of women he considered good friends of his. He wasn't going to bully intel out of her and he wasn't going to coax it or trick it out of her. She had to volunteer it, because he was here to help.

So, he sat back and waited. He had patience to spare. And since she wasn't a dummy, she'd realize that he had flown over six hundred miles to help her, and the smart thing to do was to tell him everything.

Finally, she sighed. "It's all so nebulous," she said, her voice almost a whisper.

"Uh huh." Raul kept his features without expression. "Intel usually is. We work on probabilities. On breaks in patterns, on slightly unusual activities, on someone not being somewhere he should be. On a thousand clues you have to put together, and sometimes it's 50-50 whether you're right or wrong. There is no such thing as chancing on an email that says we will hit this target on this day at this hour. Nope. What you'll have are contradictory signs, a flurry of activity here, some decrypted messages about packages and deliveries there and you have to piece it all together, knowing about sixty percent of what's going on if you're really lucky. No one ever knows a hundred percent of the intel. So then, I guess what you have are bits and pieces."

She looked him full in the face again and again he had to

work to keep his face bland. He forbade himself from studying her features because he didn't want his eyes moving. He kept his head straight and his gaze unwavering. But he was observant and could soak in the details of that beautiful face. That amazing skin, creamy and smooth. The straight nose, full lips, high cheekbones. The glowing radioactive blue of her eyes. A remarkably attractive woman who did not give off a *look at me* vibe in any way. Did not preen, did not constantly check him to see what her effect on him was, did not tilt her head coyly.

He'd been on the receiving end of all that countless times, with women much less attractive than Emma Holland.

There was none of that. She gave off the vibe of your aunt Sally, the retired librarian, low-key and engaged with the person she was talking to. But then she worked in a man's world, so would want to keep all that sex appeal under wraps.

Raul had heard the stories from the guys, and they were pretty awful. The four women had shared a period together at NSA and had had the boss from hell, and all four had gone on to other jobs and had had run-ins with sexist jerks. Felicity had confessed to him and Pierce that she never had the courage to tell her husband, Metal, about how she'd suffered sexual harassment at a think tank she worked at, very briefly, in New York. She felt that Metal would take a plane, find the man and beat him to a pulp. So, she'd said nothing.

Raul and Pierce agreed, though both of *them* wanted to go track that fucker down and beat him to a pulp themselves.

It baffled him. Felicity and Hope were so gentle and friendly. Whip smart. Incredibly hard workers, doing their very best for the guys in the field. And their best was amazing. ASI now was one of the most tech-forward security companies in the world, thanks to them. How could anyone harass them? Try to browbeat them? Do them harm? At least at ASI they were treated right. If anyone from the outside world even looked at them cross-eyed, he'd have twenty-five furious, armed and combat-ready SpecOps guys to deal with.

So, Raul prepared himself for a tale of harassment or nastiness.

But it wasn't that. It was worse.

3

Emma looked around the upscale coffee shop, with its well-dressed people speaking quietly, efficient elegant wait staff, huge pristine ultra-chic premises. All orderly and functioning. Just the way she liked things. From a young age, with a depressed mother who took to her bed with pills and a bottle of wine every time her husband told her a lie about other women—which was often—Emma had trained herself to be in control of her environment, her emotions and her life.

She liked things to be well organized and rational. Even her job was rational, understanding numbers and data.

Instead, she found herself in a maelstrom. What was happening was frightening and chaotic. From the gyrations of the market to the disappearance of Toby, she felt like she was in uncharted waters. Lost in the ocean at night, bobbing in the water, looking at darkness to infinity, and she didn't know how to swim.

But ... Raul was a SEAL.

Maybe he'd know how to navigate this.

She looked at his handsome face, soberly watching her. Serious. Earnest, even. He'd been sent by her two best friends to help her and she knew they'd choose wisely. It seems they had.

"Okay." She took a deep breath, let it out slowly, yoga 101. "I'm going to give you some blurry data points that might or might not make a pattern."

"Fine." Raul nodded without looking away from her eyes. "Let's see what's there."

Not much, she thought. "For a while now, I get the feeling that people have been coming into my office. But there's a security cam across the corridor and nobody has that I didn't know about."

"There are ways around that, Emma." Raul's dark eyes bored into hers, sober and serious. "You know that better than I do."

"Yes, I know, but –" She looked down at her empty coffee cup that had no dregs to read. Pity she hadn't ordered loose leaf tea. Maybe the tea leaves would have told her something. "I checked the log. Nothing."

"But?"

"But I think someone who knows what he's doing has tampered with the log. Someone with a high degree of access. So, it is entirely possible that someone has been in my office without my permission. And more—a few things have been shifted slightly. Not by much. More or less as if someone who wasn't as detail-oriented as I am put things back the way he or she thought they'd been. But the fact is, I *am* detail-oriented and I'm fairly meticulous about the objects on my desk. And sometimes there is a smell." She wrinkled her nose.

"A bad smell?"

"No." She shook her head. "Not at all. Slightly ... citrussy. Not a widely commercially available perfume, but a perfume nonetheless."

"Or an after shave?"

"Exactly. Not definitely female, not definitely male. I like scents but I couldn't identify it. And it was never strong because my office is well ventilated. But definitely there."

"Was it there in the early afternoon or in the morning when you first got to your office?"

"Precisely. Both." Emma met his gaze and knew what he was thinking. Someone who had come into her office over the lunch hour or early in the morning before she got to the office? "And then there's the question of Toby. I'm just not convinced that he's left. I, um, checked the agency he used to lease his apartment –" hoping Raul didn't understand 'checking' meant hacking, which she'd definitely done, "and he hasn't cancelled his lease. He isn't answering his phone or emails, and except for that one email – run – I haven't heard from him."

Raul waited a minute, watching her. When he spoke, his voice was gentle.

"You're worried. You're really worried."

She nodded her head jerkily.

"And you're right to be."

She let out the breath she didn't know she'd been holding. *Thank you, Raul,* she thought. Because she wasn't insane. Something was wrong. Very wrong.

"So ... you said you decided against contacting his family."

Emma nodded. "Toby was estranged from his family. They wouldn't know anything about his life and from what he'd said, they wouldn't care, either." She identified with that. She was estranged from her father, who knew nothing of her life, and didn't care. "He's ... not close. They don't approve of his lifestyle."

"Okay."

Emma focused on Raul. He was one of the very few people she knew who was close to his family. All sixty odd of them. How weird that must be. What would he make of someone who never spoke to his parents? But he didn't betray by so much as a flicker of his eyes what his thoughts were. "What about his friends?" he asked. "Have you been in touch with them?"

"Toby's social life is something separate from his work life. I was his work buddy. I don't know any of his friends and even those he mentioned, he only called by first names. I wouldn't know who to get in touch with."

"Okay." Raul hesitated a moment. "Is it possible he met someone and decided to take off for a romantic weekend or something?"

She thought about it, thought about how Toby talked about his love life. "Well, the weekend starts now. And Toby liked to go clubbing on the weekends, I don't know if he'd want to miss it. I'm describing him as flighty, though really he's not. I think he has fun in his social life but doesn't take it that seriously. Though ...I think he might have met someone special, from some hints he dropped. He's been looking a little like someone who has the winning lottery ticket but hasn't reclaimed it yet. But what he takes really seriously is his career. I don't think he'd disappear without a word." She took a deep breath and said aloud what she'd barely dared to think. "I'm worried about him. Really, really worried."

Raul nodded slowly. "And you are right to be. He has a high-level job he cares about. A career he cares about. People like that don't just disappear without a trace. What's your home security like?"

She blinked at the change of topic. "The building security is good. It's one of their selling points. Security guard 24/7, cameras in the lobby, in the underground garage – though I don't have a car – and in the corridors."

Raul nodded, unsmiling. "Can I take a look?"

"Certainly. When?"

"Right away. This evening if I can. You said Toby liked to go clubbing. Did he have one special club he liked?"

"He made the rounds, but I think he liked Heaven best. It's a club in the Castro. Very hip. He talked about it from time to time."

"So, it's possible that he met this person who is a little special at Heaven?"

She nodded. "Very possible."

"Let's go tonight," he said.

Emma's brows rose. "Tonight? You want to go to Heaven?"

"I do. I want to see if we can find people who knew him outside of work. Do you have any photos of him?"

"Sure." She studied him, the broad shoulders, strong hands, the angles of his face, the short haircut, above all that super macho aura that surrounded him. "It's a gay club," she said.

"Right." One side of his hard mouth lifted. "Good thing I brought a sharp suit."

———

"Hi. Come on in."

Raul had checked into his hotel and changed. They'd decided to go out to dinner before going to the club, which wouldn't start hopping until ten, or later.

Raul's jaw unhinged slightly when he arrived at Emma's apartment. She was a pure wet dream, from her fuck-me shoes to the top of her head where she'd piled about six pounds of curly brilliant red hair. In between she'd done some magic thing to her face to make it even sexier and more attractive than his memory, though he'd have sworn that was impossible. Mesmerizing blue eyes, flawless porcelain skin, ruby red mouth.

Poured into a sleek turquoise dress that hugged her curves – high, full breasts, tiny waist, round hips. Those fuck me shoes. Blue toenails.

He closed his jaw with a snap, then managed a word. One single word. "Hi."

She smiled, the corners of that red red full mouth tilting upward. Oh, man. "You're on time. I like that. Come on in." She turned and he got a good look at the back of her, walking away, all curves and killer legs and leaving behind some kind of crazy scent that messed with his head.

The fact that this woman was also crazy smart scared him, because nature had already provided her with quite enough ammo.

She said something and he'd been too far in his head to hear her. Not good.

"Sorry?" Raul wiped his mouth surreptitiously. He wasn't drooling, was he?

His hand came away dry. No, he wasn't.

She turned, smiled at him. "I said, would you like something to drink before we go? And for the record, this evening is on me."

That wiped his smile out completely. "Absolutely not."

That smiling beautiful face turned instantly outraged. She opened her mouth and he held his hand up.

"Whoa. Before you get all riled up, this isn't about me being macho, it's about karma." Her mouth closed but she was still frowning. "And survival. We're talking my physical safety here."

She did a double take, narrowing her eyes. "You're going to have to explain that."

Raul sighed. "If anyone back at ASI discovered that I let you pay for anything, anything at all, I'd have about twenty-four really angry operators plus two very angry bosses who'd want to punch out my lights. I'm good but I'm not that good. They outnumber me and outgun me."

Emma walked toward him, frowning. "What on earth are you talking about?"

"I wouldn't survive. Not to mention the fact that *I'd* punch out my own lights if I let you pay."

Emma crossed her arms over those delectable breasts. He

kept his eyes heroically glued to her face. Her head tilted, *this better be good* all over her face.

"Ok. Here's how it is. I think I can safely say that Hope and Felicity are the stars of ASI, the heart of it. It's a company of operators, mostly former SEALs, one Army Ranger puke, Luke. But all former SpecOps soldiers. That's—"

"Special operations," she said evenly. "Yes. I worked for the NSA."

She had. And he knew it. And had forgotten it. He had to up his game here.

"Yeah. So SpecOps guys are pretty ... effective. But we're like cavemen with computers when compared to Hope and Felicity, who are not only better, they are also nicer. Prettier, too. Both of them bust the balls they don't have to provide the best possible ground support to our guys in the field. A year ago, Felicity stayed up for forty-eight hours straight when five of our guys were in Nigeria, surrounded by Chinese commandos. If they'd been caught, it meant death or an international incident. They avoided death and dishonor because Felicity gave them constant intel of the enemy's movements. She didn't sleep and she barely ate for those forty-eight hours and her husband, Metal, nearly went insane. Everyone offered to spell her, but she refused because she knew how to read the data best. And she was right. Our five guys came home and walked off the plane, but they'd have been flown home in caskets if not for Felicity. That's one story. We all have a thousand. Hope has just refined an IR signal that can be read through concrete. That's going to save lives too. When you sent up the bat signal, I got lucky because I was right there but there isn't one ASI operator who wouldn't give his left nu—left, uh, pinky to help you."

Emma looked stunned.

"So, I think you need to understand that this is an immense privilege for me to be here, for me to be able to help a friend of Felicity and Hope. I have debts to those two women I can't ever repay. Dinner out and a club fee are nothing. And believe me when I say that if it ever got out that I let you *pay* ..." Raul gave an exaggerated shiver and she rolled her eyes. "They'd find my body in the Willamette."

"Well," she said, taking a deep breath, smiling. "I want you to know I booked one of the most expensive restaurants in town. And Heaven costs a hundred dollars. Per head."

He smiled. "Great. I've got simple tastes, a nice salary and I don't spend much. I've got savings. Gotta spend my money on something. This is a really good cause."

She gave a half smile. "I'm not too sure Peking Duck and house music are good causes."

He didn't smile back. "Discovering what happened to your friend? Figuring out what's going on? Making sure there's no danger to you? Priceless."

That wiped the smile off her lovely face. Because she saw that he meant every single word. When listening to her story at the café, alarm bells had rung and the back of his neck crackled like crazy. Something was going on and he would not allow it to harm this beautiful young woman, who was super bright and the friend of two women he was proud to call friends.

Not only that. A woman who powerfully attracted him.

She stared at him for a moment, her mouth slightly open. A little disconcerted by his sudden seriousness. Raul knew he could come across as a lightweight and he played that up, often. He didn't mind being underestimated, it came in useful many times. He liked to flirt, he liked to joke, unlike Pierce who was always sober as a judge and always looked like his dog had just died in a war. But under the sunny face he showed the world, Raul knew what the world was. Full of darkness and terror, some parts of it. Parts he'd walked for almost ten years. He knew precisely how bad people could be to each other, the dangers that lay in wait for the innocent.

Especially women. Raul was very fond of Hope and Felicity

and he felt a powerful attraction to Emma. They were women. They were smart as hell, helped whenever they could, were good friends. But they were women and not as strong as men. In some parts of the world, that meant they were prey for fuckheads. It was as if war had been declared on them. Raul hated that, hated what he'd seen.

Absolutely nothing was going to happen to this beautiful woman, not as long as he was there. If she'd tipped over a rock and there were scorpions underneath, they would not sting her. She was *not* going to be punished for being bright.

Raul allowed what he was thinking to be seen on his face. He was good at hiding his feelings, but he also knew how to project what was inside him.

This was one of those times.

"Ok." She looked a little shocked. "Um, ok. Um, thank you."

He slipped his easy-going face back on. "No problem."

Emma looked around a little blankly, her gaze landing on a clock on a sideboard. It was like a mini grandfather clock and looked like a genuine antique. The entire place was filled with antiques, looked like family heirlooms. The place had a nice feel to it. Like a sanctuary.

After a long moment of silence, she looked up at him. "Maybe we should be going. I booked for seven."

"Sure." He smiled. She was a little ... flummoxed. A good word. One he clearly remembered learning at twelve, asking his abuela what it meant when he read it in a book. His abuela was better than a dictionary. Her English and her Spanish were impeccable. *Desconcertado*, she'd answered. Out of balance, and that was what Emma was looking, as if she didn't quite know what to make of him.

She'd find out, and soon, what to make of him.

"But ..." She was frowning and she looked absolutely adorable with a frown. Like something you'd want to eat up with a spoon. Luscious cream with strawberry on top. "Weren't you supposed to ... ahem?"

"Yes?"

"Do a –" Her hand swept the air, indicating her apartment. "A what do you call it? A security audit?"

Again, Raul's smile disappeared. Serious business again. She needed to know he'd been thorough. "I have."

Those blue-blue eyes widened. "You have? When?"

"Coming up. I spoke with the porter who is also a security guard."

"Mike? You spoke with Mike?"

"Well, he wouldn't talk at all at first. Quite right, too. When I started asking questions about your building's security system, he clammed up tighter than –" He cleared his throat. "He was very unforthcoming. And hostile. He wasn't giving anything up, gotta admire that."

"So how did you get him to talk?"

"Step by painful step. I told him I was a security advisor acting on your behalf and gave him my card. My company, ASI, is well known. He looked at it and handed it back and said FedEx would print any card anyone asked."

"Well, that wasn't helpful of him." She looked indignant on his behalf.

"He was absolutely right." Raul smiled. "I wouldn't have given the time of day to me, let alone open up a building I was protecting to possible intruders looking for intel. So, I pulled out a secret weapon."

She smiled back. "You have a secret weapon? That's nice to know."

More than one, honey, he thought, then disciplined himself. Sexy banter was one thing. Making sure she was safe in her own home was another.

"Yeah. I saw that the building is protected by Black Home Security Systems, which is an offshoot of Black, Inc, a company my company often works with. In his presence, I called Black Inc's headquarters, asked for the name of the head of BHSS and asked to be put through to him. It turned out that Mike's immediate boss is an old buddy of mine. We've been shot at and been drunk together."

She shook her head, still smiling. "Two very soldierly bonding activities. We in the IT business usually bond over Doom."

"Yeah, guns and alcohol are the military equivalent."

"With some similarities. I mean you use guns and we wield a mouse but they are both point and click weapons."

That startled a laugh out of him. He never laughed when discussing security but here he was, a snort rising up from his belly. He had to actually cover his mouth to stifle it.

Her turquoise eyes glowed, as if there were some kind of power source behind them. There was. That amazing brain.

All of her was amazing.

"That's true." He smiled at her. "So, I got my old buddy on the line on video, Mike verified it was his boss, and his boss verified that I was one of the good guys and he told Mike to cooperate and he did. He also asked if he was in trouble with BHSS."

"I hope you reassured him he wasn't," Emma exclaimed, alarmed. "He's an excellent doorman! And always so polite. The other one, too, Charles. He's usually on night duty. They both make me feel safe here. The city's having problems and it would be easy to spill over here."

She was just so delectable when she was alarmed. Of course, she was also insanely attractive when she was serious. And happy. And sad. Raul was really looking forward to watching her express all her emotions.

"Yeah. No problem. As a matter of fact, I told him that I would recommend him to his boss for a raise. He went over your security system with me and it's good and tight. Not what our security is, but we have real enemies. I should imagine this building is full of lawyers and accountants and bankers."

She smiled. "A couple of dentists, plastic surgeons and app developers, too, but yeah. No major danger."

"Well, *you* might be in danger," he said, his voice tight. "So, I checked everything carefully. The security cameras completely cover the common areas and all the access points and exits. There is a rudimentary facial recognition program in your computer set up with all the owners' and tenants' faces registered so there is a discreet flag that goes up when outsiders enter. By the way, that was written in as policy and everyone who moved here signed up for that. You signed."

"Yes, I did. I thought it was a reasonable trade off in privacy vs. security. These days ..."

"These days, yeah." He nodded. "Both Mike and Charles have access to weapons and are qualified to use them."

She looked startled. "That's ... that's a surprise. I never realized they were armed."

Raul wasn't surprised. He would have been disappointed in BHSS otherwise. "Fire doors and emergency exits are secure. Swipe cards and fob access are state of the art. Once a month either Mike or Charles does a building walkthrough with the building manager and they check all systems. The last walkthrough was a week ago. So, for a residential building in a good part of the city, your security is decent."

"Thank you for that," she said softly.

"No problem." Their eyes met and held.

She looked at her watch and started. "We should get going. It's a nice evening. I propose we take the Number Seven. It's a tram line of old restored trams that are charming. It goes to Fisherman's Wharf where the restaurant is, and swinging back it ends up in the Castro where Heaven is. And it's a really pretty route along the Bay. We could catch an Uber back from the club."

"Sounds like a plan. You wearing that?" Raul indicated a frothy thing on the back of the sofa. It was a swirl of turquoise and emerald green, the turquoise the exact color of her eyes.

"Good guess. Yes, I am."

"Then allow me." Raul picked it up. It was light as air in his hands, bigger than it looked when he opened it up. Some kind of shawl. He hesitated. His sisters did big complicated things with shawls and scarves, twisting and turning them into what even he recognized as fashionable ... things around their necks and shoulders. He should just hand it to her.

But that pale slender neck, those delicate shoulders...they were right there. It was a perfect opportunity to touch her. It was maybe skeevy but also a temptation like no other. When he shook the thing out, it billowed like a cloud. It was soft and light. He just folded it into a triangle and smoothed the ends over her shoulders. Her skin was somehow even softer than the material.

She turned and they stood there for a long moment, face to face, his hands still on her shoulders. He stared into her eyes, fascinated. She was facing the windows that looked out over the city to the west and the slanting sunlight lit up her face and turned her eyes into gemstones. It was fascinating. He'd never seen a color like that in a person's eyes before.

He wasn't making a move and she wasn't either. He was transfixed, hand on her shoulders, looking into those remarkable eyes. For a moment, he completely forgot himself, something he never did. He was always present in the moment. But for this instant, he forgot everything. That he was here to do a job. That they needed to get going. That this was a woman he barely knew.

Didn't make any difference. His hands became bricks he couldn't move. His feet were nailed to the floor. He could barely breathe.

Time floated by and all he could do was look her in the

eyes. She had some makeup on, but it seemed invisible. All he could tell was that her eyes were enormous, cheeks high and well-shaped. Mouth a wet dream, red and moist. Hair held up by a miracle with a few locks down around her temples.

A siren went by downstairs, the loud waaah-waaaah made her blink. "We should, ah…"

"Yeah. We should," he answered. What the fuck just happened? He'd gone into a fugue state like some moron.

Emma locked the door when they walked out into the corridor of her apartment building. He'd had a talk with Mike about the key system and was reassured that the keys were hard to copy, not that he expected Emma to be careless with her keys.

Unless of course she'd given a set to a male companion. Raul repressed the spurt of jealousy that thought gave him. He had no right to be jealous, what the hell?

"Have you given your keys to anyone, even for a limited time?" he asked as they walked down the corridor to the elevator.

She looked up at him, surprised, red eyebrows drawn together in a frown. "What?"

"The keys to the doors in this complex are hard to copy. There are very few places where it can be done, but it can be done. Takes about forty-eight hours. So, have you given your house keys to anyone for a day or two? I'm asking for security reasons."

Which was a lie. He was asking because he wanted to know about her love life. Like, really badly.

It was sheer luck that Emma didn't tune into his keen interest because she answered calmly. "No, I've never given the keys to anyone. I haven't lived here long and no one's come to visit me. Hope kept promising, but the time was never right. So, no."

He blew out a breath in relief. If she'd had anything resembling a serious affair the guy would have the keys, right? He almost caught himself asking out loud and had to refrain from slapping himself upside the head.

"Good. The building supervisor has the master set of all the keys and the company that manufactures the keys is obligated to inform them if duplicates are made, but bootleg keys are possible. Hell, these days a 3D printer could make a copy. So, with your permission, I'd like to install a lock with keypad access. Maybe even biometric access."

They were in the spacious lobby now. Raul nodded to Mike, who nodded back. He held the big plate glass doors open for her.

"Well, ah, sure. If you think that would be safer."

They walked out into the balmy air. It was a beautiful evening, the setting sun making all the colors intense. They walked along Emma's street for a block and turned onto Market Street.

"Wow."

"Yeah." Emma looked up at him and smiled. "Makes the high rent worth it, eh?"

"God, yes." They were only a few blocks from the waterfront, the bay intensely blue, the Bay Bridge to the right arching over it to Oakland. The bay was filled with ferries and sailboats. He took in a deep breath, the air smelling like the sea. "Reminds me of home."

"Yeah? Where's home?"

"Right now, Portland. But I grew up in San Diego. My family made it across the border over forty years ago and have stayed on the west coast. Mostly in San Diego. I've got a cousin here in San Francisco but he and his family are away on a sabbatical, and another little cluster of cousins in Portland. I wouldn't want to settle where there isn't at least a smattering of family."

She smiled and shook her head.

"What?"

"It – it just sounds weird to have a choice of places where there's family."

"Where's yours?"

Her face closed up. She glanced behind her. "The 7 is coming now. Let's hurry."

Raul was glad the heels weren't stilettos because hurrying on stilts was not possible. Her shoes were very pretty and showed off the blue toes but the heels were reasonable. He took her arm and they rushed across the street just as an ancient tram rattled to a stop.

"Come on!" Emma's face lit up as they climbed the ancient steps into the tram. "This is my favorite! See?" She pointed to a placard at the front, above the driver. "Milan. 1933. Isn't that cool?"

It was. The seats were hard slats of wood and the tram rattled and shook but it was also charming as they powered their way to the end of Market Street and turned left along the bay.

Emma had entered first and sat by the window that looked out over the bay, and Raul sat next to her. The old-fashioned tram clanged along. It was too loud to talk easily so they watched the scenery go by. The farther along they made it toward Fisherman's Wharf, the more passengers disembarked, until they had the tram almost to themselves.

Emma turned her head to smile up at him. "Beats an Uber, doesn't it?"

"Yeah." He smiled right back at her, loving every second of this. The beautiful woman sitting close by him, the glorious evening colors of the bay, the ancient tram that had carried passengers in Europe and here and had done so for almost a hundred years. He'd never been in a mode of transport that was almost a hundred years old. Except maybe Tio Alberto's ancient Chevy, which only seemed as if it were a hundred years old.

For a brief moment, he allowed himself pure unadulterated enjoyment. He was on the clock, it was true. But there wasn't any danger right this very minute and Emma couldn't be debriefed right now, so the only thing he could do was relax and enjoy the ride. And he was. The windows were divided into two, horizontally, and the top sections were open so the sea air flowed in, mixing with the scent of Emma's perfume. Something light and floral and delightful.

Raul had spent the past week training future Black Inc operators in desert operations out in Utah. They hadn't washed for a week and sleeping in the tents was an assault on the senses between the sweat and the farts and the occasional guy jerking off.

Sitting next to Emma, on this charming rattling tram, rounding one of the most beautiful bays in the world ... well, that was pure pleasure, and he hadn't had much of that lately.

Emma leaned in close, so close her lips were next to his neck. "Next stop is end of the line."

He turned so their faces almost met, and nodded. Her eyes widened, the pupils dilating slightly. A pulse throbbed in her temple. Yeah, she was as affected by this as he was.

Good to know that he wasn't alone in this, whatever this was. It was attraction, sure, but intense. Painfully intense. He felt like in one of those movies where the camera zooms in so the only thing you see is someone's face. Emma's gorgeous face seemed to fill his entire field of vision, a cornucopia of colors. That creamy skin, bright blue eyes, red red mouth and red red hair ... for a second he couldn't breathe.

Then the tram rattled to a stop with a noisy wheeze of brakes and the world righted itself. Thank God Emma hadn't noticed anything. She was standing up, waiting for him to get up. He scrambled to his feet, a little shaken.

This had happened to him already a couple of times with Emma. For a moment there, he'd sort of forgotten about the world. He *never* did that. The world was always present to him. Not just because he was a former soldier and still worked in security, and had had awareness of danger beaten into him. But, also, because he liked the input his senses gave him. Even in battle zones, even in the shitholes of the world, he liked being able to smell his surroundings, to orient himself by the sun, to judge his surroundings by the play of light and shadows.

He was in what was considered one of the most beautiful cities in the world, San Francisco, and he'd lost it, for a second. Never even noticed his surroundings. Lost his situational awareness. Luckily, he and Emma weren't in immediate danger, but there was definitely something going on in her life and he was here to make sure it didn't threaten her.

And for a moment, he'd forgotten that.

So, from now on, Emma Holland was to be enjoyed, but without it wiping his mind out. *Hear that, Martinez?*

Raul descended the steps first. The old-fashioned tram was high and the steps were steep. He held onto Emma's hand as she descended. He didn't need to. She was nimble and lithe, but he wanted to.

Normally, Raul didn't like holding hands or walking arm in arm with a date – though this wasn't a date – because he liked keeping his hands free. But right now, there wasn't a downside to it. The waterfront was crowded, but not too crowded, with happy, sunburned tourists, out to have a good time. Not an operator to be seen, everyone loose and careless, most overweight and badly dressed and happy. Completely absorbed in themselves.

No one paid them any attention at all, which was exactly the way he liked it.

"Where to?" They were standing in the middle of the stream of tourists, flowing around them like water around a boulder.

"There. That direction." Emma nodded with her chin

toward the huge red bridge that actually looked as golden as its name in the sunset.

She set off, walking surprisingly quickly for a woman in heels. For the first time in a long time, Raul wasn't directing things. He had no idea where they were going, but he was cool with it. He was with a beautiful woman who intrigued him, in a beautiful city, going out to dinner in a city renowned for its food.

It was all good.

4

For such a macho-looking guy, Raul was surprisingly easy to be with. Emma dealt with tense alpha types all the time and you could sometimes see the waves of status anxiety coming off them. Constantly checking their surroundings to make sure they were the smartest guy in the room. Often they were, but man, at what a price.

Raul was doing his job, very aware of his surroundings. Every time someone got on the bus, Raul's dark eyes had scrutinized him or her carefully. But most people who got onto the number 7 tram line were tourists or people who loved old trams. Often they were both, because the number 7 tram line wasn't for transport so much as the fun of the antique trams. You didn't catch it to get from A to B, but to enjoy the ride.

Raul had a system. Head, hands, feet. He'd check everyone who climbed the stairs into the tram super quick, then move on to the next person. He was totally focused but also able to engage in conversation.

"I don't know Frisco that well," he'd said, talking above the noise of the tram, as they passed Pier 39. "I drove up with some buddies for a big party when I was in college. I don't remember it being so beautiful."

She smiled. "It has its problems, but yeah. It's remarkably beautiful." It was her lucky stroke in life, to live in beautiful places. She'd lived in Shanghai, Madrid, Buenos Aires and Boston. Lucky girl. She hadn't been lucky in family, but she'd been lucky in cities. She leaned a little toward him as they reached the end of the line. "A word to the wise. The locals don't like the city being called 'Frisco'. I have no idea why not. One of those mysterious things."

"Okay," he said easily. He mimed zipping his mouth. "Good to know. Will never do it again."

Their eyes met. His were dark brown with amber striations, sort of like an eagle's eyes. It had the effect of making his gaze mesmerizing, like that of a predatory animal's.

He didn't look away and neither did she. He was so very handsome but not handsome in the sense of the men she was used to. None of the quants were handsome. Mother Nature didn't hand out deep math skills to those with good looks. But the upper echelons of the bankers sometimes had twits who had been blessed with good looks. An awareness of their own attraction suffused their every move.

Not Raul. He wasn't inward focused, he was outward focused. Specifically, on her. Like being on the receiving end of a powerful tractor beam and she had to curl her hands into fists to resist the temptation of leaning into him. Though she did accept his hand when descending the steps of the tram.

How odd. She'd never needed anyone's help in her life. She was strong. She'd been a gymnast as a girl, had even contemplated training professionally before realizing she would never be that good and anyway, it would seriously interfere with school.

She didn't need any man's steadying hand. Yet, here it was.

It wasn't a skeezy attempt to feel her up, it was like a guard rail.
A human guard rail. *If you fall, I'm here*, is what it said.

Surprisingly not annoying.

Once they were on the sidewalk walking toward the Bridge,
Raul had smiled and stuck his elbow out at a weird angle. It
took her a second to realize that he was offering her his arm,
like someone out of a Regency novel. She hesitated for a
moment.

Raul smiled. "I'd really enjoy it if we could walk arm in arm
on this beautiful evening. But there's something else. I'm here
undercover, in a way. You'll be presenting me as a friend. Which
I am, but I'm also here to help you. And though there's no one
to see us at the moment, as we try to figure out what's going on,
we should make sure you're comfortable in my presence. I've
been undercover and you don't want to undermine yourself by
the slightest twitch."

Made sense.

"Put that way," she murmured, "lead on, MacDuff."

"That's a quote isn't it? From Shakespeare. I have a sister
who teaches world lit who'd kill me because I don't remember
which play. But it has a bad guy, I remember that much."

"Right." Emma's hand was right between biceps and
forearm and she thrilled to feel solid muscle. "A bad guy and
his wife."

They were walking along the waterfront, the air suffused
with the dying light of the sun, colors intense. They walked
past an outdoor crab shack and the smell was fabulous. She
realized she was hungry and was looking forward to dinner.

He glanced down at her, smiled.

"I hope they both got whacked."

She patted his arm with her free hand. "The main bad guy
was whacked. His wife offed herself. All good, and justice was
served, so a twofer."

. . .

THE RESTAURANT EMMA CHOSE WAS ELEGANT AND SPACIOUS, UP at the top of Ghirardelli Square. It was called Red Sky and the minute they walked in, it was clear why. A long mural to the left depicted one of those classic Chinese landscapes with steep mountains rising from water against a blood red sunset. It was stunning. To the right the wall was curved glass with a view out over the Bay, bisected by the Golden Gate Bridge.

A hostess dressed in a turquoise cheongsam dress led them to a table at the window and left them with an embossed leather menu. Raul pulled out Emma's chair because he was a gentleman and, he hated to admit, because it gave him a nice view down her cleavage. Yum.

He looked around the place, liking everything about it. It was stunning, there were amazing scents coming from the kitchen, the view outside their windows was world class. He was sitting across from the most beautiful and intriguing woman he'd been with in a long time. Maybe ever.

"This place is great."

She smiled, her hand on the closed menu. "And apparently the food is to die for."

He didn't really care. He was already ahead of the game, with the woman sitting across from him, the beautiful premises and the fabulous view. If the food was good, that was a real bonus. "Great." He opened the menu and didn't recognize much. "You're not looking at the menu?"

"Well, I read the reviews and I already know what I want."

"Good." He snapped the menu closed and shifted it to one side. "Makes it easier for me. I'll either have what you're having or else have you get me something you would have liked to eat besides what you're having and we'll share."

"You trust me?"

"Absolutely." He rapped a knuckle on the closed menu. "And I'm not a picky eater anyway. The Navy, and being in the field, kind of knocks pickiness right out of you."

Emma cocked her head, studying him. "What if I ordered, say, chocolate covered grasshoppers?"

"I doubt those are on the menu, but sure. I've eaten insects in the field. Good source of protein when other sources aren't available." He'd also eaten raw goat and raw snake. "Even MREs are pretty disgusting. Those are prepackaged military rations. They will outlive the zombie apocalypse and are truly awful." And gummed you up, too. On long patrols, nobody ever took dumps. They all suspected the meals were designed for that.

"Well, rest assured no chocolate covered grasshoppers this evening. I think –"

A pretty waitress glided up to them with two red drinks in martini glasses. "Two Red Skies, on the house," she said, set them on the table, then disappeared.

Emma shrugged. "Why not? We're not driving."

"Yeah," Raul answered. "What the hell."

They picked up their glasses, lightly clinked them and Emma took a sip and Raul drank his glass up in two big swallows. It was delicious.

"Whoa." He consulted his taste buds. They were baffled but delighted. "Not too sure what I just put in my mouth but it's ace. There's vodka and pomegranate juice and a couple of other things. Not very Chinese, but really good." He nudged her glass with his finger. "Drink up. You'll eat enough to absorb the alcohol."

She took another sip and smiled. "I will. I'm going to order a whole lobster."

"Yeah? Sounds good. I love lobster."

"Well, if you're paying, we can try the Angry Lobster which is spicy, and the Drunk Lobster, which is cooked in wine."

"Excellent." Raul beckoned the waitress who glided up to their table.

Raul looked at Emma, eyebrow raised. Did she want to do

the ordering? Sometimes if his dinner date was one of those babes who could never make up her mind, he'd take over and order because otherwise they'd be there forever. But Emma seemed like a woman who knew her own mind. He could leave the ordering in her hands.

She smiled at the waitress and proceeded to order in a detailed focused way that wouldn't have been out of place in peace negotiations between North and South Korea.

In Chinese.

She frigging spoke *Chinese*. And not halting pidjin Chinese either. Smooth, fluent Chinese. Mandarin. He knew enough to recognize it.

Well.

In a very upscale Chinese restaurant, with a speaker of Chinese. He was in really good hands, so he sat back and relaxed, enjoying watching her. She and the server were deep in serious discussions so he could observe her.

She had this amazingly cute little frown between her dark red eyebrows, a furrow of concentration. He imagined that would be how she looked dealing with spreadsheets. The two women were bent over the menu, Emma pointing at things with a finger and the server nodding and responding. All in freaking Chinese.

Where did she learn Chinese? Did she study it? Do a study abroad program somewhere in China or maybe Taiwan? He knew she had an advanced degree in some field of mathematics so why not Chinese too? Raul admired people who spoke languages. He was considered bilingual but his Spanish was street Spanish that his grandmother and his sister continually told him was ungrammatical and made him sound like a street thug. He found it hard to study languages. His buddy Pierce just absorbed languages, but he couldn't. Two years in the 'Stan and he'd learned only basic Pashto, enough to ask for water and say put the gun down. Not much more. Languages were hard.

Negotiations were drawing to a close. Finally, the waitress walked away, looking pleased.

Emma lifted her eyes from the menu and smiled at him. He smiled back.

"So. Chinese."

She bent her head. "Chinese. Yes."

"University? Study abroad program?" A sudden thought occurred to him, unwelcome. He coughed. "A Chinese boyfriend?"

"None of the above. We lived in Shanghai for four years in my early teens. I went to the American school, but went to an after school program with Chinese kids. I had a lot of Chinese friends and I was young. It's easy to pick up languages when you're young."

"Your dad's a businessman?"

Her face closed up tight as a fist, expressionless as a porcelain doll. There wasn't pain, there wasn't anger, there wasn't anything. This was the second time that had happened

Huh. He'd unexpectedly stepped into a mine field. He should step back but, all of a sudden, he was swamped with curiosity about this woman. He shouldn't probe but at the same time, he wanted to know everything about her, about this woman who was so smart and so pretty and was the friend of two women he was fond of.

One more try.

"Or," he said, keeping his voice casual, "maybe an academic? Or worked for a foreign company?"

He sat back, studying her face. Now that curiosity had grabbed him by the balls, he couldn't let it go. He wanted it all, even if maybe he wasn't going to get any intel right now.

But later. Oh yeah.

She realized not answering was going to be weird. Her lips curved, but it wasn't a smile. She wasn't happy.

"My, ahm, my father was in the Foreign Service. That's why we were in Shanghai. He was Consul General." And then that delectable mouth pursed shut again. Raul wasn't a dummy. Part of being a good soldier was knowing when to retreat, so he retreated. He leaned back, head cocked to one side.

"Did part of that lengthy consultation over what we're having for dinner include wine?"

She exhaled. She'd been holding her breath, waiting for him to push. He wasn't going to push, not now. Her mouth relaxed.

"It did. I ordered a decent Napa Valley wine. A good Chardonnay. I did it without consulting you and I apologize for that, but I'm familiar with the winery and with the wine and just went ahead. I hope that's ok."

"Perfect. You'll know the wines from here better than I do and I'm not a connoisseur by any means. I'm looking forward to tasting it. What else are we going to have?"

"Well, I also ordered the equivalent of some tapas—some dim sum. You're going to get a *bill*."

"Perfect. At least I can start paying down my karmic debt." Raul could have easily used his ASI company card and no one would have said anything but he really did like the thought of offering the dinner himself. He owed Felicity and Hope, but above all, it made the evening feel more like a date.

He *wanted* it to be a date.

It was business, but this was also the most fun he'd had in a long time. And she was the most fascinating woman he'd met in a long time. If he'd met her outside this situation, he'd have wanted to take her out, get to know her better.

Take her to bed, oh yeah.

"Did you like living in Shanghai?" Was it her family or the city that made her uptight?

Emma smiled. Ah. So, it was family.

"Loved it. I went to the international school but like I said, afternoons I went to a local school for extracurricular activities. I'm still friends with some of the kids. Shanghai's an amazing city. Have you been?"

He had, but that was I'd-have-to-cut-your-tongue-out-if-I-told-you classified information. And he hadn't been there for the sights. Clandestinely trucked in during the night, the team stayed hidden for forty-eight hours and left the same way, leaving several corpses behind. "Hmm," he answered. "Was it hard, learning Chinese?"

"You know how it is. Everything's easy at that age." She rolled her eyes. "Except boys. Boys were hard to deal with. They have always been exceptionally difficult."

Whoa. That startled him. "*You* had problems with *boys*? Besides having to beat them off with a stick? What possible problems could you have had with boys?"

She laughed. "Oh, man, where to start? First of all, I was, um, unattractive and awkward in my teens. I had red hair and braces and I was short and hadn't grown into my features. I was all eyes and mouth. Thank God I had my Chinese friends who considered me an alien anyway. I was so unlike anyone they knew they just took my looks in stride. I could have had two heads, for all they cared. My classmates at the international school, not so much. Also, I was a geek. Boys don't like that."

"Some of them do," he said earnestly. "Man, I love Felicity and Hope. In a totally nonsexual way, of course, because other-wise Metal and Luke would skin me alive and hang me out the window on a hook."

Emma snorted a laugh. He smiled at her. He liked making her laugh. She had a naturally serious demeanor, a small frown perpetually between her shapely dark red eyebrows, as if life were this constant puzzle. For someone like her, it probably was. Trying to figure out the underlying structures of things. For Raul,

life was pretty simple. There were good guys and bad guys. You helped the good guys and you stopped the bad guys. Sometimes permanently. You helped your friends and family. It had always been that way and always would. He didn't much think about why the world was the way it was, just about surviving it.

He suspected Emma was the kind of person who wondered why. Certainly, Felicity and Hope were like that.

A different server, another graceful woman in a cheongsam, rolled a cart up to their table and started offloading small plates of amazing food. As expected, Emma was ace at wielding chopsticks, but he was okay too, courtesy of a two-month deployment on a mission to South Korea. They'd eaten in holes in the wall where a fork and knife were unavailable and would have been frowned upon anyway.

The food was so good that conversation stopped. It wasn't at all an awkward silence, they were too busy stuffing their faces.

"Mm," Emma moaned as she put a dim sum in her mouth. "The reviews were right. This is absolutely fantastic."

Raul nodded enthusiastically, mouth too full to say anything. He scooped up more shredded Peking duck from a small plate. Oh God. So good, it should be illegal.

A young man dressed in black opened a bottle of Chardonnay – from something called Broken Bridge Winery – and made to pour in Raul's glass. Raul shook his head and pointed with his chopsticks at Emma. She'd chosen the wine, she should taste it. Without blinking, the server pivoted and poured a finger into Emma's glass. She sniffed, took a sip and closed her eyes.

Good. With her eyes closed, Raul could study her face. Such a fascinating face. She was beautiful, yes, with amazing colors. But the world was full of beautiful women. The last woman Raul bedded back in – January was it? – had been beautiful, too, but she'd also been deeply weird in bed. She'd screamed and scratched his back up, hotter than hot, and five minutes after they'd both come, she was up and out of bed, then she dressed and left without another word. He didn't even have her number and was a little hazy on her name. He was left feeling like a male prostitute, grateful she hadn't left money on the dresser.

Even dinner beforehand had been awkward, because she was more interested in real estate than in him, had tried to sell him a property in Hillsboro and hadn't even noticed the food.

The whole scene had been a massive downer and he hadn't dated anyone since. So, this evening was a real treat, even if it wasn't a date. Not technically, anyway.

Raul leaned forward. "Tell me more about Toby. Do you have any theories at all as to where he might be? Go over it again. When was the last time you saw him?"

She was quiet a moment. Felicity and Hope did that, too. You asked them a question and they took their time and when they answered the computers in their heads had run through a billion possibilities and what came out was cogent and organized and smart.

"I last saw him four days ago. We finished an internal report on commodity futures which was pretty comprehensive and detailed. He's domestic and I'm foreign. We're supposed to kick it upstairs on Monday, but that's off the cards now. We'd been working on it for a month. It was complex and we'd spent the previous week checking the details. Toby checked the math and I edited for clarity. It was a big report and was going to establish company protocol for the next semester. Toby was hoping it would secure him a promotion."

"And you?" Raul asked.

"And me, what?"

"Was it going to get you a promotion, too?"

"Oh. Well, no. I'm not looking for a promotion the way Toby

is. Toby is really ambitious and has his eye on a promotion eventually to upper management. Being in management to me sounds like the fourth circle of hell where the greedy and materialistic spend eternity scratching each other's eyes out. The next step up wouldn't be that big a jump in pay and I really don't care. I'm not –" She stopped.

Raul studied her face, trying to read her. He was pretty good at it but he couldn't tell what she was thinking. Only that she was in the grip of strong emotions.

"You're not?" he prodded gently. Any information she could give him about Toby would help. Raul was convinced that whatever was happening that might have Emma in danger ran through Toby, so all of this was necessary to paint a picture of the situation. What ASI would call intel.

But more than that ... he wanted to know what Emma thought. Why she went from being happy with the restaurant and the meal and the wine and maybe even with him, to being disturbed. Because that was definitely a frown now, one she couldn't hide.

He wanted to know more about *her*. Hope and Felicity were very tight-mouthed about their time at the NSA. The ASI guys respected that. Everyone at the company had seen or done or learned things in the military they could never talk about, ever. But even though they never ever discussed specifics, he got the impression of four young women tightly bonded, who helped each other and had as much fun as the job would allow, which wasn't much, given the boss from hell.

"I'm not ambitious that way. I already earn way more than I can justify spending. I plan on buying my own place, but not quite yet. I'm not wildly happy at PIB, but it's ok for now. I sure don't want to rise there. But Toby did. Oh God, does."

She turned stricken eyes to Raul. "What does it say that I'd use the past tense when talking about him?"

Raul put his hand over hers. "Not that he's dead. Just that you're worried that he's missing."

"Here we go." Yet another server put two steaming platters in front of them. "Who has the Angry Lobster?"

Emma smiled and lifted her hand. The server slid a platter with cracked lobster legs and lobster meat artfully arranged. It smelled amazing.

"Drunk Lobster?"

Raul lifted a finger and he got another platter. It smelled just as amazing, only different.

They dug in. Raul was pleased to notice that though Emma ate neatly, she wasn't afraid to get her hands dirty. There were bowls of lukewarm water with rose petals floating on the surface and they both used them frequently because opening cracked lobster legs was dirty work. Satisfying, but dirty.

"So," he said, leaning back for a moment. "Toby is really ambitious?" Raul carefully used the present tense. He wanted to get a sense of whether Toby was a victim here or might possibly have had a hand in what was going on. Clearly, that hadn't even occurred to Emma, but it had to Raul, who was professionally paranoid.

Bad actors disguised as good guys were all over the world. The question was – was Toby one of them? Had he done something in cahoots with his boss, say? Something that was illegal or immoral – Raul was sure that that was a fine line in the world of finance – and it was going south so he had quietly disappeared?

Possible.

It was also possible that Emma knew something she didn't want to acknowledge to herself.

Emma stared into the distance for a moment, holding a bite of lobster on a lobster pick. "Toby has a lot of layers to him. He grew up in a super religious household in the Midwest, like I said. He rarely talks about his family but you get the impression it wasn't a happy one. I don't think they had money problems but his parents were very much 'no frills' people and Toby is all about frills." She smiled faintly. "He likes travelling business and one of the reasons he wants a promotion is to travel first class. He has innate good taste, likes clothes and he's definitely smartened up my wardrobe."

Raul blinked. Her wardrobe? He opened his mouth to protest and she laughed.

"The clothes you've seen me in today? Definitely Toby. I have two sides to my closet – BT and AT. Before Toby and After Toby. Before Toby my clothes ran the gamut from beige to cream. Sometimes taupe. The After Toby wardrobe, well ... he forced me to incorporate color. And modern fashion, not just office wear. So, he's stylish and he likes the good life. People end up thinking he's a lightweight but he isn't. He's actually a mathematical genius and as soon as he works some stuff out of his system, he's going to revolutionize investment banking – or whatever it is he turns his attention to."

Raul nodded soberly. He hadn't heard anything that tipped the balance one way or another. It did shed light on Emma, though. For a woman who probably considered herself a loner, she was fiercely loyal to her friends.

"You two were close," he said. "Are close."

She nodded. "Yeah. We are. Which is why I think something has happened to him, because I just can't imagine him leaving without saying goodbye. Actually, I can't imagine him leaving without organizing a blowout evening involving lots of champagne. He just wouldn't do that. Plus, he was happy at PIB. Happier than –" Emma stopped, bit her lip.

Happier than me. The words hung in the air, as loud as if she'd said them.

Her eyes widened as she realized what she'd been about to say. Raul decided to leave it for the moment. Because he had every intention of finding out everything there was to know about Emma Holland.

Later.

"So why do you think he told you to run?"

Emma's shoulders relaxed. She was happier talking about a colleague maybe warning her of danger than of personal things.

"Well, Toby also has a taste for drama. It might have been 'run' in the sense of 'stay away from what is going on', whatever it is. I don't know. I've got nothing to go on, except for the fact that Toby has been missing for days, he's not answering his phone or his email. And that that is way out of character for him."

She was getting agitated. Agitation skewed things. Raul decided to dial it down a couple of notches. Asking about Toby's musical tastes led to a discussion of her musical tastes, which were solid.

They finished the lobster, drank the last of the wine and Raul called for the bill. Emma put her hand on his, looked deeply into his eyes, which he enjoyed like crazy. It allowed him to stare into hers. He'd never seen eyes that color, they were like gemstones. Amazing.

"Raul," she said soberly.

"Emma," he answered, voice just as serious as hers. He was going to enjoy this.

"I can't let you pay for this."

He looked down at her pale slender hand over his dark, strong hand almost twice the size of hers and smiled. "I don't see how you can stop me." He cocked his head. "Unless you're armed."

She sighed. Slid her hand off his and he nearly sighed, too. He missed the softness and warmth. "No." She rolled her eyes. "I'm not armed."

He was.

"We've been over this. I couldn't go back to Portland if I let you pay for dinner. If I let you pay for *anything*."

He'd shocked her. "Anything? I can't pay for anything? That's insane!"

"You paid for the tram tickets," he pointed out.

"Because I've got a Clipper Card. And I'll use it for us to get to the Castro. Where we're going to an expensive club."

"Excellent. I feel better already. You're a smart woman, Emma. Smart enough, I think, to know you're not going to win this battle. I've got a whole company of operators behind me. So, let's start thinking instead of how to track down Toby."

She sighed and got up from the table while he signed the tab and put his credit card in the real leather folder with a replica of the Red Sky fresco on the front. "What do we do if we can't find any clues in the club?"

"You won't like the answer," he said as he wrapped the gauzy shawl around her shoulders. It was hard to lift his hands.

She looked at him over her shoulder, startled. "What?"

Raul smiled. "We'll have to break into his apartment."

5

We'll have to break into his apartment.
  Huh.

That would never have occurred to her. But the instant Raul said it, she realized just how worried she was, because she didn't immediately reject the idea. It would be an invasion of Toby's privacy, sure. But if something had happened to him ...

And though she'd never say it out loud, Raul looked like the kind of person who actually could break into an apartment. She meant that in the nicest possible way.

Emma looked out over the Bay as they took the tram back toward the Castro. She was by the window again, Raul to her left like a living wall. He was turned slightly toward her, his broad shoulders blocking her view of the inside of the tram. She was essentially boxed in, which was something she ordinarily disliked. But not now.

Now she realized how worried she'd been, at what was going on in the financial markets, at Toby's disappearance. She'd learned to live with a low-level buzz of constant worry that sometimes flared into a deafening roar.

Now, that buzz calmed down, and though the worry was

still there, she also felt protected from it, as if he'd thrown a force field of strength around her. In theory, that was annoying. She didn't need protection. She'd spent her entire life being unprotected and she was just fine with that. If Raul had been even the slightest bit obnoxious, it would have helped to reject it. She could be aggrieved and superior. But he wasn't. He was calm, objective, clear that he was here to help her, but that she was in charge.

This whole situation might be nothing. But then again, it might be something. And if it was, she was grateful to Raul for lending her his strength.

It didn't hurt that he was incredibly good-looking, super male without being macho and was not a jerk. Or at least he hadn't said or done one stupid or jerkish thing in the time they'd been together.

Most guys she'd dated said something stupid or were jerks in the first ten minutes.

He was giving her ... a little respite from the worry and anxiety that had plagued her these past days, and she was grateful. It wasn't anything he'd done – basically all he'd done was to listen to her, and check her building's security – but, rather, simply who he was. Calm and reassuring.

They rounded the Bay and the Bay Bridge, lit up in the evening sky, appeared.

"Really nice," Raul said and she turned to him.

"Yeah. It's a really beautiful city."

"But?"

"I beg your pardon?"

"There was a 'but' in your voice."

"Was there? I don't see –" But she did. She sighed, almost sorry that Raul's perspicacity ran to emotional undertones and not just home security. Undertones she hadn't even been aware of. "Yeah. It's just gorgeous, but everything and everyone here is so – so transient."

He was listening to her carefully. "It's a tech city. Tech moves fast."

"It does. People move in, mainly make money, some lose it, and then they move out. When I first arrived, I made some friends but over the course of a year they all moved away. I made a second round of friends and they all moved away, too."

"That must be hard for someone who moved around all through her childhood and might maybe want some stability."

Emma blinked. Raul was seeing maybe *too* much. She turned her head back to the window as they rattled up Market Street. It was a ride she normally enjoyed, particularly at night, rolling up to the gaudily lit Castro district. It was a part of the city that came alive at night and as the final red drained from the sky, it lit up.

Going to Heaven was such a long shot. She was never going to find out what happened to Toby there. What was she thinking? Raul was going to throw away over $200 plus whatever they spent on drinks on a wild goose chase, not to mention the meal.

He didn't seem to mind – in fact he insisted on dinner and the club – but still. It was all going to be pointless. And – and if she did find Toby? And he had decided to take an extended vacation with some new love? Or had just accepted another job? And she turned over rocks to find him and he was just annoyed?

That would be awful. She'd have to apologize ... but no.

Toby was super serious at work. If he took a few days off, he'd have meticulously arranged things so that he was covered at work. He wouldn't leave her dangling. She'd been doing the work of two these past days. He wouldn't do that to her. And he wouldn't have accepted another job without telling her. He told her about his new hair stylist, for heaven's sake, he'd tell her about –

"Now!" Emma stood up. She'd been so taken up in her head

she hadn't noticed where they were. The tram was about to head up to Twin Peaks. If they missed the stop, they'd have to walk steeply downhill. "We get off now!"

The tram braking to a stop caught her off-guard and she stumbled a second. Just for a second, though, because Raul's strong hand steadied her. He felt so steady and secure it was like she couldn't fall, even if she wanted to.

Raul murmured something to the driver and he waited a few seconds more than usual at the stop. That was her fault, for getting up too late.

The old-fashioned bell clanged and the tram rattled off, leaving them on the busy sidewalk. "Wow." Emma looked up at him. "I'm sorry for that last minute warning. I didn't mean to make you scramble."

He was still holding on to her arm. "No problem," he said, his voice gentle. "You have a lot on your mind. I could see you chewing your way through it. So. Where do we go now?"

She looked around, momentarily disoriented. She'd never actually been to Heaven, had just had it pointed out to her one afternoon when she and Toby had had lunch at the Castro. They'd gone to that Somali lunch bar and had passed by this wildly funky umbrella shop.

"There. I remember that." She pointed across the street. Then, with an inward curse, pulled out her cell. It was a sign of how upset she was that she hadn't immediately used GPS. She pulled up Heaven's website, stylishly minimal, with the area map. She stared at the map, looked up and looked back at the screen.

"May I?" Raul stood with his hand out.

She nodded and handed him her cell. Normally she was good with tech but GPS defeated her. She had a lousy sense of direction and found GPS hard to use in cities. In the country-side, too.

He focused on the screen, looked up, and took her elbow. "That way."

"Okay. I'll definitely take your word for it. I'm hopeless at reading maps. I imagine you guys were taught map reading skills."

"Hmm." He'd established a pace that was not too slow but not too fast for her in her heels. A Goldilocks pace. "Have you thought about how we're going to get some intel once we're inside Heaven?"

"No, actually." It just now occurred to her that as the Toby-expert on their team, she had to come up with a finding-Toby strategy. But she was coming up a blank. "I don't know. Ask someone?"

"Definitely. But we need a cover. I was thinking I could pose as Toby's friend. I need to track him down."

Emma smiled, refraining from looking at Raul head to toe, but she had already looked her fill. He was like a walking billboard for masculinity. "I don't know, Raul. I don't think you can pass as gay."

He cocked his head. "I don't need to. I can be a friend who's worried. I have plenty of gay friends. A friend is a friend. Sexual orientation has nothing to do with it. Or I can be asking for my brother, who is a really good friend of Toby's. I'll see which story works best."

She nodded. "Okay. That makes sense. I don't think I'd ask the right questions and I think you would. Undercover missions are not in my wheelhouse but I imagine they are in yours. I'm a math and data nerd. Things either are or they are not. If the data seems ambiguous, it's because you're not interpreting it right."

Somehow they were walking slowly, her hand on his arm, his hand over hers. He was watching her face with focus, but he often looked up and around then refocused on her. It wasn't the looking around people often did to see if there was someone more interesting around, and he definitely wasn't looking at other women. He seemed intensely focused on her. But he was very aware of his surroundings. Probably looking for possible danger.

Emma didn't think there was possible danger but she was glad of his presence just the same. At bottom, what they were looking at was probably financial malpractice, maybe financial crimes. Serious, but not deadly.

Her sector, the financial sector, simply offered too many opportunities to make a lot of money, particularly if you were willing to cut corners. And the more you cut corners, the more you were rewarded. You had to have a strong moral core, or be basically indifferent to wealth not to be tempted. Emma was fairly indifferent. She earned well, her grandmother had left her some money together with her furniture, she was doing fine. She certainly wasn't prepared to break the law for more money.

But in the end, it was only money. That's all it was. Not that big a deal. Though there was a lot of money in play.

And then there was Toby. Toby's absence was an anomaly, an outlier.

Which was why it was comforting to walk so closely to Raul, to feel his muscled arm under her hand and to feel his big hand over hers.

She'd just carried herself back a thousand generations of evolution. Where they'd be living in a cave and he carried a big club.

"I've been undercover, yeah," Raul said and she was jolted out of her thoughts. She'd been down another rabbit-hole. "It's not always a lot of fun. But my buddy Pierce has spent half his career undercover. Sometimes he'd dive so deep into the role he almost lost himself. Not lost his sense of mission, he'd never identify with the enemy, but he'd lose his sense of self."

"That's your good friend, right? Hope told me you guys went through a hard time together."

And that handsome face just closed up tighter than a fist. Amazing to watch someone switch personality in a second.

"Yeah," he said, his voice tight. His arm under her hand tensed.

Emma was really sorry. She hadn't been thinking. She heard the story from Hope who'd heard it from her fiancée, Luke. Raul and Pierce were buddies who worked well together, had each other's back. And then they'd had the commanding officer from hell. A psychopath who loved killing innocent civilians for target practice. But he was a psychopath whose uncle was a Senator, and head of the Senate Armed Forces Committee, so the psychopath was untouchable. Raul and Pierce had reported him anyway and had paid a heavy price.

Emma understood that, down to the bone. She, Felicity, Hope and Riley had worked for the Boss from Hell at the NSA. He hadn't used civilians for target practice, but he was as toxic as they came and the four of them had had to band together in self-defense. The NSA was an institution that was top heavy with weird men and reporting a harassing boss had only gotten them demotions and warnings.

"It's over now," Raul said and she nodded. A good way of dealing with things – turn the page and start over. "And right now, we're both where we want to be." He turned his head and looked at her while squeezing her hand.

Well.

Her heart gave a thump at that.

She shouldn't flirt with Raul. He was here for work, doing her a big favor, actually. This wasn't fun, an encounter with an attractive man. This was a mystery he was volunteering to help her with.

But oh. If this had been a chance meeting with an attractive man, it would have been fun. The nicest thing to happen to her this year.

Last year, too.

They'd left the super funky part of the Castro and were walking along a recently gentrified street, with fancy coffee shops and expensive boutiques. The lights were bright and fun, some actually beautiful. The art galleries had art works that were stunning. One shop specialized in cowboy boots and had an array in the front window that reached out and grabbed you. The etched leatherwork was exquisite, some boots brightly colored. She leaned in to see one intricate design and laughed. It was a perfect replica of Van Gogh's Starry Sky.

"Great, isn't it?" Raul said.

"Fabulous." She looked up at him. "Can you see yourself wearing them?"

"Cowboy boots are for riding horses and I don't do that. And I'd be scared of ruining the artwork. But I would buy them and frame them. Or maybe buy them and give them to a cousin who'd love them."

He was serious.

The next shop was something else. They both instinctively stopped and stared. It was a decorating shop and was perfect if you were the Sun King and had just dropped acid.

"Wow," she said finally. Even in the evening light, you'd need to wear sunglasses to fight the glare from thousand-bulb chandeliers and shiny brocades and a billion mirrored surfaces. "Some people really like their glitz."

"Speechless," Raul said. "Though I'm tempted to go inside and see what other wonders there are."

"My glitz quota just maxed out," Emma said firmly, and tugged at his arm. "And we're close to Heaven, right?"

Raul gave another deep look at the window. "Yeah, close to Heaven for Liberace. But we're also close to the other Heaven, too. Let's go."

Heaven was on a very short side street, basically taking up one whole side of the street. They stopped and took in a long, low structure made of concrete that seemed to stretch forever. In the middle was a wide entrance with two bruisers standing on either side in that 'at ease, men' stance, hands covering genitals. Satin cords forming a corridor for when the line got long, but it was early and there were only a few people lined up.

The crowd was young, well-dressed, hip and happy. Mostly men, some women. She and Raul lined up and moved to the head of the line in under ten minutes. Emma had fun listening to the chatter of the people around her. She learned about two awesome hairdressers and an ace asshole bleacher and was almost sorry when it was their turn to approach the bouncers. The bouncers took one look at them, then turned their heads forward and stared straight ahead again.

They'd passed the chic test.

There was a sort of antechamber, a big room where another loose line waited to pass by a guy with neon green hair sitting at a plexiglass table. When they got to the table, he smiled brightly at them.

"Well, hello!" He looked Emma up and down and then Raul, lingering over Raul. "Entrance for two?"

Raul had his credit card out. "Yeah. Two, thanks."

The green haired guy passed a cellphone-like device over the card and it beeped.

It showed a sale of two hundred bucks. They each received light blue bracelets.

Emma turned to Raul. "Are you sure …" she began uneasily.

"Hey." Raul snaked an arm around her waist and bent to kiss her. It was brief but hard and left her completely shaken. He walked to the door keeping his arm around her waist, bending to speak directly in her ear. "We're a couple, remember? And I don't want to hear another word about money."

He stopped at the door, one hand clasping her waist, the

other on the door, about to open it. He looked down at her and at her nod, opened the door.

They walked through and Emma forgot everything.

"Oh my God," she breathed.

It was – it was *amazing*. The huge space, an ugly squat concrete box on the outside, was magically transformed into a beach on the inside. Not just any beach, either. A beach on some magical tropical isle, the kind of beach that was on tourist brochures and never corresponded to reality.

The lighting somehow recreated the effect of sunlight on rippling water, light blue evanescent lights on the walls and ceiling. There were seating pods everywhere, the couches like on a chic beach, with lightweight cotton canopies and walls. You could arrange some privacy for yourself by pulling the curtains closed. It was early in the evening and the pods were all open. Very handsome waiters with amazing hair, dressed in lightweight trousers and aloha shirts and sandals, circulated with drinks. At the end of the huge space was a plexiglass wall forming a bright blue pool. Two young guys frolicked in the pool in tiny little swimsuits that left nothing to the imagination. They were gorgeous and had tiny breathers allowing then to spend time underwater.

Heaven was a day at the beach. And not just any beach. Bali-Maldives quality beach. No wonder Toby came often.

Toby. Their reason for being here. Emma turned to Raul to find him looking at her, not at the amazing décor of Heaven.

"Something else, eh?"

Dance house music hadn't started up yet. The music was light and New Agey. Exactly what you'd expect in heaven.

"Maybe this is what heaven is actually like. Beautiful surroundings, beautiful music, beautiful people." Well, if you had to be dead, and you'd gone to heaven, you'd want this. Where everyone was young and pretty and fashionably dressed. Even the smells were heavenly. Very expensive colognes, excellent liqueurs, some kind of ocean breeze smell.

"Maybe." Raul smiled down at her, the skin around his eyes crinkling. Something a woman would hate, but on him – man. It looked good. "We should try to be good people, then. Here, let's find a place to sit down before the crowds arrive."

About twenty people had arrived in just the time they'd taken to look around. If they wanted some privacy, they'd have to find a spot soon.

The underwater effect was mesmerizing, exactly like standing on the beach at noon on a cool summer's day, watching colors ripple and wash over the sea, which was actually the floor of a club. Emma felt like she could stand there forever, just enjoying the scene.

"There." Raul pointed to a small cabana—two loungers and a beach bed, half enclosed by the lightweight cotton panels billowing around it. "Let's grab those seats."

Good choice. There were technically two other seats in the enclosure, but as long as the place wasn't crowded, no one would intrude on their privacy. They sat down facing the back wall and the two beautiful men cavorting in the water, like mermen but with strong lean legs.

"So, this is the guy, right?" Unobtrusively, Raul pulled out his cell and showed her the screen. On it was a photo of Toby, taken from PIB's website. They'd laughed at their company photos. Hers looked like a hostage photo and his looked like he ate small children for breakfast.

"It is, but I can't imagine anyone recognizing him from that photo. And he sure wouldn't look like that when he was here in Heaven. Here ... hold out your phone."

He did and she pulled out hers. She scrolled quickly and found three photos where Toby was laughing or smiling, the Toby she knew, and tapped her phone against Raul's and saw the three she had chosen appear on his screen.

"Those are the photos you'll be needing. So, what are we going to do? Stop random people and ask if they know Toby?"

He stood and gave her a hand. "Let's start with the bartenders. Let's leave my jacket and your shawl. We can keep an eye on them as we ask the bartenders."

"Sure." She stood, leaving her shawl on the cushion. Raul had shed his jacket and loosened his tie and he looked absolutely delicious. The breeze off the bay had tousled his hair and a lock curled over his forehead. In any other man, it would have been ridiculously pretentious, someone preening in a mirror, making the lock of hair fall just so. Instead, she'd seen the wind ruffle his hair and he probably wasn't aware in any way that he looked so handsome and ... and dashing.

It was just something about him, the way he carried himself, the long, lean, strong body that moved with an athlete's precision, the sober expression he had when he wasn't smiling, that air of readiness – someone willing and capable of reaction if something bad happened. He probably wasn't aware of it, but she was.

Others in Heaven were, too. As Raul made his way to the bar that had been made to look like the tiki bar in some exclusive resort, heads swiveled in his wake. She smiled secretively and tightened her hold on his arm. *Sorry guys, he's mine.* For the evening at least.

They leaned on the bamboo bar and Raul signaled the bartender. He came over. "What'll it be, folks?" He tapped a QR code on the counter. "Here's the drinks menu."

"We're sitting over there, so I guess we'll wait for a server. But in the meantime, my brother asked me to look for a friend of his, Toby Jackson. My brother didn't have an address or a phone number, but said Toby came to Heaven a lot, so I thought I'd try tracking him down here." He looked slowly around the cavernous space that also somehow was gorgeous and welcoming. "I'm glad Rob told me to come. This place is great. Isn't it, sweetheart?"

Raul smiled down at her.

Well, she was the sweetheart, so she'd better answer. "Fabulous. I don't think I've ever seen such an attractive club. Congrats."

The waiter was very good-looking, dressed like all of them were in white slim cut pants and an aloha shirt. He had sleeve tattoos that echoed the colors of his shirt.

"Thanks. I don't think I know any customers named Toby."

"Oh!" Raul gave a very good imitation of a man just thinking of something. "I have photos that Rob sent me. Here."

They both bent over Raul's screen, the bartender touching Raul's hand, moving it when Raul scrolled to show all the photos. He seemed genuinely reluctant when he shook his head. "Sorry. Good looking guy. I'd have noticed him if he came in often."

Emma leaned on the counter. "What's your shift? Do you get off before Heaven closes?"

The bartender cocked his head. "I study, so I have a light shift. I work from 7 to 11, what we call the 'early bird shift'. Heaven closes at 4 am and I couldn't do the whole shift. I have classes at 8 in the morning."

"Are those official shifts? I mean is there a general turnover at 11 in the evening?"

He pursed his lips. "Yeah, for some. If you can make the whole shift, the money is good but it's hard to do anything else with your life. So, for those who are studying, or modelling or trying to get into acting, it's not viable. I'd say about a third of us do half shifts and two thirds work the whole shift. Management's really easy. As long as the work gets done, they don't care."

"Cool place," Raul said, pocketing his cell. "We'll keep asking around. My brother won't forgive me if I don't track this

Toby down. We're sitting over there. Do I order here or wait for a server?"

"I can send your drinks over," the bartender smiled. "So, what will you be having?"

Emma was a little worried. They'd had a lot of wine over dinner. Granted, that was some time ago, but still. But Raul was cool. "We drank a lot over dinner, so I think we should start out slow."

"Gotcha. I'll get a server to send you over two Mojito Mock-tails. Absolutely delicious, but without the rum. How does that sound?"

"Perfect. Thanks." Raul gave a huge smile that made Emma's heart beat faster and made the bartender blink. Some-how, and she had no idea how he did it, twenty bucks were left on the counter. He took her elbow as they walked back to their cabana.

"Smoothly done," she said admiringly. "Did they teach you how to do things like that in the SEALs?"

"Yeah, we had training in undercover work. This is Under-cover Lite, though. Beautiful woman, chic nightclub, fabulous food ... it wasn't always like this in the Navy, believe me."

Beautiful woman ... well, he was undercover, after all. But there'd been a little renegade spurt of pleasure at his words. *Down girl,* Emma told herself.

They reached the canopy and sat down. As soon as they were settled, a very handsome man appeared and deposited their drinks. If they were as good as they looked, they'd be great. Tall glasses with bright mint in clear liquid.

"There you go," the server smiled. He had an elaborately cut hair style that probably required weekly cuts with precision tools, and was wearing a brightly colored aloha shirt with blindingly vivid turquoise parrots. "Whose bracelet do I take?"

For a moment, Emma didn't understand, but Raul did. He held out his wrist without taking his eyes off her. The server had a tiny metallic wand that beeped when waved over Raul's bracelet. Raul was taking care of the drinks, as well. She sighed.

Something ethereal floated across the room. Silvery, shimmering, with tentacles ... "Oh my God!" she laughed. "A medusa!" It traversed the room slowly, evanescent, nearly transparent.

"And look." Raul turned her face slightly. Something was rippling across the ceiling. She laughed when she realized she was seeing a hologram of a school of silver fish darting here and there. It wasn't hard to imagine that it was what you would see from the deck of your superyacht anchored in the Bahamas.

Then holograms of a silvery octopus and a shark joined them. By the time they floated across the ceiling, other creatures took their place.

"Drink up." Raul was holding her mojito mocktail up. She took it and drained it. It was incredibly refreshing. She'd been thirstier than she thought. Being undercover was thirst-making.

"That was refreshing." He put the glass down on the bamboo table and turned to her. Genial Raul was gone and Dead-serious Raul had taken his place. But only she could see the change. He was good.

Raul leaned in, keeping his voice low. No one could have heard anything from a foot away and there was no one nearby. "I'm going to make the rounds of the first shift baristas. Let's try it solo, and we can try in tandem on the second shift. Can I leave you alone for a while?"

She smiled at him. "Sure, mom. I'll be fine. I don't think anyone will attack me in Heaven. You're more to the crowd's taste than I am."

"Good girl." Raul rose, cell in hand, and made his way to the long tiki counter. Emma watched his back, more out of pleasure than to keep her partner safe. She wasn't the only one watching. Watching Raul walk was a delight, no matter your sexuality. Those broad shoulders, lean hips, long legs ... yum.

And the way he moved was all man. Totally unselfconscious, full of grace and power, the walk of a man who knew where he was going. He got to the counter, leaned on it and beckoned a smiling barista. Maybe word had got round that he was leaving a nice tip, because they engaged in conversation as Raul showed his cell screen. Finally, the barista shook his head and Raul moved on.

Emma sat back. Raul was doing his thing well, better than she could have done. She was a terrible liar, had never learned the knack. As a matter of fact, her entire university and work career rewarded her for discerning reality, analyzing and reporting on it. Lying about anything – trends she was seeing, reassuring people when things were actually going badly – carried terrible consequences in her world, including the possibility of massive losses.

In her private life, too, Emma had never seen the point in lying. And anyway, there was never a real temptation. In the few times she'd been in a relationship, however brief, she never strayed. Never wanted to. So, she never had to lie about what she was doing. Lying to Felicity or Hope or Riley – the very idea was repugnant. Their friendship was based on being open and kind to each other.

Professionally, she got her info basically from bots and never had to coax anything from anyone. She'd make a lousy spy.

Raul, on the other hand ... She watched him make his way down the long counter, chatting with the bartenders, seemingly entirely at ease. She thought she could see money exchanging hands discreetly but it was done with great finesse. At one point he seemed to blur. The mocktail was alcohol free so it had to be something else. Clouds of fog. Somewhere a dry ice machine started up, pumping out just enough to blur contours and give everything a mystical look.

Raul was doing his thing. She stopped looking in his direction, sat back and relaxed. It was actually the first real relaxation she'd had in days. Since Toby disappeared, in fact. Not that she'd found Toby, but she had found an ally. Someone who believed she wasn't wrong to be worried. Someone who was actively helping her find him. So, she could stop the anxiety-scrolling waiting to hear from him and do something.

The vibe of Heaven was changing. More people flowed in, laughing and chatting. Mostly men, some women. All beautiful. The tempo of the music speeded up too. Later there would be house music, presumably, but for now they were covers of popular songs. A few couples were out on the dance floor. The music segued into salsa and more couples drifted out to the dance floor. Some had serious moves.

Servers walked by with really interesting-looking drinks. Some pale and cool looking, some in neon colors that screamed of summer at the beach, some inside fresh pineapples. A few had little retro paper umbrellas. Another server walked by with a tray of four drinks that had layers of colors.

After a lively cycle of upbeat rhythms, the music slowed down.

"Come." Raul appeared out of nowhere, big hand held out to her. "Let's dance. We'll try to fit in."

Oh *yeah*. Emma hadn't danced in … forever. She'd spent a lot of years in Hispanic cultures and loved dancing. Raul would make a wonderful dance partner. He was physical grace personified. Oh man, this was going to be fun.

Not.

Sigh.

Raul turned out to be the only Latin male in the world who couldn't dance. They ended up in a dull two-step completely out of rhythm with the music. One-two. One-two. Repeat. But after a minute or two she wasn't noticing his lack of skill as a dancer. Who cared when she was up against the strongest body she'd ever felt?

He curled his hand around hers and gently brought her right up against his chest and oh my God, that felt so good. He felt good and smelled good. It was utterly natural to rest her head against that broad shoulder, close her eyes, and just relax against him. No need to think of any fancy steps.

She didn't have to think, she didn't have to do anything but sway and breathe. Her body was taking care of her, drinking him in.

Raul bent his head down to her, speaking directly into her ear. His breath against her ear gave her goosebumps. "Not much of a dancer, sorry."

Emma smiled against his chest. "They should take away your Hispanic last name and call you Jones. The Dance Police should just cart you away."

There was a deep rumble in his chest it took her a moment to recognize as laughter. "You have no idea. My sisters and female cousins make fun of me. No one wants to dance with me at weddings and quinceañeras. It's one of the tragedies of my life."

How could any woman not want to dance with Raul? Never mind the boring things their feet were doing. Above the ankles, it was sheer heaven. Her legs brushing his, chest to chest. Holding one hand, the other around her waist. Basically, she was in Raul's embrace.

Maybe the two-step was underrated? Because it was lulling, like being rocked to sleep. Except sleep was the furthest thing from her mind, even though her eyes were half closed. The two step was basically swaying, back and forth. She felt him against every inch of the front of her body. Like being pressed against a warm wall. Except one part wasn't a wall. With every movement, their hips met and he was becoming aroused. He wasn't obnoxious about it, not pressing against her in any way. It was just so natural, feeling him swell and start to rise.

Because, well, she was feeling aroused too, only in a way

that wasn't obvious. Her entire body had turned into an eroge-
nous zone, her breasts and sex glowing with heat. The only
place where their skin touched was her hand in his, everywhere else was covered with clothes.

But her body didn't care. Her skin prickled all over and she
was filled with heat, like a bonfire had been lit inside her. With
her face pressed against his shoulder, she could barely see the
rest of Heaven, and didn't care. More people had come onto the
dance floor and she had a vague impression of crowds now.
Buzzing noises of voices came to her dimly. She herself was in a
cocoon of intense pleasure and heat, in Raul's arms, gently
moving to a beat she was barely aware of. Her entire world was
Raul, her senses weren't sending her messages from the outside
world, they were sending her messages from Raul. His strong
steady heartbeat against the ear pressed to his chest was louder
than the music. His scent – soap and somehow leather – was
stronger than the scent of bar food and liquor. Somehow, he'd
brought her even closer to him, and he rested his cheek against
the top of her head, completing the Raul Force Field.

Was dancing supposed to be like this? Why hadn't she
known? All those dance classes and it had all been in her head
and her feet. Memorizing the moves, counting steps. Her
partner had been secondary in all this. Now it was all her partner, who was turning her on, making her feel so alive, while
moving slowly.

The music stopped but they continued their slow shuffle.
After a moment, Emma lifted her head. They were almost
alone on the dance floor, people in a circle looking at them like
the dorks they were.

A sultry tango started up and she looked up hopefully at
Raul, hips already moving to the beat. A tango with him would
be really sexy. He smiled down at her and oh God, he was so
sinfully handsome at this moment. The lock of black hair
falling over his forehead, dark eyes dancing, firm mouth lifted

up at one corner. He brought their clasped hands to her face and stroked her cheek.

"Sorry honey, the tango's too –"

The words were lost. Emma was ripped from his arms by a smiling, horsey-faced guy dressed in blinding white, with gelled bleached white hair.

"You should be ashamed of dancing like that with this fine woman," the guy said, laughing, and swept her into his arms.

And just like that, she was in the tango.

6

_____

Raul was sorry to see Emma go. He immediately missed her warmth and softness in his arms. But he'd been well on his way to a full woodie, on a dance floor, no less, so maybe it was for the best. Not having her plastered to the front of his body was a loss, but life was full of them.

Plus, he got a front row seat to Emma dancing the tango and *man*. He wouldn't miss this for the world.

She was a natural.

The guy who grabbed her was a little odd-looking, but you forgot that immediately once he started moving. And Emma ... wow. Just fucking wow.

The music was all instrumentals at first, the tune vaguely familiar. Emma and the guy somehow fell into this instinctive thing, circling around each other as if they'd known each other forever. Movements sinuous, echoing. Tango had a whole vocabulary to it. His second cousin Jorge, who fancied himself a ladies' man, had tried to explain it to him once, with the *sacadas* and the *ochos* and the *giros*, but Raul lost interest after about a minute. If you had to learn something physically complex, well then shooting fit the bill. Raul was really good with guns. That was enough for him.

But watching Weird Guy and Emma, well. Maybe there was something to it. They couldn't possibly have worked out the moves beforehand but they moved in instant sync, just like in the Teams, where if you zigged, your teammate zagged. Only his teammates weren't as pretty to watch as Emma and the guy.

The steps were complex and perfect, and perfectly in time with the music. How the fuck did they *do* that?

And then a woman started singing the song and Raul laughed out loud. *I Bust the Windows Out Your Car.* A song that had been imprinted on him at the age of nineteen when a casual girlfriend who mistook his signals actually broke the windows of his ancient Fairlane he'd bought with high school graduation money.

Emma heard him laugh, looked over her shoulder and smiled at him. While executing some ridiculously complex steps. He was frozen solid to the spot as she twisted and twirled and let the music run through her while he felt a wave of desire so strong it nearly brought him to his knees.

He wasn't the only one watching. The other dancers had moved to the periphery of the floor and most had stopped dancing to watch two masters at work. It was like the ceiling opened up and a huge spotlight lit Emma, a star so bright he couldn't see anything else. Just Emma, an incandescent woman moving to the music, moving with the music. She *was* the music and she was so desirable he could barely breathe for wanting her.

The two were twirling, using everything in their bodies— arms, legs, head, chest--the steps becoming incredibly fast. Emma hooked her leg around her partner's leg – there was a word for that but Raul was so blasted with lust he could barely remember his own name – and flung her slender pale arms in the air, arching backwards, the guy's arm around her waist for balance. For as long as he lived, Raul would never forget the picture she made, pale skin, red hair, body flung out in abandon and he had a sudden image of how she'd look during sex.

It bloomed in his mind—Emma under him, in bed. Arms flung up over her head, eyes closed, coming around him, buried deep inside her.

Fuck! Now he had a massive hard-on. In public. Shit shit *shit!* The last time that had happened to him was when he was seventeen and Mary Knudson bent down in class and he saw her nipples. But he wasn't seventeen now, he was thirty-four, and used to controlling his dick. Men didn't have woodies in public, they saved it for when they were alone with the woman.

He pinched his nose and looked up at the ceiling where silvery gray stingrays were flapping their wings and thought of bad things. Of his last commander, aiming at a pregnant woman on the streets of a dusty town and firing. Aiming at the woman's pregnant belly and shouting *Two for the price of one!* Grinning.

Only he and Pierce saw that one and they'd looked at each other, horrified. Knowing they were going to have to report it. Knowing they were in for a world of hurt, but not as much as the poor woman writhing on the ground, whose movements were becoming slower and slower until she stilled.

Yeah.

That brought his woodie down.

The song was coming to an end. Emma and her partner were only a few feet away. The guy wrapped her up in that complicated embrace that led to a spinout and let her go. But instead of holding her hand to stop the spin, he let go and Emma spun right into his arms, perfectly, as if they'd rehearsed this a thousand times.

She was warm, panting with the exertion, so very alive in his arms. With that last spin she landed hard against him.

Instinctively his arms went around her. It felt like he'd caught her, that life had thrown her at him, his very own prize. His.

There was no thought and no planning. If he'd put a little thought into it, he might have stopped. Or not. Right then, stopping seemed insane. He was aware of the reasons for not kissing her. He was here on a job, or rather a mission for friends, which made it even more important to do it well. On missions you kept your head, you didn't get blindsided by a woman. He was overstepping bounds ... those thoughts were like pesky flies in his head, completely overwhelmed by the heat as he brought his mouth to hers, like iron filings to a magnet.

She tasted wonderful. She'd been laughing, her mouth uptilted so their mouths were not quite aligned. But then she got into the kiss, and oh yeah, she was kissing him back. Raul licked inside her mouth and felt her tongue touching his and it was electric, almost painful — a line of heat running straight from his mouth to his dick.

Emma was clinging to him and he was clinging to her harder, as if someone were trying to wrench her away from him and he was set on never letting her go. Holding her tightly, he plunged into her mouth like finding salvation there, the source of heat and light. Needing to breathe, he thought briefly of lifting his mouth for a second from her but then tossed that idea aside as ridiculous. What was breathing next to kissing Emma Holland?

Nothing.

And anyway, somehow he was breathing through Emma, and she was breathing through him.

There was some weird sound he couldn't place. The part of him that wasn't a man but a soldier – a part that would be with him for the rest of his life – forced him to open an eye. He didn't want to. Eyes closed was the way to drink in Emma, so he could focus on the taste of her, the feel of her. But he was hardwired to pay attention to strange noises so he cracked one eye open and then the other.

He stepped back a little, enough to make her step a little back too.

They were surrounded by clapping club goers. The guy who'd danced with Emma gave a sardonic salute off his forehead. Most were smiling, some were laughing. He and Emma had been a momentary distraction, but there were many others and they drifted off after a moment or two. A few smiling over their shoulders at them.

Heaven clearly approved of romance.

"Whoa." Emma looked a little stunned, off balance. "That was, that was –"

"Something," Raul said. "Yeah, it was something." He looked at her narrow-eyed. "You okay? I mean, did I overstep –"

"No!" She huffed out a breath and lowered her voice. "You didn't step out of line. Maybe I did. Got too much into the spirit of tango."

"Well, I am really grateful." He grinned at her. He thought she was with him every step of the way during the kiss, but maybe that had been his hopeful dick talking. He sketched a little bow. "You are amazing. Where'd you learn to tango like that?"

"Buenos Aires," she said. "*Viví allí un par de años y me encantó. No puedes vivir allí y no tanguear. Todo el mundo lo lleva en la sangre.*

I lived there for a couple of years and loved it. You can't live there and not tango, it's in everyone's blood.

Something shorted in his brain, sparks flying. She was the most beautiful woman he'd ever seen, incredibly brainy but fun, a good friend to his good friends and ... *she spoke Spanish*? This was just too much.

She'd spoken Spanish to him. He should answer. Yep, he should. He opened his mouth but nothing came out. She cocked her head, those brilliant blue eyes fixed on him like blue headlights.

"Raul?"

He shook himself, cleared his throat. He needed to answer her, but the truth was that his Spanish sucked. It didn't suck if you were white bread because you couldn't tell. But she could.

"Ah, that's amazing. Ah, that you lived in Buenos Aires. That your Spanish is so good. And you also speak Chinese. That's, uh, amazing."

Her head cocked the other way and she studied him. No other word for it. Like he was a spreadsheet she had to figure out. Trying to understand why he didn't speak Spanish to her. She was smart, she'd get there. He'd spoken in English because her Spanish was better than his.

She was going to point this out and he'd be embarrassed.

But all she did was smile at him, touch his arm and change the subject. "Raul. It's past eleven. Do you think we should check the second shift bartenders? We need to find someone who knows Toby."

That snapped him back to the present. They were here for a reason. Not for him to admire her tango or for him to kiss her – though that had been fantastic – but to find Toby and begin to understand what was going on. Because there might be a danger to Emma here. And if, before, he was determined to protect Emma because she was Felicity and Hope's friend, now it was his absolute priority. To keep Emma safe.

Because Emma was special. And no harm was going to come to her while he was around. And he was going to be around for a long, long time.

That conviction settled into his bones. He didn't know he'd been looking for her, but he had. And now he'd found her. And he was going to stick to her side like glue until they solved the mystery and then afterward he was going to stick to her side like glue because ... because.

"Get your stuff, honey. There's too big a crowd to leave that pretty shawl or your purse on the table. I think we should both talk to the bartenders."

"Okay." She bent immediately to gather her things and turned her face up to his, utterly trusting. "You're the expert."

"I am." He wasn't. He had no fucking clue if it was better to have Emma with him. The fuck did he know? He had some experience prying intel out of sullen insurgents but none in gay nightclubs. All he knew was that he wanted Emma by his side. It was like she had some magic force field around her that made him feel better – smarter and more alive. "Let's just go down the line and see if we can find someone who knew Toby."

"And Colin," she said. "The guy he was excited over. Toby told me his name was Colin." At the mention of Toby, her face became serious.

"And Colin. Yeah. Someone's bound to know something if Toby came here a lot."

Raul put his arm around her waist and they walked together to the south end of the long counter. He palmed some twenties and Emma looked at his hand and opened her mouth.

"Not. A. Word." He spoke without moving his mouth and she gave a big sigh.

The first bartender was medium height, rough looking with gym muscles and prison tats. He didn't seem to fit into Heaven's super hip vibe. But he was pleasant enough as he sidled up when Raul crooked a finger. "What'll you have?" he asked in a pleasant tone.

Raul bent his head toward him until their foreheads almost touched. "Information."

He opened his hand to show the twenty and the bartender cocked his head. "Sure," he said. "Unless you're a cop."

"Nope," Raul answered. "Not a cop. I'm here on behalf of my brother, who's looking for a friend of his who seems to have disappeared." The bartender took the twenty and looked down at the photo on Raul's cell screen. To his credit, he studied the photo carefully. He looked up into Raul's eyes. "He in trouble?"

"Don't think so. But don't really know. He was supposed to meet my brother in LA, but he didn't show up, and my brother – he's really worried. This guy, Toby Jackson, came to Heaven a lot, apparently, and my brother told me to look here for some info."

The bartender looked carefully at Raul, at Emma, back at Raul and clearly got the message Raul was sending. Gay brother asks straight brother to do him a solid. Raul had been undercover and he knew how to project vibes. If he wanted, he could be very intimidating. But he could also project harmlessness and that's what he did now. The man had been slightly tense but he relaxed. There was a story there, of drugs maybe or something else, but Raul didn't care, just wanted to know – on behalf of his brother – if Toby was okay, and projected that.

"He came to Heaven often, huh?" the man asked.

Raul nodded. "Most nights apparently, the last couple of months or so. Was a regular."

"So, you don't want me and you don't want most of the guys on shift right now. Most of us are new. You want Rick. Farther down. Tall, thin, Goth. Can't miss him."

"Thanks." Raul slid the twenty over but the man slid it right back. "Give it to Rick, and a couple more if you can. Rick's mom is sick and he's been moonlighting in the morning at a Star-bucks." He bent forward, scanned to his left. "Okay, he's here. Fourth man down. Good luck finding your friend. Your broth-er's friend."

"Thanks," Emma said quietly and the bartender looked at her for the first time. A sure sign of his orientation. If it had been Raul, he wouldn't have been able to keep his eyes off Emma. Well, less competition for him.

They went directly to Rick. There was no missing him, as the other guy had said. He had to run at least six five, was rail thin, had black eye makeup and black lipstick and had dyed black hair in blue-tipped spikes. He sort of looked like an elongated Penguin.

Rick sauntered over. "Hi. What'll it be?"

"Some info," Raul said. "If you have the time."

Rick cocked his long head. "Yeah. Well, no emergencies, not at the moment. What do you need to know?"

Raul showed the photos to Rick, watching carefully. Rick was good, kept an impassive face, but there was a flicker of his eyelids when Raul showed him Toby's photo.

He launched into his spiel. "His name is Toby Jackson, works at a bank. He's a really good friend of my brother, who lives in New York. When my brother heard I was coming to San Francisco, he asked me to look him up. But he's sort of disappeared. My brother said to ask around, said to come here, that Toby came often."

Rick was still looking at the photos.

"So—do you know him? You seen him around?"

Rick handed his phone back and sighed. "Yeah. I've seen him around. Didn't know his name was Toby."

"I understand he was often with a guy called Colin. Don't know the last name."

Rick's face just closed up. No other way to describe it.

"I just serve drinks, man. I don't follow people's personal lives."

Emma stepped up. "I appreciate you want to protect people's privacy. But we're worried. I'm worried. I worked with him and he has disappeared. We don't mean any harm to Toby, swear to God. We just want to know if he's ok. If you've seen Toby lately, or if you know who this Colin is, we'd really appreciate you helping."

Raul remained silent. Emma was doing a better job of it than he was. She radiated worry and honesty. He'd had a lot of training in interrogation. He had a pretty good grasp on when people were telling the truth and when they weren't. What most people didn't grasp is that truth-telling is very powerful. Subconscious signals are sent when people told the truth that relaxed, gave a little dopamine hit. Rick definitely got a dopamine hit.

He searched Emma's face, then Raul's, gave a small satisfied nod. "Okay, Toby used to come in a lot but I haven't seen him in a few days. I have seen a very unhappy guy he was always with. Don't know his name, but they seemed happy together.

"Is he here now?"

Rick paused, straightened, scanned the room. "Yeah." He pointed. "See that pillar over there, looks like ice? On the light blue couch next to the pillar. Tall, black hair, blue eyes, silver shirt, lilac tie. That's who your guy was with. Been here every night this week." He brought his gaze back to Raul and Emma. "I hope this is for real. I hope you're not going to disturb a good customer for some lover's spat."

"No," Emma said softly. "It's a serious matter. Thanks for your help."

She started making a bee line for the guy Rick had pointed out. Raul stayed behind for a second. He held out his hand and when Rick took it, the original twenty and four more Jacksons exchanged hands. Rick looked surprised at the feel of several banknotes.

"I have a mom I love, too," Raul said and turned to follow Emma.

HE WAS RIGHT WHERE RICK SAID HE'D BE. CLOSE UP, COLIN WAS A good-looking man, very lean, with dark hair and deep blue eyes. He was speaking with another man and looked up when they approached.

Emma wondered if eyes that red hurt.

"Colin?" Raul asked.

He nodded, wary. "And you are?"

Raul looked at her then back at Colin. "We're friends of Toby. Can we talk to you for a moment?"

At Toby's name, Colin's face froze. No, his features froze but his red eyes flashed temper. "Go away."

"It's important. We wouldn't bother you if it weren't important." Raul's voice was quiet but firm. The club now was noisy, with hundreds more people, house dance music throbbing. But Raul's voice carried, without being loud.

Colin turned his head away. "I have nothing to say to you."

The man he'd been speaking to twitched in his seat, uncomfortable. "Hey, I should leave you guys –"

Colin shot out a hand and gripped his wrist. "Stay. I have nothing to say to these people."

Emma touched Raul's elbow, moved past him and sat down next to Colin. "Colin. It's Colin, right? I feel like I know you, Toby's talked about you so much."

Colin frowned and focused on her out of those blood-shot eyes. "You – you're Emma? Emma Holland? Toby's work partner?"

She smiled. "Yeah. I work with Toby. Worked with Toby. I haven't seen him in days. It's just not like him to disappear. I'm really worried about him." Emma leaned forward and addressed the man on the other side of Colin. "Do you think we could have a private conversation? We won't be long."

The other man nodded, shot to his feet and made a beeline for the bar. Colin watched resentfully as he left.

"So." Emma tried to keep her voice low, like Raul had, but she was almost drowned out by the music and the raucous laughs of a party two tables down. But she desperately wanted to keep this confidential. She looked around. "We really need to talk. Is there somewhere we can go to have a little privacy?"

Colin's mouth set and he was going to refuse. She touched

his forearm. His arm was tight with tension under her hand. "Please, Colin?"

He blew out an alcohol-laden breath, picked up his Negroni and stood up. "Come with me, but then you leave me the hell alone."

Emma exchanged glances with Raul. His face was sober, serious. He indicated with his hand that she should go first. In this exchange, he wasn't looking for a friend of his brother. She was looking for a missing colleague and friend and she would be taking the lead.

This wasn't in Emma's wheelhouse at all. As they followed Colin's rigid, angry back, she whispered, "Let me know if I'm making a mistake."

He briefly gripped her elbow and squeezed. "You're smart. You won't make any mistakes."

Hmm. Nice thought but not true. Still, it did make sense for her to do the interrogating. But she wasn't used to doing things she wasn't good at.

Colin crossed the giant space and led them into a long, broad corridor. Though there was no door, the walls must have been insulated because the noise level dropped by several decibels. He was checking rooms to his left and right and finally entered a room to the right. If she'd thought about it, Emma would have imagined separate rooms at a sexy club to be remakes of Victorian bordellos, but this was modern, elegantly furnished without the beach motif, a perfect place to have a conversation. In fact, there were several couples in little seating pods scattered around the room. The music that had been deafening out in the main part of the club was pleasantly muted in here, a lively background noise.

Colin walked across the large room to the back wall, to a seating arrangement that could fit six people. A small white leather couch for two, four white leather armchairs, a round transparent plexiglass table in the middle.

Instead of sitting, Colin downed the last of his drink, set the glass on the table and walked to a brass and glass bar set against the wall. He got another glass, poured himself another Negroni, placed his bracelet against a reader and held it until it beeped.

Raul looked at her. "Something to drink?"

Colin was so hostile, maybe it would help if they all had a drink in their hand. "Yes, thank you. White wine, please. Preferably Chardonnay, but any decent white wine will do."

He smiled at her. "You got it."

She watched him get a glass of white wine for her, a finger of Scotch for himself, and imitated Colin, pressing his bracelet against the reader.

Colin sat in the middle of the small couch, making it clear he didn't want anyone beside him. Okay. Emma sat in one of the armchairs, Raul sat right next to her. He was quiet, leaving this part to her. The ruse of looking for his brother's friend was over.

Luckily, Emma wasn't going to have to lie, she was so bad at it.

Colin gulped down half his Negroni and leaned back, scowling. He was like a Pantone wheel –pupils bright blue, the white of his eyes stoplight red, black and greenish bags under his eyes. Complexion pale gray. Silver silk shirt, lilac tie.

"So." He was belligerent, looking at them out of half-closed eyes. But Emma suspected it was more because he was drunk than hostile. "The fuck you want? Talk."

Emma could *feel* Raul bristling beside her and laid a casual hand on his knee.

Down boy. Colin was not only drunk, he was hurting.

Emma leaned forward, trying not to wince at the smell of alcohol rising from Colin like a miasma. "Colin. When was the last time you saw Toby? Do you remember?"

"Do I remember? Do I *remember?*" His face tightened. "Yes, I fucking remember. I saw him seven days ago. Last Friday evening. We spent the night at my house. We had agreed to move in together. Otherwise, with my job we weren't seeing each other enough. It was Toby who suggested that he move in with me. My place is larger, a house on Alamo Square. It was a big step for him, a big step for me. I don't usually like people in my space, but with Toby – well, it works. Worked. So, we agreed that he'd break his lease, but he'd plan on starting to move in over the weekend. I'd asked for the weekend off."

"What do you do, Colin?" Raul leaned forward too as he asked.

"I'm an emergency room physician. At St. Francis Memorial. As you can imagine, I work long hours. It cuts into your private life. I was so happy when Toby suggested moving in. It works. We – we work." His mouth twisted. "No. We worked. Toby changed his mind, clearly. He was going to start boxing things on Saturday and I planned a really nice meal at home to celebrate on Sunday. Catered because I don't cook but I have good china and silverware. I had two bottles of Veuve Clicquot chilling in the fridge. Candles. He was supposed to be at my house with his suitcases by 7 p.m. Seven came and went, eight, nine. He doesn't do what I do, I couldn't imagine an emergency in banking. I started calling at eight but his phone was off. He doesn't have a landline. My calls became frantic, I called the emergency wards of all the hospitals. Around midnight I started to get a clue. I'd been ghosted. He'd ghosted me. *Me!* I didn't call his office on Monday because I didn't want to embarrass myself. But the fucker never called, didn't even try to explain himself."

Colin's voice broke and he looked sharply away in a vain attempt to hide his emotion. Emma could see he was suffering. "And you haven't slept since, have you?" she asked softly.

He shook his head jerkily. "Maybe an hour or two, here and there. My work was starting to suffer. Yesterday and today, I took the day off. I'll get over it. But I thought –" He blinked rapidly. "I thought we really had something, you know? Nowadays it's really rare when you connect and I thought we had."

"Colin." Emma waited a moment for his extreme emotion to pass. She needed to have his full attention. "I don't think Toby ghosted you. In fact, Toby is missing."

Colin blinked, face slack in shock. "*What?*"

She nodded sharply. "Toby is missing. He hasn't been in to work this week. No one knows where he is. I've called him time and time again and get voicemail. We answer our phones, always. We're in money markets and they move fast and it's unheard of for a quant like Toby to just ignore his phone for days. I'm really worried. I think –" she glanced at Raul, "we think something might have happened to him. That he is in danger. He was working on something that has enormous implications, that is possibly a huge criminal conspiracy. I don't have all the details, but I think Toby does. We're talking a lot of money and Toby knows what it is, but we don't, not yet."

Colin was sitting up straighter. "You think he's in trouble. Over something he found out, doing his job."

"I do." Emma nodded. "We do. I'm not entirely certain what it is because Toby put it all together and then disappeared. I don't have his data. But I think he knows something is going to happen and there are people who stand to make a lot of money who don't want him talking. Plus — maybe I'm not as close to Toby as you are, but I have been working with him for a while now and I think I know him. Toby does not have a streak of cruelty. He wouldn't treat you like that. He wouldn't disappear. He wouldn't make you worry. He wouldn't make me worry. If he hasn't contacted us, I very much fear it's because he can't."

Colin was silent, staring in the distance. Clearly piecing things together in his head. Finally, he nodded. "It seemed really weird to me, too. Not like Toby at all. Have you been to his apartment? Maybe there'd be something there that would tell us where he is."

Emma glanced at Raul. "We were thinking of going tomorrow morning. See if Raul can break in. Raul is former military."

Colin shot Raul a penetrating glance, and Raul gave him a blindingly angelical smile. Colin looked down at his empty glass. "Not really necessary," he said.

"Bad security? Good security?"

"I've got a key."

7

Emma glanced at Raul sitting beside her in the backseat of the Uber, but he was watching her so intensely she swiveled her head back to stare blindly out the window at the Castro streaming by. His focus felt like hands on her skin.

When he turned his head to stare out the front, it was like someone had unplugged her.

They'd made plans with Colin to meet at the front entrance of Toby's building tomorrow morning at nine. Colin had stumbled away and suddenly Emma was left with Raul. When she whispered that they should be leaving, mission accomplished, Raul simply put his big hand under her elbow and rose, taking her with him. He hadn't spoken a word since. They simply walked out of Heaven and an Uber was waiting for them. She had no idea when Raul could have ordered it, but like Cinderella's coach, there it was, waiting.

Orange, too.

He'd given her address and continued his brooding silence. Emma had no way to interpret his mood. Happy they'd gotten a clue, so he could move forward and resolve this issue and get back to his life in Portland? Angry that this wasn't going more quickly? Bored? What?

One thing for sure, he wasn't talking. His face was tight, deadpan. He looked like a smile – one of those easy smiles he'd given her all evening – would break his face.

Even looking the other way, she was so intensely aware of him sitting beside her, his big body radiating heat. A bigger than life presence in the quiet, dark car.

He slid his hand along her arm and interlaced his fingers with hers. His hand was large, broad-palmed. He had calluses. She'd never held hands before with a man with calluses on his hands. Her father had never been the type of dad who'd hold his little daughter's hand as she skipped down the street. And anyway, his hands were super soft, now mottled with age. Totally unlike Raul's strong, sinewy hands with that luscious olive skin.

And the few guys Emma had dated before coming to San Francisco weren't hand-holding types either. Most of the men she'd dated were data guys or finance guys and they weren't into romantic gestures. And even if they wanted to hold hands, their hands were for keyboarding, not hard and callused like Raul's hand. Raul's hands were for – what? Shooting? Fighting?

A sudden image of his hands on her, on her naked skin, bloomed in her mind and she was grateful for the darkness in the car as blood rushed to her face.

Emma felt his hand against hers but she also felt him all along her body, like a force field. One of those science-fictiony ones that shimmered and crackled, full of energy that might explode.

She might explode. It felt like there was nitroglycerine under her skin, just waiting to detonate. Each moment driving down Market brought the vehicle closer to her place. No idea what to do once they arrived.

In any other circumstance, with someone who'd gone out of

his way to help her, inviting him in for a nightcap would seem like the polite thing to do. Emma knew exactly how to keep something like that impersonal. Stand at a distance in the elevator, maybe stay standing while pouring a drink and reviewing the day. She didn't think Raul would be anything but a gentleman. Not worried about that.

She was worried about herself. Because she didn't know if she could trust herself to be a lady.

How foolish she'd been not to have taken to bed the few guys who'd asked. Not interested. With a couple of them, she'd been actually repelled. To the point where she wondered whether she'd precociously used up all her hormones and was drying up down there. Imagining her vagina as a desiccated desert, full of tumbleweed and cacti.

Well, those were foolish worries because no, she wasn't drying up. She was *burning* up. Skin tingling where Raul touched it, aware of his presence beside her with every cell in her body.

Every hormone she had woke up, after having been dormant for so long, the traitors! Emma was sure she could feel her ovaries, little bright points of heat deep in her belly. It was impossible, of course, but still. Raging ovaries was not a good place to be with someone who had been sent to help her and whom she'd first met today.

The vehicle passed New Montgomery, the Ferry Building all lit up at the end of Market. The turnoff to her street was coming up and she lived just a block down. What the hell was she going to do? Thank him and go up alone?

That was definitely a possibility or would be if her hormones hadn't reacted in horror. So okay, her whole body wanted to spend more time with Raul. It hadn't been this excited in ... huh. Forever.

But – invite him up and then what? Raul might be a perfect gentleman but she worried that her entire body was sending out pheromones by the ton and she wouldn't be smooth.

Women had a playbook for this sort of thing. She used to master it, but hadn't really had the occasion to use it since she'd moved to San Francisco. The guy makes a small move forward, you contemplate it, after a sufficient amount of time has gone by, you make a countermove forward. Friendly, but at times distant. Open to whatever, but prepared to shut it down in an instant. Cool but not cold.

The playbook went right out the window and her mind, usually her most trusted organ, one that had never let her down, pooped out on her.

The vehicle stopped right in front of the big glass doors of her lobby. The lobby was lit so brightly it cast light into the vehicle. When Emma turned to Raul, his brown eyes were lit up, reflecting the light.

With no idea what to say, she opened her mouth. Then: "Would you like to –"

"Yes," Raul said.

In a moment, he'd exited from the door, rounded the back of the vehicle and opened her door. He stood there, one big hand out.

She still had no idea what she was going to say, but maybe he did. Whatever it was, he was on board with it. She took his hand and it was natural then to tuck her hand in the crook of his arm. Halfway across the big shiny expanse of her huge lobby, Raul stopped. "Wait here," he said and made a beeline to the desk with the night security guard. Emma knew him. Nice kid, mixed race, very polite. He and Raul conferred, heads together, for a minute or two. Raul brought something out of his wallet and the guard nodded, face sober. Raul straightened, rapped his knuckles once against the granite counter, gave a brief nod and in less time that it would have taken her, crossed the lobby, took her arm again and walked them to the elevators.

Emma frowned when they got into the elevator. "What was that about?"

"I introduced myself, gave him my affiliation with Black Home Security, and asked him to keep an eye out for suspicious characters." His eyes bored into hers. "I don't know if you're in any real danger, Emma. Until we find Toby and debrief him, we have to take precautions."

Toby. A missing Toby and small earthquakes in the market. Small earthquakes going on inside her at Raul's nearness as they rose up to her apartment to ... to what?

It was so hard to think with Raul so close. Hard to plan, hard to think of what was next. What was next was in the future and the here and now took up all of her hard disk.

She was overwhelmed with sensations, had no idea what to do, what to say. She was silent as they exited the elevator as one, Raul's hand on her lower back, his other holding her key. He'd held his hand out in the elevator and she'd instinctively known what he wanted. He opened her door, ushered her over the threshold, flicked the light switch.

She felt heavy, could only move slowly. She moved a few steps into the living room, eyes falling on the silver platter holding a few bottles of good liquor.

"Do you – do you want a drink?"

He nodded, his hand falling from her back.

She poured them both a few fingers and handed him his glass. He brought it to his mouth and she did, too. But they both stopped before sipping it. She put her glass back down on the sideboard.

"This isn't what I want," she whispered.

"God, no," he said, putting his own drink down and pulling her to him.

This was what she wanted. This. Putting her arms around that strong, lean body, his mouth on hers. No one around them, nothing to interrupt them. Raul felt so good, tall and strong and so solid.

He was kissing her so deeply, it felt like she'd never been kissed before. Certainly it was the first time she'd been kissed like this, as if they would both die if they were pulled apart.

He held her head between his big hands, but it didn't make her feel controlled. She felt infused with some strong hot wind that would carry her away if she weren't held to earth with those hands.

Raul pulled away, head tilted back, eyes closed. His head fell forward and he opened his eyes, heat blazing from them. "God," he said, blowing out a breath. "I don't know where to begin."

She understood completely. She wanted to continue those kisses that made her feel dreamy, untethered, ready to float away. At the same time, she wanted to rip his shirt off and touch that strong chest all over.

"Start from the top." She smiled at him, loving every second of this. She felt excited, as if her skin could barely contain her. But she also felt crazy relaxed, safe in his arms.

She'd spent the past week scared and worried, anxiety thrumming beneath her skin. Nothing like that now. Holding Raul, being held by him, was to sink into a state where nothing bad could happen to her. Just insane pleasure allowed. The closer to him she got, the more intense the pleasure.

"The top," Raul whispered, and pulled the pins anchoring her hair to the top of her head. Her hair tumbled to her shoulders.

Raul tunneled his hands through her hair, lifting a strand to his face. "It's cool. I keep expecting it to be hot."

His hands moved to her neck and unzipped her dress, leaving the two panels open. Her skin was so hot she welcomed the slight coolness of the air on her bare skin. But then he placed his palm between her shoulder blades and her skin burned again. Even the air she was breathing burned her lungs.

Kissing her, Raul opened her dress further, slipping it off her shoulders, slipping it to the floor. She felt the light linen pool at her feet, standing in a strapless bra and panties, glad she'd splurged on the pale green lacy underwear. Watching Raul watching her was worth it.

His eyes were narrowed, nostrils flaring. He was affected, but so was she. His gaze was like hands touching her. Her breasts felt swollen, between her legs it felt like a furnace had been lit.

Raul's eyes met hers. "You're so fucking beautiful," he said, his voice raw, as if he hadn't spoken in days.

Emma had been told she was beautiful before, but not like this, not as if the words had been wrenched out of him. Before, it had felt like a polite compliment, almost a rote compliment. Something that had to be said, essentially, to get into her pants.

This wasn't like that. This felt like it came from someplace deep inside Raul, like a confession.

His hands went to the back of her bra and stilled.

"Is this what you want?" His voice was strained, hands frozen. She was sure that if she said *no, I don't want this,* he'd stop. But the last thing she wanted was for him to stop.

Emma's hands were on his chest and she wanted to rip that elegant jacket and starched white shirt right off him. All evening she'd wondered what he'd look like naked, whether he had heavy chest hair or light chest hair. She'd have taken a bet that he didn't manscape.

She pressed a kiss over his heart. "It's what I want but not where I want. I think we should be in the bedroom, don't you? We – oh!"

He'd picked her up and was carrying her, with no apparent difficulty, down the corridor. She'd never been carried as an adult and oh God. It was luscious, liberating, like flying. No wonder it featured in so many movies and books. Like being queen of the world, a *sexy* queen of the world. Though there weren't that many men who could carry a full-grown woman without breaking a sweat.

Without it changing his breathing, either, as she discovered. Because Raul was kissing her and kissing her and kissing her, eyes closed.

How to get him to her bedroom without running into a wall?

Emma improvised a primitive guidance system, tugging on his right arm when she wanted him to turn right, on his left arm when she wanted him to turn left. They made it to her bedroom intact and he let her legs slide gently to the floor. It had been wonderful being carried by him but held closely to him felt even better. The entire front of her touched him everywhere and it was amazing. She tightened her arms around his neck, clinging to that super strong body.

He was fully erect, she could feel him through his pants against her bare belly.

Raul lifted his head and looked at her. The room was dark, the only light source back in the living room, barely enough to see by. His face was drawn tightly, mouth swollen from their kisses. Her mouth was swollen too. Her mouth, her breasts, her sex.

"You have too many clothes on." Those words came out in a sultry purr and she nearly looked around to see who said them. She had. She'd said them, in a voice she barely recognized as her own.

"God, yes," Raul muttered, taking the tiniest step back so he could undress. He undid the buttons of his shirt so fast it was like waving his hands over his front and presto! Buttons undone. Shirt off. Belt buckle unfastened, pants unfastened, unzipped, off. Briefs, socks and shoes. Like a dream. He was naked in front of her and oh, God. Before he could take a step forward to her, she shot out a hand, palm against a pec, to hold him there for a second so she could get a good look.

She'd thought he was strong, built, but the clothes hid a lot. Naked, he was like a poster for male beauty—hard, lean planes of muscle, fitting together perfectly. Graceful, strong. A male animal in its prime.

And his penis. Ah. A real champ. Thick and hard, unlike any she'd ever seen and she realized that the men she'd had sex with had had basically semi-erections, nothing like this. A couple had needed their hands to enter her.

Raul wouldn't.

"We okay here?" he asked, voice strained. "I'm not getting any younger."

Instead of answering, Emma stepped forward and lifted her face to his.

It happened all at once. He got rid of her bra and panties in an instant and pulled her to him, while kissing her deeply. The whole front of her body was against a warm, hairy wall with his erect penis against her belly. As his tongue moved against hers, she could feel it move against her, becoming impossibly harder.

And she got softer, heat melting her from within.

The world tilted and she found herself on her back on the bed, his heavy weight feeling so delicious on her, anchoring her.

Strong hairy thighs opened her legs and he entered her with one heavy thrust.

"Ahhh." Raul let out a big breath. "God. Did I hurt you?"

Did he hurt her? She consulted her body but ... nope. The only thing she felt was heat and then she surprised herself as her vagina convulsed. It usually took her a long time to climax. So long that half the time she faked it just to get it over with. But now her body just went ahead and climaxed and oh, God, it was so delicious.

"Not hurting, no," she gasped as he lifted her legs, pressing them back so he could enter more deeply. Her head pressed back against the pillows as she kept up contracting, a climax so hard it almost hurt. Raul was kissing her neck as he started moving in her, short jabs that somehow rubbed right over her clitoris, giving her almost electric jolts of pleasure.

The thrusts were heavy now, their bellies making slapping noises, the headboard beating against her wall, faster and faster ...

She came again with a wail, vagina clenching against his penis which swelled and then he was over the edge, too, teeth clenched against a deep moan.

They stilled. Emma because she had no more energy. The tight hold she had on him with her legs and arms loosened. Her thighs fell forward and her arms fell to the bed.

She was completely undone, her body having taken over, all flesh and sensation.

Raul sprawled on her, face on her pillow, lips close to her ear.

"God," he breathed and goose pimples broke out all over her body at his lips at her ear.

"Mmm."

"My condoms are still in my pants pocket," he said sadly. "Lotta good they did us there."

"Oh. Um." Condoms. Something about condoms. So hard to think while little shocks of pleasure were still running through her body.

"I'd say I'm really sorry and I am but ... I just lost control there. Trust me when I say that never happens."

Condoms. Now she remembered. "I was having ... problems. My doctor prescribed a monthly shot which is also a contraceptive. So ... it's ok. I'm also disease-free."

She was staring up at the ceiling, eyes half closed, blinded from pleasure. But she could hear him smile.

"Oh, man. We have tests all the time. I have a clean bill of health, too. So, um ... Emma?"

She was fast falling asleep. Literally. She could feel herself fall into a deep well of darkness.

He nudged her shoulder with his. "Emma?"

"Yeah?"

"You ok?"

"Oh yeah," she breathed.

He pulled out of her partially, then slid back in. Once. Twice. She was pulling away from that deep well of darkness, back into light and heat.

"We're not done here. We have barely begun."

8

_____

"Wake up, sleepyhead," Raul said and lightly kissed Emma's cheek. It was amazingly soft, just like the rest of her. He watched as she slowly opened her eyes, taking in him, the room, the morning sun around the drawn drapes. Then she closed them again.

Not an early morning person, then.

He was. He'd been awake since dawn. Instead of jumping out of bed for a quick run or a workout in his home gym then a shower, though, he'd simply lain in bed, Emma's head on his shoulder. It felt really good, all that bright red hair spread out over his arm and chest. It still surprised him when he touched it that it was cool and not hot as flame.

He'd stayed put and listened to her breathe, stared at the ceiling and marveled at what he was feeling.

Happiness. That's what he was feeling. So odd he hadn't even recognized it at first. Life as a SEAL had never been happy. Fulfilling and challenging, yeah, but definitely not happy. Happiness wasn't the point. Then there'd been the fury and sadness of betrayal and the almost court martial and then he'd landed at ASI. He loved ASI, loved his teammates, but what he felt there wasn't what he was feeling here, right now, with this beautiful woman sleeping on his chest and ... he lifted his head a little at the sound. Yep. Snoring.

He grinned.

She was sound asleep so he figured he could get out of bed without waking her up. She didn't even stir when he made his way to the bathroom to shower. Raul rarely stayed over so he wasn't used to soap that smelled of something spicy, shampoo that smelled of something flowery and towels that smelled of lavender, but it wasn't a hardship. Considering what the barracks at the Utah outpost had smelled like. Like sweat and piss and cum.

He put on pants and shirt. They weren't fresh, but he had fresh clothes back at the hotel, and padded barefoot in the kitchen. Hmmm. She was neat. He liked that. And she had a fully stocked kitchen which he liked even more. A woman he'd dated briefly when he first arrived in Portland had had the saddest kitchen he'd ever seen. Gleaming marble, shiny, expensive stainless steel appliances and absolutely no food and no sign that the kitchen had ever been used for actual cooking.

Emma's kitchen was used, a lot. He snooped shamelessly, suddenly curious about this woman who intrigued him more than anyone he'd ever met. The fridge was full of food and leftovers. Really good leftovers, too. He hummed a little as he brought them out to the small table of the breakfast nook. Banana bread. Half an omelet. A quarter of a loaf of whole-wheat bread and salted butter. Several jams that looked home-made. Small jars, hand labelled. Strawberry, blueberry, orange and lemon. Yum. Those all went on the table. And, in a cookie jar, some real cookies, homemade. There was a big enameled bowl in bright colors filled with apples, pears and bananas on the counter. That went on the table, too.

The espresso machine was one he was familiar with, plus

there was a French press. Which would Emma prefer? Both, he decided.

Humming, he made an espresso that came out perfectly, with a little foam on top, and a big mug of French press coffee that looked dark and enticing. Putting both on a tray, he walked into the bedroom and looked down at her.

Mornings after could be hard. He'd had his share of them. Awkward silences, smudged makeup. Sometimes that awful feeling of wanting escape from a mistake.

Not this time, nope. He looked down at her, delighted with her, eager to discuss finding Toby and to find out more about her. The morning felt fresh, full of things to explore, mainly her.

He took the espresso cup and waved it under her nose. Her nostrils flared, eyes tracking right and left under her eyelids, coming up out of deep sleep. A caress of her cheek with the back of his forefinger did the rest. She opened her eyes. Women with eyes of a beautiful color had unfair advantages over everyone else. Raul's eyes were a perfectly dull dark brown, with lighter streaks. But Emma ... Some stray ray of sunlight fell across her face and lit those eyes up an unearthly shimmering blue, like two shards of ice in a summer sky.

It took her a moment to catch on. Raul watched the stages. First the blink. Looking at the coffee, steam drifting up from both cups, big and little. Gaze travelling up his arm to his face. Another blink. And suddenly she realized she was naked under the covers. Looked at his face again, remembered last night, and turned a stoplight red.

Raul imagined she hated that her fair skin signaled emotions like a billboard. His skin was dark and he never blushed. And he knew how to keep a poker face. It never betrayed anything he didn't want known.

"Hey," he said softly. "Good morning."

"Good – good morning." Sadly, when she sat up, she pulled

the duvet up over those luscious pale breasts. Raul mourned the loss briefly, but knew that he'd see the girls again as soon as humanly possible. Her head swiveled, as if looking for an exit. "I um, we um ..."

She couldn't find the words. But he could.

"We sure did." Raul bent to kiss her forehead then her luscious open mouth. "And we will again. Or at least I hope we will."

She blinked again and that lovely mouth curved in a smile. "We might."

Yesss! Raul did a mental fist pump. But alas, he'd been a SEAL and once a SEAL, always a SEAL. The unofficial SEAL motto was *do the hard thing first.* What he wanted was to crawl back into bed with her for a repeat of last night, but what they needed to do was get going to Toby's apartment.

He bent to kiss her again, lightly. Because if he gave her a real kiss, he wouldn't be able to stop. "I didn't know which kind of coffee you liked so I brought both. I'll drink whatever you don't. Plus, I raided your kitchen, which has some mighty fine stuff, and put breakfast on the table. How far is it to Toby's place?"

"About a quarter of an hour I think, if we have wheels."

Tight, but doable. "I'll have coffee and a slice of the omelet I found and go get my car at the hotel. If you can be downstairs waiting in half an hour, we can make it by nine."

She downed the espresso. "I'll have another one of these, thanks." She twirled her finger and he obligingly turned his back. He'd seen it all last night but that was at night. They would definitely get to the point where she was comfortable with being naked with him during the day, but apparently now was not that point. He could hear rustling behind him and two slim arms snaked around his waist. She squeezed. "Thanks."

He brought one of her hands to his mouth and kissed the back of it. "No problem."

Emma walked out from behind him dressed in a bathrobe, walked into the kitchen and sat down at the breakfast table. He slid another espresso in front of her and she looked up with a smile and a nod.

"Have you given a thought to what happens if Toby isn't missing but just went off grid for a while? If we walk in on him? It would be embarrassing."

Emma scrunched up her face in thought, then shook her head. "No. I've been thinking about this a lot. I think the worst thing that could happen is that the apartment's empty and we have no clue where Toby is. He was infatuated with Colin and I don't think he'd ever ghost him. Toby wouldn't ghost anyone. I think he was really sick of the mind games his family played with him. And I can't imagine him just not showing up for work without telling anyone. Toby loves his job at PIB, but above all, he loves his career. He wouldn't jeopardize it for anything. I don't think we're going to walk in on him chilling on his couch watching TV or with a new lover. I think – I think something's happened to him."

The face she turned up to his was worried, drawn. Raul erased the wrinkles between her eyebrows with his thumb. "Well, we're going to do our best to find him. And when we do, maybe he'll still have his boyfriend to come back to."

She smiled wanly. Emma was worried and Raul thought she was right to be worried. Every description of Toby was as a serious man and serious men don't disappear without a word. There were all sorts of nasty scenarios – ranging from a kidnapping to murder. Raul's job was to find him and keep Emma safe. Though now his priorities were – keep Emma safe and find Toby.

"So, I'll be in front of your building in forty-five minutes and we'll meet Colin at nine. And we'll start looking for Toby in earnest." She nodded, still looking worried. Raul dropped another kiss on her lips. Fast because she was sinfully sexy, sitting there with flame-red curls tumbling around her shoulders, the bathrobe with a sexy gap in front.

Raul was a SEAL so he had the fortitude not to look. But it wasn't easy.

Emma turned her head, soft hair shifting on her pale shoulders. "We should synchronize watches."

"How do you check the time?" he asked.

"On my cell."

"Exactly. And our cells show the same time. So, we're good. We'll go to Toby's and decide what to do afterwards. So, see you downstairs at –"

"Eight forty-five. I'll be there," she said softly.

He nodded. Yeah, she'd be there. Emma was solid.

He was used to moving fast. He caught an Uber right outside Emma's building to his hotel and changed into jeans, boots, shirt and jacket. Suitable for working. It was warm enough to be without a jacket but he wanted to be armed. He had a Glock 19 in a pancake holster. And there were more weapons in the vehicle Black Inc had made available. Upon arrival at the airport, the Black Inc office texted him the license plate of the vehicle he would use and what he could find inside. It was a pretty exhaustive list, including weapons hidden inside the door panels, and drones. Everything he might need for a mission with no parameters.

Raul had no idea what the nature of the danger might be, but where there was a lot of money involved, there were bad things and bad people. So, he was glad he was loaded for bear.

He didn't have to speed and pulled up right on time outside her building. And there she was. It had been a long time since he'd felt a rush at seeing a woman. They were going to try to find a missing man who might have been kidnapped. Serious stuff. But he had Emma at his side. Dressed in straight legged black pants, a light green cotton sweater and a dark green vest. Sneakers. Hair pulled back in a messy pony tail.

She looked good enough to eat and there was no place else in the world Raul would rather be. As she walked toward him, smiling, he leaned over and opened the passenger side door. She opened it up and bent down with a smile.

"Hey," she said.

"Hey," he answered, as something in his chest gave a hard knock.

9

"*Todo hecho.*"

    "*Bueno.*"

He had had no doubt that his man, Guillermo De la Vega, would do what had been ordered, do it well and on time. After all, he'd been a colonel in Mexico's *Fuerzas Especiales*, Special Forces. He was just as disciplined and efficient working for Marin as he'd been working for the Mexican Army. Maybe more so, since he was being paid fifty times as much as he'd earned as an officer.

He was reliable and smart. A *soldado* not a *sicario*.

Jorge Marin de Herrera put down the phone –landline conversations were less vulnerable to interception than cells – and became Blake Rutherford again. Jorge Marin was on track to accomplish perhaps the single most deadly attack on US soil in a generation while making enough money to live out the rest of his days in supreme luxury. He could possibly buy his own small country.

Blake Rutherford would continue to live his life as the last of a long line of patricians who'd been in California for generations. Thanks to his mother's genes prevailing over his father's, he very much looked like an Anglo patrician – tall, slender, fair, facial features straight out of the English peerage.

Jorge Marin de Herrera was a Mexican criminal who ran a drug cartel and whose identity was a closely held secret. He was El Quìmico, specialized in fentanyl. But across the border, he was his alter ego.

Across the border, Blake Rutherford was a respected U.S. citizen who as far as anyone knew, lived off a trust fund and had a spot on several corporate boards. It was a pity that the Rutherford money ran out in his mother's generation, and he basically inherited fair skin, fine features and dark blonde hair instead of a trust fund.

Luckily, Jorge Marin de Herrera took care of the money.

And all his men had been promised small fortunes, so they were motivated. A successful end to this 'mission', as he liked to think of it, and his men would all retire rich.

It was his secret, his superpower. The ability to think ahead to the end game. To not be distracted.

Marin leaned back in his reclining office chair, pleased with everything. He often wondered whether it was the American in him that had allowed him to look at the drug trade and realize that all the cartels and cartel bosses were doing it wrong.

So shabby and downmarket. With mindless thugs as employees. Using terror and not money to incentivize. So much money to be made and they did it in the dirtiest, bloodiest manner possible. Making the entire thing untenable in the long run. The life expectancy of the cartel bosses was short and they usually died horribly or in a cell.

So stupid.

Well, he wasn't stupid. Neither of his personas were stupid.

He was Jorge Marin de Herrera, El Quìmico, head of the Cabo Cartel, about to make a stunning financial coup and become, quietly, one of the richest men in the world.

He turned a little in his Tuscan leather office chair, on the twenty-fifth floor of the Heiman Building, head of a small successful business that would disappear on the tenth of June. As would he.

He would sell his fentanyl manufacturing business – labs and all – and retire. Not too sure where. Maybe Switzerland, where the food was good and the streets were orderly and the police protected the rich. It was an expensive country but if you had all the money in the world, it didn't matter, did it?

Marin prided himself on his speed. From gaining precious intel from a captured DEA agent to a plan to make more money than God had been the matter of a week.

And he could do it only because he had a cadre of intelligent soldados under him. And, of course, because he knew a very greedy banker.

COLIN WAS WAITING FOR THEM DOWNSTAIRS, AS PROMISED. HE was an entirely new man this morning. His eyes were less stoplight red and he'd shaved and was dressed soberly in dark pants and a light blue shirt. Above all, he'd lost that traumatized look and was now sober and serious. He looked every inch a physician.

"Hey," he said as Raul and Emma walked up to him. "I spoke with the porter and explained the situation. The porter knows me, so he's good."

"When was the last time security saw Toby?" Raul asked.

"Saturday evening, coming in. I was on night duty at the hospital and Toby said he was going to stay in and go over some work stuff. I haven't seen or heard from him since."

Raul nodded. "Can we have a look at the security tapes after we've seen Toby's apartment?"

Colin looked startled for a moment. "Ah, sure. I think so,

anyway." He thought for a moment, then nodded sharply. "Yeah. Yeah, that's a good idea. Sorry I didn't think of it first."

Raul didn't smile. "Why should you? That's not your business, it's mine. Your business is saving lives."

"Your – your business?" Colin glanced at Emma, who nodded. "Sorry?"

Emma touched his elbow. "I was really worried about Toby, Colin. So, I called in a – a friend of friends who works for a big security company. One of the best. If anyone can help us figure out where Toby is, it's Raul."

Raul had completely morphed from charming dinner companion and passionate lover into serious security guy. Everything about him was vastly reassuring. Face sober and serious, seemingly aware of everything around him, that tall broad-shouldered body ready for anything. Emma realized how safe she felt with him. How anxious she would have been searching for Toby on her own. Something about Raul made her feel that they would solve the mystery of his whereabouts, no matter what.

Poor Toby. He'd been missing for six days now. A long time if he was sick or in distress. Enough time for him to be …

Nope. Not going there.

Emma drew in a sharp breath. "Okay. Let's go on up. Colin, lead the way. I've never actually been to Toby's apartment. When we wanted to unwind, we'd have a drink at my place. Or out."

They crossed the large marble lobby, Colin nodding to the porter behind a U-shaped desk. She saw Raul's eyes flicker to a discreet plaque affixed to the side of the desk.

"Are they –"

"Yep," he said softly. "Black Home Security."

Okay. That was going to be helpful. They trooped up together. Somehow, without being in the slightest obnoxious,

Raul managed to make them feel under his protection. Even Colin looked relaxed.

Toby had chosen a really upscale apartment building which was upscale in a different way from hers. Her building was sleek, minimal. His building was ostentatious, all dark wood and brass, elaborate lighting fixtures, decorative tiles on the floors, brightly enameled planters.

He lived on the tenth floor, just off the elevators. Colin swiped a card and put his hand on the brass handle. Raul held his hand up. "No code?"

Colin shook his head and Raul pushed the back of his hand on the door.

A hallway light turned on as soon as they walked through the door. Inside, Toby had decorated his apartment fully, and Emma was ashamed of the many unopened boxes in her own place. They'd moved to San Francisco and started work within the same week. She still felt impermanent, like she could take flight any day, but Toby had put down roots. Heavy, deep ones.

Colin went to the wall to push the button to open the heavy brocade drapes but Raul stopped him. He fished out latex gloves from his jacket pocket and gave a pair to Colin and to her.

Emma and Raul put their gloves on but Colin just stood there, holding the gloves in one hand. "This might be a crime scene," Raul said gently and Colin turned pale, nodded and put the gloves on.

It *could* be a crime scene, Emma thought and sent up a quick prayer to the patron saint of funny, quirky math geniuses that Toby would be found, safe and sound, soon.

Raul stood in the center of the room, looking around. Emma could almost see the gears grinding in that handsome head of his. All his attention was directed outward, to what he could see and feel and, for all she knew, smell and taste. This was so different from her world. Most of the people she knew imported digital data into their heads and processed it. It was intriguing to watch a man process data from the real world.

Well, she corrected herself, it was intriguing to watch *this* man process data from the real world.

"Hit the button," he instructed and the heavy drapes slowly slid open. It was sunny and light flooded Toby's living room and dining room. "Okay. The curtains were closed, which means either that Toby left here – willingly or not – while it was dark or very early in the morning." He kneeled, looked at the lush nap of the living room rug. "Looks like boot prints, several of them."

Raul began a systematic search, clearly working on a grid. Colin stood still where he was, by the window, looking stressed. Emma moved to the kitchen, which was pristine – Toby once said he couldn't cook – and entered the large corridor that, like in her own apartment, would lead to bedrooms and studies. She stared at the flooring, beige ceramic tiles.

"Raul," she said quietly. He looked up and came quickly to her side. She pointed a shaking finger at the ground and the baseboard.

Blood.

Blood in elongated teardrop shapes. Not great gory stripes but definitely blood.

"Not arterial, thank God," Colin said. He'd come up behind them. "Arterial blood splashes in a very specific way."

Raul nodded. They followed the blood trail into the master bedroom. Raul and Colin both followed the trail to a spot near the bed where blood had soaked the carpet. They were going to be better at this than she could be, so she wandered around Toby's bedroom, trying to understand what had happened.

The bed was unmade, big gold green duvet thrown back, gold pillows strewn about the bed. A marble and wood bedside table held a lamp on its side, an Echo, two books in disarray and a third on the carpet.

"He'd been asleep, or at least in bed," she said. Both Raul and Colin were hunkered down studying the bloodstain, but both looked up at her. "Toby was pretty neat. He told me once that he literally couldn't leave a bed unmade because he'd been beaten as a child if he didn't make his bed. He wouldn't leave the bed unmade. Whoever took him, dragged him out of bed."

"Early in the morning, or at night?" Raul wondered.

"Alexa. What was your last command?" Emma asked the air.

Alexa's eerie voice answered, "My last command was 'Play lo-fi music.'"

"When was the command given?"

"The command was given at midnight oh five."

"Taken at night, then." Raul stood, looked around. "They dragged him out of bed. He put up a fight and they must have clocked him one, badly enough for him to lose blood. But not enough blood loss to be dangerous, right Colin?"

"Right." Colin was pale but composed. "No major blood loss, but if it was a head injury, he might be concussed."

God, I hope not, Emma thought.

"There were two guys," Raul said grimly. "One wearing a size eleven boot and one wearing a size thirteen boot."

"Big guys," Colin said. His jaw muscles were working. "Toby weighs 140 pounds. It was no contest."

"No," Raul said. "And kidnappers tend to be armed."

Emma shot a warning glance at Raul but he'd turned away. But then again, Colin was an emergency room doctor. He'd probably seen more bullet and knife wounds than she'd had hot meals. And they had to be realistic if they had any hope of finding Toby.

"They took Toby's computer, I think." she said. She'd been subconsciously looking for it in the living room. It wasn't in the bedroom. "Let me check."

There were two other rooms in Toby's apartment, one set

up as a study and another as a guest bedroom. She checked the rooms, the closets and the two bathrooms, then walked back into the bedroom.

Emma touched Raul's arm. "Yeah, his computer's missing. All his devices are. He has a couple of iPads and two normal laptops and I can't find them. And there's one he always has with him. It's a beta prototype someone gave him, with revolutionary software. It's unmistakable, with a swirly purple and cream cover. I can't find it anywhere."

Raul thought for a moment. "Would it be easy for just anyone to operate?"

"God no. It took him a couple of days to tool around it and familiarize himself with the operating system. And anyway, he'd have very good security. His tablets are all password and thumbprint protected."

"Then they need to keep him alive if he has actionable intel on that computer."

Actionable intel.

"Yeah. I hadn't thought of it that way, but yeah." A breath she hadn't realized she was holding whooshed out. Colin looked relieved. Then he frowned. "Unless they try – they try to torture it out of him."

Raul's face tightened, but he said nothing. "Okay, let's finish checking the place. Notice what should be there but isn't. Or something that's there but he should have taken with him. Basically, just take notice of anything unusual."

They let Colin take the bedroom. Emma took the study and the bathrooms and Raul took the living room and the kitchen. After half an hour they met in the living area.

"Okay, sitrep," she announced and smiled sweetly at Raul's raised eyebrows. "I love thrillers. Colin, you go first."

"The suitcases I'm aware of are all still in his closet and it doesn't look like any clothes are missing. The hanging clothes have been swept to one side. I imagine they were looking for hidden panels, but this place doesn't have anything like that. They checked the drawers of the nightstands but it doesn't look like anything was taken. The same for the drawers of his dresser. He's neat and the contents of the drawers were disturbed, so they searched them. No way of knowing if they took anything, but I doubt it." His mouth tightened. "I did find some blood on the sheets. I think they might have hit him while he was sleeping."

"And dragged him out of bed," Emma said, appalled at the picture in her head. Two men breaking into her friend's apartment, striking him while he was asleep and dragging him, bleeding, away.

Time for her report. "Both bathrooms are intact, his travel trousse is on the sink counter, toothbrush is in its holder. In his study, I found two old tablets but not the laptops, and as I said, not his special one. Like Colin said, I think they checked the contents of his desk drawers and the closets. In the living room, everything is intact. It wasn't a robbery, that's for sure. Besides the electronics, there's a really expensive TV, a bunch of silver frames and those two framed lithographs on the wall are a Matisse and a Giacometti. Originals. I remember when he bought them. Nothing of value besides his electronics was taken. Is his wallet here?"

"Yes," Raul said. "I found it in an enameled jar on a table near the door. His wallet and a slim leather holder with four credit cards. Inside the wallet was about two hundred dollars. And there were the keys to the house."

"He emptied – empties his pockets the instant he comes in the door," Colin said softly. "He says he likes to get rid of the day as soon as possible."

"What about his car?" Emma asked. "He's got the latest model of the Elektrica, that electric car. He loves that thing. It doesn't have a key but it's got a card."

Raul strode over to the enamel bowl and stared down. "No cards. Just credit cards in his wallet."

"Should we go down to the garage to see if his car has been taken?"

"No need." Raul picked up the intercom and pressed five. It had a little printed legend, Lobby. "Hi. This is Raul Martinez. We just spoke. Do you have video cameras in the garage? Yes, excellent. Can you check to see if Toby Jackson's Elektrica is in its parking slot? Yeah, I'll wait." Raul held the receiver against his chest. "We should also ask if we can see footage of the night he was kidnapped. Sunday."

Emma drew in a breath. "Um. Really not necessary to ask. I can, um, find out more quickly than he can, probably. I could have found out if his car is in the garage, too."

Raul looked at her. "By 'find out', do you mean hack?"

"Um. Yeah."

"Excellent. Yes." He straightened as the security guy in the lobby came back on the line. "No? Thank you very much. So –" He took in a deep breath. "The car's gone. I imagine that one of the guys drove it away. Probably to make anyone looking for Toby think that he'd taken an unexpected trip. I don't think they imagined anyone would actually come here, to Toby's apartment. Not too sure how to find Toby. Hack into the traffic cams during a period we think he might have been taken but that's not going to be easy if it was nighttime."

Emma had seated herself on the couch, her laptop on the coffee table. Her laptop didn't have the visual flair Toby's did but it was pretty cool. "I have an idea about how to track down Toby's car, but before that, I think we can say that Toby was taken at 3 a.m. Tuesday night. And we can say that sort of by default because that's when the security cam system in the building was hacked."

"Wow." Raul sat beside her, shaking his head. "I can't

believe a system set up by Black Home Security would be hack-able by anyone outside the system. I'll have to tell them."

Emma did a little digging. "Well, your precious Black Home Security's cred is safe. The condo management must have decided on lobby staff and door locks from Black Home Security but decided that the video security system from Black was too expensive and opted for a cheaper system." She looked up and gave a little smile. "Penny wise and pound foolish, as the Brits say. I expect the Black video security system would have been harder to hack into than this one, which was like punching your way into a paper bag."

"Black Home Security videos are absolutely unhackable," Raul bristled. He was incredibly cute when he was miffed, dark eyebrows drawn over dark eyes, jaw clenched. The thing was, there was very little that was unhackable, but she didn't say so, just made a little humming noise.

"So, the Elektrica seems to be a pretty neat vehicle. I don't have a car and was looking into it because Toby was so pleased with his. One of the things he loved about it, since he was, as he said, 'mechanically challenged', was that the company took care of routine maintenance. They would schedule check-ups for you and if you couldn't make it, a company mechanic would pick your car up, take it to their operations center, check every-thing, and drive the car back. It's in the sales contract. And one of the things they do is keep track of tire pressure. One of their selling points is that you'd have to drive over spikes in the road to get a flat tire, because since they monitor tire pressure, you know when you're about to get a flat."

Emma sat back, pleased. Raul and Colin shared a puzzled glance.

She sighed. "Don't you see? To transmit data, there has to be a transponder which –"

"Which can be tracked," Raul said.

"Exactly." She turned her laptop around so both Raul and

Colin could see it. "So, I have Toby's last location." In the search field was a long line of GPS coordinates.

"Where is that?" Colin peered closely at her screen.

Raul was trying to do calculations in his head, but he didn't have to do that. A moment with her GPS app and she had the site. "That is at 22645 Ross Way. I have no idea where that is, I haven't lived here long enough. Let me check a map."

"I know where it is." Colin tapped the map with a tear drop over a specific point. Emma still couldn't figure out where it was since she didn't recognize anything on the map. "It's in a bedroom community outside the city limits. That's a road that winds up into the hills and it's a very wealthy area. I once looked at a property in that area and there is nothing under five million dollars. It would be more now."

"Well, that's weird." Emma started another search and came up with a Facebook page. "It belongs to a Russell Stewart, a lawyer specializing in corporate law, especially franchise law. Living just outside Philadelphia." She tilted her head as she studied the Facebook page then clicked through to a website that turned out to be the website of his law firm. Wolper, Wolper and Stewart. The law firm was busy, litigating seventy-five big lawsuits in the past twelve months, Russell Stewart being lead counsel for most of them. All of the trials held in the Philadelphia area. She tilted her head the other way, trying to make sense of this.

"I'll see how many other properties this Stewart owns. Maybe they are all rental properties."

"High end ones," Colin said.

"Yeah. Maybe that's his investment portfolio."

Emma dug. "I think it is. He has eighteen similar properties scattered throughout the country, mostly in popular expensive cities. San Francisco, San Diego, Los Angeles, Chicago, Boulder, Boston and New York. The properties are managed by something called Sundial Property Management and he is –" she tooled around a little, "he is the majority owner, but has a manager. Leyla Cartwright, lives in Philadelphia, and whoa. She's his wife. All in the family. The average rental is $10,000 a week. He's making more from his real estate business than he is from lawyering. Wow."

"Wait a minute." Raul reached out and turned her laptop around. His eyes widened when he saw the initials at the top of the page. IRS. "Jesus, Emma, you hacked into *Internal Revenue*?"

She sighed. So many people had small minded views about data acquisition. Data wanted to be free. "Well …"

He pushed his hands against the air, as if pushing away some thoughts. "Great," he declared. "I'm all for getting as much intel as you can as fast as you can. And you're the fastest I've ever seen. Faster even than Felicity and Hope and I thought they were the Usain Bolt of data."

Emma waved away the compliment. "I'm not faster than Felicity and Hope. I'm just more used to getting economic data. It's what I do."

This time Raul's eyes bugged. "You hack into the IRS for a living? How –" he waved his hand. "Never mind. Don't want to know. Just grateful you're on the side of the good guys. So, is Toby's car still there?"

She switched screens. "Yes. Hasn't moved since Sunday night. Which I think means he is still there." She didn't even want to think of him not being where his car was because that could mean that – Nope. Not going there. Not not not.

Raul drummed his gloved fingers once, hard, on the glass surface of the coffee table. "Colin, you know the area. How far is it from here?"

Colin frowned. "Depending on the traffic, I'd say between forty-five minutes to an hour."

"Okay, we'll let you know what we find out –"

Colin stood abruptly. "Oh no. If you think you're going

without me, you're crazy. Apart from anything else, Toby was wounded. I'm a doctor, in case you've forgotten."

Raul clearly wasn't happy with the idea. "I haven't forgotten. It's just that I don't know what we'll find."

"Exactly." Colin nodded sharply.

"And I don't know what it will take to get to Toby. I'm not happy with Emma being with me, either, but I'm even more unhappy with the thought of leaving her behind. I've had medic training, don't worry about that."

"Fine if Toby's got a bullet wound." Colin rolled his eyes. He stood straight, shoulders back, feet set apart, as if ready for Raul to knock him to the ground. He was an emergency room physician and you don't get to be one of those if you are easily discouraged or lose your nerve easily, Emma thought. "Though I see about three bullet wounds a day on duty. At least. But suppose he's concussed? Severely dehydrated? Been drugged? Could you tell the difference? I won't be in your way. If there's any fighting to be done, I'll definitely leave that to you because you're trained and I'm not. But I've been trained in medical emergencies which are not bullet wounds. Not only that, I care for Toby and you don't. You've never even met him. Toby's a means to an end for you, but for me he's someone dear to my heart. I have a right to be there if Toby is being held a prisoner and needs help."

Emma could quite literally see Raul vacillating, something she imagined didn't happen often. That handsome head was weighing the pros and cons, bouncing around in his brain. Colin clearly wasn't someone who would be helpful in a fight, if it was a fight that awaited them. But he *was* an emergency physician, if immediate medical aid was necessary. Walk through Door Number One and you'd have deadweight in an emergency, and Emma was already deadweight. Walk through Door Number Two, and you could conceivably have a wounded Toby dying in their arms for want of immediate medical care.

Colin stood there, arms across his chest, clearly not going to take no for an answer. Raul did the right thing.

"All right." Raul sighed. "I'll go get my vehicle which has some equipment we might need. Emma will come with me. You have the GPS coordinates, but it would be best if you follow me. We'll stage off site."

Emma didn't really know what that meant but if there was one thing she'd learned in the money market, it was to follow the experts because they always had inside information. Being wrong about the financial experts could make you lose money but being wrong about Raul could make you lose your life.

She batted that thought away immediately. There was something about Raul that made her trust him, instinctively. Unlike most experts, he didn't glide through life smugly, convinced he knew best. Though he'd worked in the most elite team of soldiers in the world and was undoubtedly competent in a number of fields, there was no celebration of self, no posturing. Just quiet efficiency.

She was in good hands.

All of a sudden, an image of those hands on her, stroking her breasts, holding her hips, flashed through her and she could feel herself going stoplight red.

Thank God no one noticed. Raul was making the rounds of the apartment on a last-minute check and Colin was quivering in place, staring at his watch, impatient to get going.

Five minutes later, Emma was alone in the two-story atrium, looking out over busy Post Street. She was sitting on a raffia leather-covered bench, with her laptop out, calculating the best route to the address where Toby's car was. Maybe Toby, too. She copied the route on to her cell, which pinged just as Raul pulled up. While walking out of the building, Colin pulled up behind Raul. Colin's car was electric, sleek, sky blue, completely silent.

Fumes were coming out of the exhaust pipe in Raul's

Escalade, and she felt like he was driving the twentieth century and Colin and Toby the twenty-first. On the other hand, for some reason, she couldn't see inside Raul's SUV at all, the windows weren't tinted rap-star black, either. Very cool. Particularly since Colin's windows were all completely transparent and his scowling face and anxiously drumming fingers on the steering wheel were clear as day.

"Cool windows," she said when she was seated in the vehicle and they took off. "Couldn't see inside at all. Usually that happens when they are tinted illegally dark and you're a rock star or drug dealer."

Raul shot her a glance. His hands were easy on the steering wheel, movements smooth and efficient. He was a good driver, even in a city that wasn't his. If Emma could avoid driving at all, she did. She'd moved so much that having a car was a handicap, and in most of the cities she'd lived in the public transportation was so good driving was silly. Or where public transportation was bad, taxis were cheap.

"It's a special film that lets in light but doesn't allow anyone to see inside. We all use it to coat the windows of our homes, too. Or at least those who own their homes. But the SUV's tricks don't stop there. It's a James Bond car, got lots of special features."

A billion movies and thrillers shot through her mind. She turned in her seat excitedly. "Oh man, don't tell me, let me guess."

"Okay." Somehow Raul had perfected the art of paying close attention to a conversation while also paying close attention to driving. Something she herself had never managed. Once in Boston with a colleague who'd done a study of the Mumbai Sensex, she'd driven her car in a ditch. Luckily a very shallow one, but still. Her colleague was still angry at her.

"Let me think. Can it fly?"

He gave an easy smile. "No."

"Does it have like a power assisted engine so you can super-charge it and go at 200 mph?"

"Yep. But just 150 mph."

"Oh." She blinked. She'd been semi joking. "Ahem, does it have headlights that fold back into the chassis and machine gun barrels come out?"

"Not quite, but close. More yes than no."

Wow. Okay. "Does it have its own ventilation system like the president's, so that if you drive through poisoned air, the air doesn't penetrate?"

"Nope. That kind of system adds considerably to the weight of the vehicle. It would be counterproductive. But it is armored and has bullet resistant windows."

"Huh. My imagination is running out of gas. What else does it have?"

"Well, Black Inc is pretty well equipped. There's a small arsenal in the trunk, it has a sat phone just in case we go to a place that doesn't have wifi coverage. Spike strips. Run flat tires. It's good to go."

"It certainly is." Emma couldn't remember ever being in such a comfortable vehicle. Incredibly smooth and incredibly quiet. It looked like a standard SUV but felt like some expensive European car made for royalty. She looked around, out of those specially tinted windows. They were starting to climb. She glanced at the GPS map on the monitor. "I think we're nearly there."

"Uh huh." Raul pulled smoothly to the curb and saw in his rearview mirror that Colin had pulled in too. "It's around that curve and about half a mile up the road."

Emma simply looked at him, confident that he knew what he was doing.

Colin rapped at the window, looking tense and worried. Raul buzzed his window down. "I know the house is just up the road. But we can't walk in blind," he said before Colin could open his mouth.

In a moment, Raul opened the back of the vehicle where there were four big plastic cases and one smaller one. He opened the smaller one, pulled out two strange looking metallic things about as large as his fist. Underneath was a ruggedized laptop which he pulled out as well.

He pulled at elements of the metallic things and she instantly recognized what they were. "Drones," she breathed. Exactly what they needed.

"Yeah." Raul opened up the laptop and she nudged him out of the way with her hip.

"This is my domain."

He held his hands up and stepped back. Emma placed the laptop on the top of one of the large plastic containers, essentially turning the back of the vehicle into a makeshift office. She quickly ran through the program, familiarizing herself with the commands and features. In the foam casing holding the drones was a joystick. She picked it up, relishing the familiar feel of it in her hands. She'd spent thousands of hours operating joysticks. This one was simple and fit well in her hand.

First things first. The drone lifted quietly and hovered above them. Emma saw that it had a range of fifty kilometers and could operate for five hours without recharging. A text said that with the addition of small, powerful solar panels, the autonomy could be extended in daylight to twelve hours.

Neat. She brought the drone down gently.

She turned and saw Raul's face. "What?"

"That is –" He cleared his throat. "It took us two morning seminars to master use of the drone software and guidance system."

"Well, frankly, it was pretty straightforward. Do you trust me with the joystick?"

"Absolutely." Raul said fervently. "You're much better at it than I am. But follow my directions."

"Sure." Made sense to her. He would know where to send the drone and she knew how to send the drone. Partnership. "Let's start now."

She toggled the joystick and the drone rose back up easily, hovering in the air like some gigantic hummingbird. It was eerily silent.

"Got some excellent noise abatement there," she said as she sent the drone up, down, to the right, to the left. Its movements were smooth, almost graceful. "If we're careful, no one will know it's there."

Raul shook his head. "First time I tried this particular model, I crashed it. You're making it fly like a bird."

She smiled. "What can I say? I have an affinity for tech."

"An understatement. So, switch on the cameras."

A second later, the tablet pinged to life. The image was hi-def, very clear. There were two images. One from a minicam in the belly showing images it flew over and one mounted higher up that showed the path ahead. Emma practiced enlarging first one then the other. The images remained crystal clear. This was top rate gear.

"What do you want, the belly eye view or the forward view?"

"Forward."

"Forward it is."

She touched the controls and the drone shot up and disappeared over the trees. But everyone was watching the monitor, including a fascinated-looking Colin. The drone was zippy, so it was at the coordinates in no time. They'd flown over three large estates, all lawns and pools and red tile roofs. Nobody seemed to be home in any of the estates except for one gardener. A small insert in the upper right-hand corner of the monitor showed GPS coordinates.

"You're close, maybe you should slow down," Raul said, unhelpfully.

She shot him a glance and he held his palms up. "Sorry."

He should be. As if she didn't realize that stealth was required now.

"Do the cameras have IR?"

"Yep."

"Can you get me my laptop? I left it in the truck."

"Sure." Raul loped over to the front of the Black Inc vehicle and came back with her laptop.

She opened it up, got the floor plans she'd found earlier on the drive over and set her screen next to the monitor. "Okay. So, what we have here is the floor plan of the house, the one that was authorized. I have no way of knowing if changes were made, but it will at least give us an idea."

"Smart thinking." Raul flipped through the schematics and she could see he got a good grasp of the house. Better than her, probably. She wasn't good spatially. "Okay. Rise up high and let's get a bird's eye view. A drone's eye view. Slowly. Movement captures the eye."

She lifted the drone slowly until it was about fifty feet high, high enough that the camera could take in the entire estate in one glance. It wasn't a huge lot, and was mostly filled with a monstrous McMansion, bloated in the middle. The house had about five feet of dusty lawn all around it from the house to a stucco wall encircling the property. She took the drone around the perimeter, dropping very quickly to see under a portico.

"There," she said softly, even though they were so far away her voice couldn't possibly carry. Sitting on a wicker armchair was a guard. He was dressed in black. A weapon was slung across the arms of the other wicker armchair. He was smoking, and an ashtray full of stubs was on the wicker coffee table. She lifted the drone up immediately.

"I saw him," Raul's voice was soft, too. "Armed, but a moron.

His weapon isn't in easy reach. Switch on thermal imaging. Let's see who else is in there."

Emma switched to thermal and again ran the perimeter of the house, only with the cameras turned inward. "Gotcha," she said softly as the fiery outline of a person appeared. She checked the floor plan. "He's in the kitchen."

All three of them put their heads together watching as the fiery figure, trailing wisps of red, moved around the kitchen. Not cooking so much as pulling things out of the fridge and nuking them. No signs of weapons but the thermal imagery wouldn't pick up on them. While the red figure had its back to the window, Emma placed the drone outside the window and switched on regular vision.

Whoever built the house didn't even think of cloaking the windows. Emma resolved then and there to try to have her windows always cloaked. It was eerie looking inside this house.

The man in the kitchen wasn't overly tall but was very broad, with the kind of muscles that looked impressive but probably got in his way. Gym muscles, totally unlike Raul's lean panther-like build. Dark haired, longer on top, shaved along the sides. Tattoo sleeves on his arms. Tee shirt a size too small to show off those pecs that almost needed a bra. On the counter was a gun and a cellphone. She didn't recognize the gun but she recognized the cell. It was good, expensive. She glanced briefly at Raul. He was going to have to take these men down without them drawing their weapons or reaching for their cells.

If he was worried, he didn't show it.

"Go to the roof," he said softly. "Use thermal."

The drone covered the roof in a grid. And on the southwest corner room they hit the jackpot. A man, lying down on a bed. One hand stretched over his head.

Without being asked, Emma directed the drone to the window of the southwest corner room. Colin was bending so close to the screen, his nose was almost touching it. She gently pushed at his shoulder and he moved back. But he was fixed on the screen.

"Damn." Raul let out a small breath of exasperation. Venetian slats covered the window. "We really need to see inside."

"Let me see what I can do." Emma focused tightly, sending thanks up above for the thousands and thousands of hours she'd spent gaming. She wielded a joystick like a surgeon wielded a scalpel.

First, she ran the drone as close to the window as she could without crashing it. But there wasn't much to be seen, except that the room was in semi-darkness. She pulled away, angled to the right side of the slats. There was a gap, but nothing to be seen except dark wall and ... she zoomed in.

A mirror. Angled to catch the bed with someone on it.

Colin took in a deep breath.

There, unmistakably, was Toby, lying on his side. He was unmoving, eyes closed. The outstretched arm was because his hand was handcuffed to a bedpost. Emma studied his chest. *Please God,* she prayed. *Let him be alive.*

"Goddamn." Colin's voice was shaky. "Is he – is he ... yes! He's breathing! Oh my God, he's *alive*! Let's go!"

Raul's hand shot out and grabbed his arm. "Not so fast. I understand how you want to go to him, but we need to neutralize those two body guards and I'm the best one to do that. We can't give them a chance to notify whoever paid to have him kidnapped and whoever is paying for those guards. We won't be doing Toby any favors by rushing in and alerting the bad guys. They might even have instructions to eliminate him if they are discovered. So, we have to do this quiet and we have to do it smart. We on the same page here?"

Colin struggled briefly with himself but gave in. Raul was right. Rushing in wouldn't help Toby. The only one who could rescue him was Raul. Emma would be hopeless in anything resembling a fight, let alone a firefight and Colin didn't look built for a fight, either. Right now, he was trembling head to toe, arms wrapped around his middle.

Emma was a little shaky, too.

Raul sure wasn't. His movements were swift and sure. From the back of his vehicle, he removed a bullet proof vest, a handgun and a holster, a baton, restraints and two pre-loaded syringes.

"Those are...?" Emma nodded to the syringes.

"I hope they are filled with cyanide." Colin's voice was vicious. "They hurt and kidnapped Toby!"

"Colin, you're a doctor and you're sworn to heal," Emma told him, then turned to Raul. "You can't kill them," she said seriously.

Raul splayed a large hand over his heart. "I won't. I won't even dent them, if everything goes right. They won't even know I've been there. It's Rohypnol, will put them out and they won't have any memory of it."

"Date rape drug," Colin nodded.

"Hmm. No intention of raping them," Raul said. "But they need to wake up and find Toby gone and not understand how it happened. Honey, can you kill their video feeds? Where we're parked there are no cameras. But we can't leave any way to trace back to us."

"Sure. And I'll set up a loop so they won't even know when it happened. How long will they be out?"

Raul checked the syringes. "Colin, 1 mg of flunitrazepam. How long will they be out?"

Colin's jaw tightened. "At least five to six hours. Depending on body mass."

"Great. Okay, Emma, can you?"

"On it. Video feed all along the street down. I sent a mirror drone feed to your cell so keep it out."

Raul gave her a big smack on the mouth. "My girl. We're a great team."

She barely had time to turn red and he was gone. But he was right. They were a great team.

Colin hadn't noticed. He was pacing up and down by the side of the vehicles.

She sighed and stared at the drone feed as Raul went to rescue her friend.

10

Raul loved the night.

Like most SEALs, he operated best under cover of darkness. If he'd had the choice, he'd have waited for the early hours of the morning to raid the house, knowing most people's defenses were at their lowest at about 3 a.m. But his hand was being forced. No way to know what the guards' instructions were regarding Toby. They could be ordered to get rid of him at any moment. Toby needed to be rescued now. Right now. Murphy's Law dictated that it be in broad daylight. Mr. Murphy always had his say.

But still, he didn't anticipate too many difficulties.

SEALs trained and trained hard to maintain situational awareness at all times of the day and night but these jokers didn't seem to be the sharpest tools in the drawer. They were essentially goofing off. Even two to one was no contest.

He made his way quickly down the street. It took him a minute studying his cell to realize what Emma had done. She'd traced a map of his trip according to the neighbors' vidcams she'd disabled. As soon as he passed the field of vision of the cams, they'd turn back on. The homeowners would have to be staring straight at the monitors to realize they'd been turned off for a moment and, if anything, would write it off as a glitch.

Having Emma along on a mission was amazing. God. She should join ASI and work with Hope and Felicity at making the life of ASI operators better, safer. Yeah.

For a moment Raul stopped and listened to himself.

Oh God yes! Emma in Portland, working for ASI. Yes yes yes! He knew perfectly well that workplace romances were frowned on, but Hope and Luke and Felicity and Metal made it work. Mainly it worked because Hope and Felicity were so great.

Emma was great, too, just like them. Super smart without being obnoxious. And she was beautiful, there was that. But not beautiful in a high maintenance kind of way. Raul had dated a model once and it had been like dating an Irish setter. Lovely to look at but dumb as a rock, and very high maintenance. The instant he was out of bed, he wanted to escape. It wasn't like that at all with Emma. As great as they were in bed, he loved being with her out of bed, too.

If she was in Portland, working for ASI, he could see her *every day*. Man. ASI gave its new employees use of a studio apartment and his own house wasn't far from the ASI place. He could see her every day after work, too. Sex and smarts. And she was nice. She cared enough about her colleague to be doing all of this. She was very good friends with two of the finest women he knew.

He needed to grab on fast.

She was a woman in a million. She was –

"Raul." Her voice was in his ear. Was she telepathic? What the fuck? "Raul, you're veering too far from the path I set. There are some peripheral cameras that could catch you."

Fuck. He had on earbuds and she was telling him nicely to get his head out of his ass. "Copy that." And he wrenched his mind away from Emma and on to the mission.

Not often he had to do that. He was intensely mission-oriented all the time. All SEALs were. Emma was messing with his head.

"You're almost there," she murmured. She must have been worried that he'd had an attack of idiocy.

He couldn't let on that the team leader had had his head up his ass. So, he just repeated, "Copy that."

He was about ready to ask for the drone to confirm that the outside guard hadn't moved, when she flew the drone over the rooftop and down the side of the house, without moving into view of the terrace. The drone switched to IR and yep, Asshole 1 was still sitting in the lounge chair. He hadn't moved except to get a bottle of something. The bottle was on the round table next to the lounge chair.

Raul hoped it was beer. No special operator he knew would ever *ever* drink alcohol while on a job.

But he didn't underestimate taking the joker down. It had to be done fast and completely silently, without giving him a chance to sound the alarm. He scaled the stucco wall easily and dropped silently to the dead grass.

'All war is deception.' Sun Tzu. Who also said to 'stomp the grass to scare the snake'.

"Emma, send the drone in fast toward the man's face from his right." Raul was on his left. He subvocalized into the mike, knowing the sound wouldn't carry more than half a meter.

"Copy that," she answered. And she did it just right. The drone was silent enough but any noise would carry in the silence of the afternoon, so she went in fast. By the time Asshole 1 realized he was hearing something, it was too late.

The drone zipped out from the terrace roof and flashed to the guy's face. All he'd perceive is something dark, moving fast toward him. He shifted toward the drone, flailing his arms and Raul was behind him in a second, putting him in a chokehold.

Chokeholds were great. Raul loved them. They downed an enemy without blood or guts being spilled. He was really tempted to make the chokehold last long enough to make the douchebag's unconsciousness permanent, but after a moment, he relented and left the man on the ground, head lolling. He jabbed him with the preloaded syringe and put restraints on his wrists and ankles and tied ankles to wrists.

He stepped up, looking at his handiwork. Bad guy # 1, restrained. He took the man's Glock 19 and stuck it in his waistband. Weapon, removed. Using his foot, he turned Asshole 1 over and took several shots of his face and sent them to Emma.

"Can you send those to Hope and Felicity for ID?" he asked Emma.

She clucked her tongue. "Please."

He had no idea what she meant until his cell flashed a photo ID badge. Martin Safire. Currently employed at Sierra Security Solutions, a security company based in LA that had a bad rep. Not that its agents were bad at what they did, but that it was a company that was willing to stretch the limits of what it was willing to do.

The other guard was probably also Sierra Security Solutions, which recruited from the military. Two former soldiers guarding a financial analyst. That wasn't good.

"Going after the second one," he subvocalized.

"Roger that," she answered quietly. Raul grinned. She really did read a lot of thrillers.

The drone made the round of the house, lifting up over windows, then dropping back down to skim the side of the house. The kitchen was on the other side of the mansion. The drone stopped outside the kitchen in IR mode. Asshole # 2 was eating, just finishing up. Raul imagined that his task would be to guard Toby, and the other asshole was supposed to guard the perimeter.

He had to act fast. It would be standard procedure for the two to check in on each other periodically. They were sloppy but if that was protocol, they'd follow it. Raul had to take

Asshole # 2 down before he alerted to the fact that something was wrong. The element of surprise was his best weapon here.

Fiery Asshole #2 stepped away from the table holding something. Something cold and inert which didn't show on IR. No points for guessing a weapon. He was armed, but then so was Raul.

"Emma, show me –"

He didn't even finish the sentence and the mansion's floor plan was on the screen of his cell. He absorbed the plan and waited. If the man went to the left, he would take a route to the right. If he went to the right, Raul would take a route to the left. Either way, he could see how to stage outside the room Toby was in and how to get there before the guard.

The guard went left.

The door to the back was unlocked, which was bad tactics. No doubt they thought themselves super safe and keeping the door unlocked made it easier for them. ASI would have kicked out any operator who made such a sloppy mistake. In the Teams, that would have been enough to have you kicked out.

Raul kicked the guy trussed on the ground just to make sure he was still out. Not even his eyelids moved.

He eased himself into the house, quiet and fast, and stood with his back to the wall, at the corner where the bedrooms began. Unfortunately, the bedroom where Toby was being held was two doors down. It was going to be tricky.

Asshole # 2 came walking down from the end of the corridor. Emma had put the IR image back on his phone so Raul could follow. Asshole # 2 walked to the room Toby was in, opened the door, checked on Toby, closed the door. Toby hadn't moved in all this time.

"Emma," he murmured. "Create a distraction."

Almost instantly a loud thump came from the wall at the end of the corridor. Asshole # 2's head swiveled and he started walking toward the sound. It was all Raul needed. He was fast when he needed to be. In under a second, he was behind the man with his baton swinging to the back of his head. He didn't hit hard enough to break skin but enough to ring his bell. Another chokehold and syringe and the man sagged in Raul's arms. He eased him to the ground and trussed him up like he'd done with Asshole # 1. He took a photograph and sent it to Emma.

"Going in to Toby now. Don't see other heat signatures, you guys are good to come in. I found the house system. The gates and the front door will be open. I'm going to go to Toby."

"We're on our way." Emma's voice was ragged. She was running.

Raul slipped into the room where Toby was being held. He stood by the bed for a moment, letting anger flash through him at the sight of the young man shackled to a bed. He had a badly bandaged head wound. His face was waxy pale and drawn. The one arm that was handcuffed had blood around the handcuff where he'd tried and failed to wrench himself free.

He looked like a hostage in a terrorism video, a young man kidnapped and tormented, basically because he was too smart.

Raul hated this. Hated the fact that the thugs of the world thought they could punish the smart and the bright because thugs weren't afraid of using violence. Well, neither was he.

He'd gloved up because he wanted the fuckheads who'd done this to wake up to find their hostage gone and no clue at all as to what had happened.

The first thing was to unshackle Toby, give him back some dignity, even if he was unconscious. Luckily Raul had received extensive and expensive lessons on how to do this, courtesy of Uncle Sam. In a moment, the handcuff was open and Toby's arm fell to the bed. He moaned, the pain reaching down past the drugs he'd been given. If he'd been handcuffed for four days, it was lucky he hadn't dislocated his shoulder.

Raul put a hand on Toby's other shoulder and gently shook him. "Toby. Toby. Can you wake up?"

The eyes under Toby's eyelids tracked right and left. He moaned again, sighed.

The door slammed against the wall as Colin rushed in, carrying a doctor's bag, followed by Emma.

"Toby!" he cried.

Well, the cavalry had arrived. Raul stepped back. Colin's gloved hands were assured as he efficiently checked Toby for further injuries, the steady hands of a surgeon. Quickly, he checked Toby's blood pressure, opened his eyes and checked the pupils, counted heartbeats. Toby's eyes stayed open of their own accord, unfocused, mouth slack. Suddenly, he blinked and seemed to realize what he was seeing.

"C-Colin?" Toby's voice was a hoarse whisper, raw and filled with hope. "It's you? Oh my God, it's you! You came!" He let out a great, wrenching sob.

"Oh, honey." Colin's face melted. "Of course, I came." He bent and hugged Toby who leaned his head against Colin's shoulder and started crying.

Toby had been through a lot and Colin had been worried sick. Raul met Emma's eyes and they turned their backs on the couple, to give them a private moment.

Emma leaned so close to him that she was practically in his embrace. He didn't want to cry but he did want to kiss her. Later. There'd be plenty of time for that later.

"So." Emma's voice was barely above a whisper. "Those guys work for a security company. Like yours. That's pretty heavy ammunition to point at Toby."

It was.

"It's not like my company. Sierra's known for cutting corners and they hire people who would do anything if the price is right. But you're right. Toby must be really dangerous to someone if he – or she – is willing to sic a security company known for its lax morals on him. I hope he's capable of reporting what it is he found. I don't know what they pumped in him."

"We will know," said Colin, and they both turned around to see Colin untying the tourniquet around Toby's arm, and putting a plastic stopper on a beaker. He held the beaker full of blood up. "I came prepared. I know a lab where they can analyze this in less than an hour and tell us what they shot Toby up with."

Toby's head hung loosely. "Shots," he mumbled. "Lots of shots."

Colin's arm tightened around his shoulders. "I know, honey, I know. But Raul and Emma are going to find them and make them pay."

"Damn right," Raul muttered. The fuckers. "Colin, we can debrief later. I'm anxious to get Toby out of here, as soon as we can."

Toby's features tightened with alarm. He was still slurring his words, but some clarity was coming back with each passing moment. "Out! Oh God yes, get me out of here!" He grabbed onto Colin's shirt sleeve. "Don't take me to the hospital! They'll find me! I couldn't stand going through this again, I'd die."

Colin put his hand over Toby's. "I won't take you to the hospital, unless I feel you need an MRI. But your pupils are the same size. I think you are suffering more from the drugs that were injected into your system than any physical injuries. So yeah, we'll take you to my house." He looked up and met Raul's eyes. "Right?"

"Right." Raul nodded. No way would he let Toby be taken to Emma's apartment. They didn't know about Emma but he wasn't risking her. He liked Toby but he more than liked Emma and ... no. No danger was getting near her. She could work the case at Colin's place and on her computer. "Let's get going."

"Come on, honey," Colin coaxed, pulling Toby's pajama

clad legs to the side of the bed. "Stand up. Let's get you out of here and get you safe."

Toby nodded, pushed off with his hands, tried to stand and collapsed. He would have sunk to the floor if Raul hadn't grabbed him. He had Toby under the arms and could feel his legs shaking. No way could Toby make it back to the vehicles under his own steam. Colin was thin, spindly. Raul didn't think he could carry an adult male that far. Raul could, no problem. SEALs regularly trained with packs weighing 50 lbs. They'd trained carrying fellow SEALs weighing 220 lbs. If Toby weighed more than 140 lbs. he'd be surprised.

He strengthened his hold on him. "Toby, I'll carry you to the car. Will you let me?"

Toby nodded, breathing heavily.

Raul bent forward and slid Toby into a fireman's hold, one forearm holding Toby's legs down against his chest. He could have carried him in his arms but he wanted at least one hand free. They'd eliminated the guards but there was no guarantee other men weren't coming. Now that they had Toby, they had to get out as fast as they could. Emma was holding the drone.

Raul looked around carefully. "You sure you guys didn't leave anything behind that could identify us?"

Emma and Colin both shook their heads. They were smart people. Raul trusted that they were leaving a clean environment that would mess with the heads of the fuckers who had kidnapped and drugged Toby. He wanted it to appear that aliens had beamed in from outer space, grabbed Toby, took out the security guys and left.

"OK then. Let's go."

Toby weighed nothing at all. Raul broke into a trot back to the Black Inc vehicle. He couldn't wait to get out of there. He trusted Emma to have done a good job of blocking out all vid cams and of looping the cams back at the house where they'd been keeping Toby, but the less time they stayed, the better.

Colin placed Toby carefully into the front passenger seat of his car, strapped him in, gave them his address and took off.

Emma watched them go with a frown. She looked worried. Raul rubbed the frown away from between her brows. He hated seeing that look on her – anxious and lost. They'd made progress, mainly thanks to her, but the heart of what was going on – that was still a mystery.

"It'll be OK," Raul said. "Toby clearly has some knowledge they want and when he tells us, we'll know, too. Only we have two big security companies on our side, all made up of good guys, and ties to the law enforcement community. Nobody will come after Toby again. We'll figure out what Toby knows and stop whatever he's found out and everyone can go back to their lives." *Except you*, he thought, but didn't say. Emma was never going back to that bank.

She was going back with him.

Whoa. That thought again. Where was it coming from? From some place deep inside that had been doing its own thinking and planning without him even being aware of it. Because the image sprang straight to his brain, fully formed. Like a shot time-travelled straight from the future. Emma, at ASI, working with her best friends, Hope and Felicity. She'd be treated like a queen and he'd make it clear to all the horny unattached operators at ASI that she was *his*. He loved his teammates but he wouldn't trust them around a beautiful unattached female, right there in the office.

She wouldn't be unattached. Nope. He'd be sitting right next to her long enough for the notoriously hard-headed operators to get the message.

"Okay. I hope you're right." She still looked worried but climbed into the SUV. "I'm hoping they didn't zap Toby's knowledge right out of his head. He looked pretty out of it."

Raul hoped that, too, but he didn't say so. With civilians, bitter truth had to be doled out carefully. SpecOps warriors were used to looking at reality, no matter how harsh. By instinct, by nature, and by training they were never dismayed, no matter how bad the news. There was always a Plan B and C and D. And if not – shit happens. Move on. Civilians got discouraged easily.

Still, if Toby could remember nothing at all, then they were up shit creek.

They took off and travelled in silence until they arrived down off the hill. Emma was checking something in her Magical Mystery Computer. Raul glanced at the screen a couple of times but all he saw was streaming data, which he'd never understand, not in a million years. He'd once asked Hope about some data that was streaming on her computer and when she replied, he understood one word in ten.

Emma looked up from her screen when they turned into Van Nuys. "Where are we going? Didn't Colin give you his address?"

"Yup." Raul leaned forward and tapped the GPS. "But first I was thinking we might grab a bite to eat. What do you say?"

She looked at him for a long moment before answering. "Grabbing a bite to eat sounds good. It would also give Colin and Toby a moment, and maybe allow Toby time to get his head clear and maybe clean up."

"That, too." They were on a timeline but nothing that couldn't allow the two some private time and maybe let Toby get his mojo back.

"That's very thoughtful of you," she said, looking puzzled.

"You sound surprised. I can do thoughtful." Particularly when the side effects were more time alone with Emma and maybe avoiding some drama in the Colin household. He didn't say that, though. Emma was looking at him with admiration in her glance so he wasn't messing with that. No way.

They were driving down toward Market. He pulled to the

curb. "That looks like a nice place. Japanese fast food. Unless you know someplace better around here?"

She shook her head.

He narrowed his eyes suspiciously. "You speak Japanese, too?"

"Nary a word," she said cheerfully. "Your manhood is safe."

Raul gave a crack of laughter. The lady was sharp. Luckily, his manhood was truly safe.

11
———

The food at the Japanese place Raul stopped at was great. Emma took their business card. It was a hole in the wall but scrupulously clean. They shared a bowl of edamame. She had a fabulous huge bowl of Udon noodles and Raul had tempura, sukiyaki, they shared their dishes and drank tea.

As she'd seen the evening before, he wasn't a fussy eater and liked everything. She'd had a couple of dates this past winter with a food snob and she'd spent evenings with the guy – Mitch? Mark? – who delighted in sending back dishes that weren't absolutely perfect. Luckily, she hadn't slept with him because she wondered whether he'd send her back, too.

And also luckily, Raul hadn't shown any desire to send her back after a night in bed.

Raul was absolutely right. They needed to eat. After a night, umm, a night of very little sleep, and rescuing Toby, she needed sustenance. Though she imagined that in the military, Raul had operated for long stretches of time without eating at a nice Japanese eatery. Another reason she was glad she did what she did and not what he did.

"So," Raul said, finishing his tea and planting his forearms on the table. "Toby and Colin."

"Toby and Colin," she agreed.

"You think it will last?"

Emma sighed. "I don't know. Colin feels like a solid person. Toby's a bit more ... flighty I guess. But he seemed over-whelmed with joy to see Colin. I'm hoping it lasts, for both of them. It needs to last at least as long as Toby's still in danger. We need to keep Toby safe and hidden."

Raul's face tightened. "Damn right. I don't know easy it will be. I don't know how badly whoever it is who kidnapped him wants him to stay out of circulation. And we don't know how long the situation will last. What the end game is, and when. We can keep Toby hidden for a while, but he has a job, rent to pay, commitments."

She sighed. "Yeah. Toby can't just disappear. He has a life. A career he cares about."

Raul put his hand on hers, large and warm. "Friends."

"Friends." She nodded. "But I guess now comes the hard part. Figuring out why all of this is happening."

"While keeping you safe. Don't forget that part." Raul didn't let go of her hand, curling his hand around hers. Heat from his hand rose up her arm. "This is what we're going to do. We're going to have Hope and Felicity keep an eye on PIB to see how they are reacting to Toby's disappearance."

She smiled at him. "And to how SSS reacts to two of their operators being found trussed up with no memory of how that happened and how Toby escaped their grasp."

"That's right." Raul smiled back. "Someone won't be happy."

"And we have to find that someone, right? Find out who Toby is threatening."

Raul lifted her hand to his mouth and kissed it. His beard was heavy, already growing out. There was a small bite of beard when he kissed her hand and she liked it. "My money is on you. And Hope and Felicity. You guys are amazing."

They were nice words, and he seemed to mean them. He'd stopped smiling and gazed deeply into her eyes, completely serious. But there was a misreading of the situation here.

"*You* saved him, Raul. You were the one who went in, overpowered two men and saved him."

"I would never have found him, not in a million years if you hadn't done your magic trick. Following the tires. Man, that was just genius. Plus being so good with the drones."

"But once I was there, I couldn't have overpowered those men."

He shifted, took her hand in both of his. Closed his eyes in pain. "No. Fuck no. That's not your thing. Your thing is figuring shit out, my thing is to knock heads and kick down doors. Together, we're quite a team."

A team. Emma hadn't been a team in years, not since the NSA. And even then, she and Hope and Riley and Felicity hadn't been a team in the sense of working on the same things. They each had their field of specialization and were working on different projects. They were friends, though, and they banded together mainly in self-defense against the head of the department, the Boss from Hell. Not even she and Toby were a team at work. She was specialized in foreign markets and he was specialized in the domestic market. She'd always done her own thing, on her own.

So, the idea of teaming up with Raul was really enticing. But Emma was also a realist and didn't want to read too much into the situation. They were teamed up temporarily because Raul had been sent by Hope and Felicity and his company to help her on this one thing. She couldn't even read too much into the night spent together having sex, though that was spectacular. It was spectacular in her memory because she'd never had much of a sex life. Maybe from Raul's point of view it was nice, but that was it. So, she would embarrass herself if she got too attached, thinking that by 'team' he meant 'couple'.

Looking away from him was hard and it felt like turning her head away from a tractor beam. She looked at the walls of the hole in the wall diner, covered with cheap prints, then out on the colorful street, then brought her gaze back to his. "We'll do our best, that's for sure. Because I think there's something serious here. Something that is dangerous."

"Agreed." He nodded. "Okay, we're all fueled up and we've given Toby some time to recover. And Colin probably has something to get the drugs out of his system. Should we go?"

"Text Colin. Tell him we should be there in about twenty minutes."

Raul texted, then looked at incoming messages. "Colin's expecting us. And Felicity has a report on SSS. Put that away." Because she'd been trying to sneak her credit card to the pretty Japanese waitress.

"Can't blame a girl for trying," she said and he rolled his eyes. "We'll take Felicity's report in the car. I really want to see Toby, make sure he's ok. And see if he has a grasp on what's going on. Why he would be kidnapped."

"He was kidnapped for what's in his head." Raul stood and scrawled his signature on the bill.

No shit, Sherlock, Emma thought, but didn't say. Raul had done nothing but help and it was entirely thanks to him that Toby was safe, though dinged. Raul was kind to want to share credit but there was no way she and Colin could have freed Toby on their own. That was entirely thanks to Raul's bravery and skills.

Emma stood, too. "So, let's get what's in his head out into the open."

"HE'S GONE," CHRIS RICKS said on his cell.

Whitaker Hamilton III had been scanning a tech company's prospectus with an eye to investment. That was what he told himself. Actually, he'd been daydreaming about the island just off Bali where a Russian mobster had built himself a palace worthy of Kublai Khan and hadn't lived there more than a few weeks before being offed by a Belarusian mobster. Hamilton had bought it last week for a song because he'd been able to offer cold hard cash. Quite literally. A courier specialized in these transactions had hand delivered two suitcases with twenty-five kilos each of hundred euro bills, having flown in from Singapore on a private jet. Seven million euros. A steal.

The mansion was spectacular. A little gaudy, to be sure, and Hamilton was going to have to strip some of the gilt and replace the real zebra skin couches but those were minor details. The compound had three swimming pools, a spa, a gym, ten bedrooms and ten bathrooms, all waterfront property. The assistant who'd taken care of the transaction was so intent on cashing in on the property that he'd thrown in a small yacht as a sweetener.

The property had a staff of twenty, including a chef lured away from a five star restaurant in Hong Kong, a trained butler, cleaning staff, gardeners, two chauffeurs and the crew of the yacht. The agent had assured Hamilton that the staff would stay on and the most strenuous thing Hamilton would have to do was get out of bed in the morning and walk down to the terrace overlooking the ocean and consume his breakfast buffet.

Hamilton could feel the sun on his skin and smell the scent of fresh tropical fruit and was daydreaming about the parties he would hold when his cellphone rang and wrenched him away from the images.

It was ex-detective Ricks' ring. Saying that Toby Jackson had escaped.

Fuck. *"How?"*

Ricks' voice was somber and emotionless, but not defensive. It wasn't his fuckup, it was SSS's.

"Nobody knows, sir. I'm at the house right now and all we have is two operators in restraints and no memory of anything. One minute they're guarding the asset and the next they're trussed up like pigs without a scratch on them otherwise. And the asset is gone. We don't even have a time frame."

"Video cams?" Hamilton's skin prickled. For weeks now, his quant, Jackson, had been asking for in-house data, digging deeper and deeper. Hamilton had had a feeling that Jackson had discovered something.

This wasn't in Ricks' wheelhouse. But he'd heard rumors of a good security company that, for the right price, could be persuaded to do whatever you needed. For the right price. Music to his ears. He'd contacted Sierra Security Services and the vice president of operations hadn't turned a hair. Toby Jackson had been taken out of circulation smoothly and quietly.

After the tenth, he'd be dumped on his doorstep with pharmacological amnesia and no clue where he'd been. They'd wiped his work computers. With no incriminating evidence, it would be too late for him to say anything. If he hadn't figured anything out ... well, he'd had a vacation of forced rest. Hamilton had even planned on giving him a hard time for going AWOL from the job and then firing him. Because Toby wouldn't have anything like a legitimate explanation and would never suspect his boss.

"All video cams were down for half an hour. That's including all along the street. It was someone who knew what they were doing, both with the cams and in overpowering the two operators."

This was awful. "So, we're talking one person or several people?"

Ricks' voice was sober. "No clue, boss. But definitely

someone with serious computer skills and capable of getting the drop on two experienced operators and getting a captive man out slicker 'n snot."

Hamilton ground his teeth. Ricks could sometimes be distressingly redneck.

This was potentially very bad news, so close to Day One. Hamilton tried to soft pedal it in his head. Because pushing the panic button, so close to victory, could be disastrous. Should he tell Marin? Hamilton entertained the thought, briefly.

We had a small hiccup, sir. One of our quants has gone ... missing. He hasn't reported in for work in five days and no one knows where he is. He might, ahem, have drawn inferences from some of the data coming from ...

No. It was unthinkable. Toby had nothing, nothing concrete.

Maybe Hamilton had overplayed his hand, actually. Maybe he should have just let Toby be. What could Toby have done, after all? Contact the authorities? Who? The SEC? Hamilton had been very careful not to break any laws. Short selling was, yes, frowned upon, particularly at the scale he'd done it, but it wasn't illegal. And anyway, no one could trace the trading back to him anyway.

For all anyone would know, a couple of trillion dollars would be sucked out of the system, down a black hole no one could follow.

Even if Toby managed to interest someone in his story – maybe some financial blogger – it was too late now. He could yap all he wanted afterward. No one would believe him anyway. Or ... maybe *he* could be accused of some of the short selling.

Now that was an idea. Set up some accounts in Toby Jackson's name, put some money in his accounts, gently nudge the SEC in his direction...yes that would tangle him up in knots, and the more accusations he made, the more the authorities would think he was covering up his own work.

Hamilton turned his voice mild. "Well, Ricks, keep me informed. And keep an eye on his apartment. And continue keeping an eye on Emma Holland. She is his friend and she didn't turn up for work, either."

Holland was as smart as Jackson and perfectly capable of adding two and two and coming up with five as well.

"Grab her tomorrow, interrogate her ..."

The relief in Ricks' voice was audible. There'd been a screw up. He wasn't responsible in any way but screw ups had a tendency to tarnish everyone close by. And he had been given a new mission.

"Yessir. Will do, sir."

THEY DROVE TO THE ADDRESS COLIN GAVE THEM AND PARKED outside. It was a steep road and he had to park on a slant. Any vehicle Black Inc provided would have perfect brakes, but still.

Emma stared at the building that looked like it could have housed the Addams family, except it was in various pastel colors. "A Painted Lady," she said, surprise in her voice.

Raul looked around. No ladies in sight, painted or otherwise.

Emma laughed. "That's what they call these Victorian homes in San Francisco. Wooden homes built during the Victorian era in the Queen Anne style. They are usually painted in three colors or more."

All Raul saw was a façade that looked rickety, with gables and turrets, fussy and over decorated and yes, painted in light blue, dark blue and yellow and green. He had no idea what Queen Anne was and didn't care. The place looked like where the witch took Hansel and Gretel. Like it would blow over in a strong wind.

He glanced over at Emma so they could make fun of it together, but she had stars in her eyes.

"Colin lives in a Painted Lady," she sighed.

Chicks.

You had to walk up a steep stoop to get to the door, which seemed to Raul weird right there. A curtain twitched, he saw Colin's pale face and the door opened.

Raul walked behind Emma, turned and took a good look around the street while she greeted Colin. He knew how to look and what to look for. He searched the street in quarters, 180°. A quarter view, blink to black, another quarter view, blink to black. Nothing suspicious, nothing overtly out of place. Very few people on the street. A middle-aged man walking a remarkably ugly dog with a fancy sweater, a kid skateboarding, an elderly Chinese gentleman carrying bags of vegetables, tufts of green poking out of the top of the bag.

Most people were working. No one had tailed them coming here, he'd made sure of that. They were good to go. He turned back around.

"Raul." Colin nodded.

"Colin." Raul nodded back. Colin looked stressed.

Inside, the place was better than outside. It wasn't full of knickknacks or overly precious. You could walk in a straight line for more than a few steps.

Raul had an aunt, Tia Matilda, who lived in an ancient house in LA and inside it was a nightmare clutter of things to trip over or knock over. He wasn't clumsy, so he never broke anything, but it was always a miracle. Everybody hated going to her house except for the fact that she was a fantastic cook.

Colin's space was open and not cluttered. He led them down a wood-paneled corridor to a bedroom-study. Bookshelves filled with books, mostly medical texts, a desk with two computer monitors, and on a couch, Toby popping to his feet.

"Toby!" Emma rushed forward and embraced him. He was her height, both of them short in comparison to Raul and Colin. Their coloring was different but they could have been siblings. Same height, slender build, super bright, vibrating at a higher level than most people, like hummingbirds.

Tears tracked down Toby's face as he clutched Emma, more a gesture of desperation than affection. He was white-faced, shaking. "Thank you so much, darling Emma. Colin told me you went looking for me, wouldn't give up until you found me." His entire body gave a big shudder. "Who knows what would have happened to me if you hadn't done what you did."

Emma pulled back. She patted him on the shoulder, gently smiling. "I think you have Raul here to thank for saving you. I just found you. If it had been just me and Colin, I think you'd still be back in that place."

Toby lifted his eyes, looked at Raul. Clearly, he didn't remember him. "Thanks, man. Appreciate it. Who are you?"

"A friend," Emma said.

"Emma's friend," Raul said firmly, making it clear that he was her friend-friend. More than casual. "Why don't we all sit down and do a debrief?"

"Raul's former military," Emma offered.

"Sure." Toby looked like he was happy to sit down because otherwise he'd fall down. He sat on the couch and Emma sat beside him. She kept her arm around his shoulders and he leaned into her a little. That told Raul a lot. Toby clearly felt that Emma was someone a person could rely on. Raul was, too. He didn't like people who collapsed at the first difficulty. Emma wasn't that kind of person. Neither was he.

Raul sat down in a spindly chair that looked like it could barely carry his weight. There was an office chair too but he imagined Colin would use it once he came back into the room.

Colin arrived immediately, angling sideways through the door, carrying a tray.

Raul's head went up hopefully, but it was tea. He'd have preferred coffee but presumably Colin knew Toby and knew what Toby would like. Emma too, was happy with the tea.

Emma and Toby were the stars here. They were the ones who had to be comfortable.

Colin poured out four mugs. The tea looked strong and black – none of that straw grass nonsense – and smelled good. There was a serving plate piled high with scones, small croissants, fruit-topped pastries, looking good enough to be worthy of the Queens of IT back in his office. It had been all of an hour since he'd last eaten. Raul was hungry.

"Looks great," Emma said enthusiastically, picking up something with a slice of kiwi on top.

"Thanks, babe," Toby said, picking up a scone. His hand trembled.

Emma noticed, too. She looked at Colin. Their eyes met.

There was a rhythm to interrogations. Interrogating a terrorist was very rapid pace, quick-fire, never allowing the terrorist time to think, to make up plausible lies. This was the opposite. This was to elicit memory and it required time and finesse.

Emma's territory.

Raul sat back and sipped.

"Toby." Emma's voice was very gentle. "What's the last thing you remember?"

"Going to bed Friday night." He met Colin's eyes. "After we spent the evening at Heaven, remember?"

Colin nodded.

Emma leaned forward. "And nothing after that?"

"After that, what I remember is seeing you, Colin and that guy –" he nodded to Raul, "bending over me. I felt like I was swimming out to sea. Like I wasn't even in my own body. Like I wasn't even me."

Colin's voice was grim. "I told you guys I dropped off a sample of Toby's blood to a friend of mine who has a lab for analysis."

Raul's skin prickled. "Was it an official test? Is Toby's name going to appear anywhere?"

"No. Absolutely not. My name wasn't on it, either. The owner of the lab knows me and owes me and expedited the results. Here. Here's the analysis." Colin held out his phone.

Raul and Emma bent over it, then both looked up at Colin. It was a string of chemical products. Raul had a passing acquaintance with street drugs and incapacitating drugs, but the numbers baffled him. "Can you interpret that for us, Colin?"

"Yeah," Colin said tightly. "He was perfused with enough fluni-trazepam to keep him docile but aware enough to drink to keep hydrated and to void bladder and bowels. Carefully calibrated so they wouldn't have to hydrate him intravenously and clean him. Also, enough to stop the creation of memories so he wouldn't remember what happened to him. Another couple of days of this, though, and they would have created permanent neurological damage. They knew what they were doing. They were neutral-izing him in a way that created the least mess for them. I don't think they cared that they might be creating lasting damage."

No, they wouldn't have cared. Two operators for SSS? They wouldn't have given a shit.

Toby reacted as if they were talking about the weather on Mars – nothing to do with him. He sat, shaking slightly, staring down into his cup of tea.

Emma touched his shoulder lightly and he started. "Toby? Tobe? Are you up to talking about what happened? We might be on a ... on a timeline here."

He put the mug on a small table by the side of the couch. It rattled for an instant. "I don't know what happened, Emma. I can't remember anything after Friday evening. I told you."

"Uh huh. Yes, you did tell me. Let's try something else. You didn't show up for work on Monday. We had the files on rare earth mineral mining corporations to go over, do you remember that? We were supposed to discuss them and take a decision whether to recommend or not."

Toby's eyes widened. He sat up a little straighter. "Yeah. Yeah, I remember that. I was projecting a possible five-year 27% return. I was about to recommend a sizable investment."

"The day you didn't show up, I pored over the data and you really called it, Toby. I waited for you to kick the recommendation upstairs but ..."

"But I disappeared." Toby sighed and stared at his hands, frowning.

Emma leaned forward a little. "Toby, you'd been a little agitated lately, and not because of rare earth minerals, either. Both of us had seen those anomalous data, together with some massive shorting. Here, let me show you –"

Emma took out her laptop and opened it, screen turned toward Toby. She pressed a few keys and the screen lit up with coursing data, the Matrix-like configuration. Raul thought she was maybe pressing this too soon, but Toby snapped to attention, like a recruit suddenly spying his commanding officer.

Nerds, he thought, with a wry internal smile. Hope and Felicity were the same. If something caught their attention, they forgot tiredness, hunger, thirst. They were like dogs with a bone until they got to the heart of it.

Emma put her head next to Toby's and they started speaking some special language Raul couldn't follow. Some words were in English, many were in math. He couldn't understand any of it but it was intense. Toby was taking the lead, pointing things out that were incomprehensible.

The only thing Raul could do was wait and finish his scone. Luckily, it was really good. So was the tea, which surprised him. He was more a coffee guy, himself.

He glanced at Colin, who was patiently waiting, too, while Emma and Toby did their thing. He and Colin exchanged a wry glance, two men whose partners had completely forgotten about their existence and were immersed in apparently fascinating nerddom. Toby even had regained a little color in his face.

It took them about an hour. Emma had supplied the data she had which she shared and it turned out Toby remembered he had copied much of the data he'd studied to a secret place in the cloud.

Raul didn't dare make small talk with Colin because he didn't want to disturb them. Though in truth they looked like it would take a nuclear explosion close by to jog them out of their focus trance. After a while, Colin got up, cleared the cups, and went to do something in the kitchen.

Raul was a sniper. He had endless wells of patience. He'd once hidden in a hide for three days, not moving, barely breathing, pissing in a bottle, holding back dumps, waiting for a high value target to come in his sights. The fucker finally appeared, Raul snapped into high alert, smoked him and left fast.

Patient waiting was his friend. And since what was being figured out wasn't his circus, he was free to get lost inside his head. Normally, he defaulted to work mode. ASI was in the process of evaluating renewing its weapons. An upstart tech company was offering a series of handguns that were made out of a new kind of ceramic that was used to coat modules landing from the space station. The ceramic had amazing heat resistance, strength, but was very lightweight and didn't show up on metal detectors. The weapons became slightly fragile after the 100,000th round had been shot, but they were easily replaceable, since they cost a tenth of an ordinary firearm. His colleague Jacko was the company armorer, but Jacko had brought him in on the considerations.

Raul had spent a lot of time and effort and thought on the issue.

But right now? Nah. He'd rather think about Emma. Beautiful, fascinating Emma. Raul was starting to understand his buddies Metal and Luke, the partners of Felicity and Hope. Partnering with a really smart woman was dangerous stuff, but both of them seemed off the charts happy. Raul knew them from their military days and would have described both of them as tough, no-nonsense guys. Guys without a romantic bone in their bodies. And yet, when their women were around, they were reduced to puddles of goo. It would have been weird, borderline insane, if it weren't for the fact that both Felicity and Hope were really fantastic. They were beautiful and smart, both of them. But, also, kind and hard workers and a ton of fun to be around. Both of them geniuses with computers and data and not one operator at ASI, not even one highly trained SEAL or Ranger, in Luke's case, had ever beat them at Mortal Kombat or Street Fighter. Not even close.

You had to admire that. Raul sure did.

And now, he was close to a woman who was as beautiful and as smart as Felicity and Hope. Actually, though he could never say so to either Metal or Luke, she was more beautiful than either woman. Metal and Luke both said loudly and often that their woman was the most beautiful/smartest/most fantastic woman in the world. They didn't say it in each other's company, though.

The thing was, Raul secretly thought that was bullshit. Emma was more beautiful than Felicity and Hope were and was certainly as bright as, if not … no. Not going there, not even in his head. But Emma was really bright.

She shared with Hope and Felicity the fact that she was easy to be with. No games at all, just fun when it was time for fun and serious and focused when at work, and never high maintenance. No maintenance at all, really. Emma didn't pout for attention. As a matter of fact, right now she probably wasn't even aware he was in the room.

She hadn't once been morbidly curious about his career. SEALs sometimes were catnip to women, for all the wrong reasons. Some women liked the thought of a violent man, without realizing SpecOps screened out for violence. For violent natures. Violence was a tool. They'd missed with Buchanan but, generally speaking, SEALs weren't violent men. They used violence as a precision tool. Plus patience, an ability to improvise, ability to work in a team. Violence didn't define them, effectiveness did. They did what they had to do to establish order. Sometimes that was investigative work, sometimes that was persuasion, sometimes that was, yes, violence.

Some women liked that, liked a hint of violence, as if he could ever hurt a woman. If he ever hurt a woman, he'd have his grandmother, his mother, his two sisters and a billion female cousins on his back. They were all tough women and they'd make him pay.

That was one end of the spectrum. The other end was women who treated him like a barely literate thug.

Emma did neither, she treated him like a highly trained professional, just as she was, only trained in other disciplines. She seemed to respect him for who he was, not a person who only existed in her imagination, to be lusted after for the wrong reasons, or hated for the wrong reasons.

There was a real ease to being with her, like a ... a flow. Like the kind he had with his teammates at ASI, only with sex.

Spectacular sex.

The kind of sex he was really looking forward to tonight ... Pleasant images filled his head and then Raul saw something on Toby's monitor when he shot a casual glance their way and thoughts of sex flew from his mind, to be replaced by a shot of pure terror.

"Stop!" His voice was loud, hoarse. Filled with horror. Three puzzled faces turned his way.

12

Toby's computers had been wiped clean. All they had was the data he'd shared and some he'd saved to the cloud. His memory was almost shot, and it was as if he were seeing the data for the first time.

He hadn't ever had a chance to lay it all out for her before his kidnapping, he'd only given hints of unease, coupled with the fact that she too could see that something originating inside their bank was distorting the market, in a way that was hard to see, let alone understand.

But though Toby was visibly suffering, was pale and was fighting nausea and a headache, he ran through the data set with her. Whoever had taken him had underestimated him. He was beaten down but not broken.

Emma followed him as he went over his investigation. After a week worrying over data, it became a real investigation. He even laid out the dry wells he dug. She loved it that he was secure enough to point out where he'd made mistakes. He hadn't made many though.

"So," she said, after reviewing his data with him, "it looks like this started two months ago. The placing of short sell orders."

"Two months and ten days ago. March 28th is the first order. I haven't been able to follow this any further back than then. So, I am just assuming that late March, early April is the starting point of whatever this is."

"And the shorting grew." The figures had been astounding.

He shrugged. "Almost exponentially after the first week. That first week everything was tentative. Then the floodgates opened, but most of it in the dark pools."

"How much are we talking here? In total?" She was speaking to him, but keeping an eye on the data streaming from his monitor.

"About a hundred billion."

That jolted her. She had a sick feeling in her stomach. "Looking at the shorts, and we can't be positive we're seeing it all, if the stocks do decline suddenly, we're looking at –" she stopped.

"A trillion," Toby said. "We're looking at a trillion leaving the market. Like after 9/11."

She blew out a breath. It was an unspoken fact that in the immediate aftermath of 9/11 several trillion dollars exited the economy. Most felt because of short selling, which meant someone knew that 9/11 would happen. Of course, the terrorists knew 9/11 would happen, but the trades weren't international. They were domestic. No one ever discussed this but it was commonly believed. But if you asked anyone at the top levels of the stock market infrastructure, they would look uneasy and say it was merely an urban legend.

Right.

You had to be low or middling on the totem pole to believe that.

"There's more. I just remembered something else."

Emma didn't see how there could be more but she sat and looked at Toby who'd been so brilliant to pull all this together. If he'd been an investigative journalist, this was Pulitzer level work.

"Yeah?"

"I think it might be naked shorting." Naked shorting was when the trader had not borrowed the shares. Was operating in the blind.

She closed her eyes and imagined it. Millions of shares being traded and when the date came due ... nothing. Naked shorting meant putting enormous pressure on the market because there was no guarantee that the shares being shorted actually existed.

Which was, of course, illegal. And massively disruptive.

"What are they shorting?"

Toby sipped his tea, thinking. "Well, that's the thing. I looked and looked and nothing jumped out at me. Not like the short selling of airline shares before 9/11. The risk is spread out over tech, commodities, general corporate shares. Agrifood corporations, the energy sector, the automotive sector. Hell, even entertainment. So, there is nothing there."

Toby had set his computer to project on to Colin's big screen TV on the wall. As they talked, data was scrolling. Emma could see some patterns, and was hoping they would spark Toby's memory, since this was data Toby had already studied.

"So it started end March?" As Emma interrogated Toby, Colin was staring into space, uninterested. He'd get up periodically and feel Toby's pulse. He was only interested in the state of Toby's health. Raul was paying attention, gaze switching from the wall mounted TV to their faces. He probably wasn't getting much of what was being said or of what was scrolling from Toby's computer, but Emma trusted him to be able to interpret Toby's body language.

Toby was scared, weak, shaky but determined. And, underlying it all, angry.

"And it all originated from us?"

"Most of it, yes." Toby looked her in the eyes. "A set percentage originated from Hamilton himself. He tried to hide his tracks, and he was fairly decent about it, but–" he shrugged.

Emma knew what that shrug meant. Toby was the best.

"And we're talking ..."

"We're talking maybe half a billion. From him."

That closed her down. Her boss came from a well to do family but not billionaire class. He earned well but nothing like what would allow him to gamble half a billion dollars. He was dipping into bank funds. Embezzling. Hoping to make the money back before it was discovered.

"Wow." It was all she could say.

"That's not all. Other shorts came from bogus accounts. Accounts that hadn't been active for more than a month. And they, too, originated from Pacific Investment. A lot of effort was made to cover that up, but ..." He shrugged again. "Most in dollars, some in Bitcoin and Ethereum."

Emma found it hard to breathe. She was used to dealing with massive amounts of money, but this – this was an order of magnitude greater. That's what governments bet.

"So, again, if they were made with some kind of insider knowledge, how much are we talking about if the shorts are successful?"

"A trillion dollars, a billion more or less."

Emma met Raul's eyes. For better or worse, a trillion dollars was a scary sum of money. The kind of money that wrecked markets, moved governments. The kind of money won or lost in wars.

"When were these bets made?" Raul asked, his voice sharp.

"Technically, they aren't bets, they are shorts," Emma said. "Though of course, they *are* bets. Someone is betting that something will happen to throw the market in disarray. Enough to earn a trillion dollars."

"That's a lot of disarray," Raul answered. "Centered around your bank."

She nodded. Yeah. It was. "Maybe I should go in on Monday and try to see if –"

"No," Toby said loudly, then brought a hand to his head as if his own voice had hurt him.

"*Fuck* no!" Raul nearly yelled the words at the same time.

"Whoa." Emma paused. This was one of the very few times in her life that someone had said 'no' to her. It was true her parents hadn't ever said 'no' to her because they were too wrapped up in themselves to care and in school she'd always been a top student and why would the teachers say no? Even at work at the NSA, the Boss from Hell had never told her what to do, only criticized bitterly work that had been done.

So, she didn't ordinarily take kindly to being told what to do.

But something about Raul's tone, his clenched jaws and fists, told her he was genuinely worried. And after a second, she realized he was right to be worried. If something really was going on at Pacific Investment Bank, and that something involved a massive amount of money then, yes, she should be staying away.

Staying away put her job at jeopardy. Oddly enough, that raised no emotions with her. With her skills, a job at another bank or hedge fund or analyst firm would be easy to come by. The best thing about her job was Toby, and he was never going back.

"Emma." Raul stepped toward her then stopped, visibly trying to control himself. "You shouldn't—"

She held up her hand to cut him off. "You're right. Sorry." Turned to Toby. "Tobe, do we have a timeline?"

Raul looked taken aback. He'd been planning on working

to persuade her, waiting for her to push back, but she didn't need persuading. She reached out with a finger to close his lower jaw and turned back to Toby.

"We do." Toby ran through some data, created a chart. It was visually clear. The short-selling began, in small quantities, at the end of March. Rising, but in tiny spurts, like an experiment. Someone or maybe many someones trying something out. By the morning of the tenth of April, however, the short selling was massive. A tsunami, but done cleverly, in a way that didn't attract immediate attention.

Most waves of short selling were focused on a single sector and, though no one would admit it, short selling was most often linked to insider knowledge. Wildly illegal but if you made enough money you weren't sent to jail. You got maybe a slap on the wrist. So, there would be short selling of airline stock or oil or the energy sector, depending on whether there was knowledge of problems at airline manufacturers, or of an unannounced oil leak or a hidden break in the electricity grid. But what she was looking at was across the board, as Toby said. All sectors. She'd never seen anything like it.

"Do we know the end game?"

Toby winced and held his head. "God, Emma. I don't know. I tried to calculate it out, but the variables just exploded. Oh God. My head hurts so much."

She felt instantly sorry for pushing him. They were on some kind of timeline, and the clock was ticking. But Toby had been knocked out and kept a captive. He was at his limits. She shouldn't expect him to be able to try so hard. Understanding the endgame of something like this was difficult. She switched tactics.

"Hey, Tobe." He was shaking. She put a hand on his shoulder and repressed a wince. He'd lost weight in the past few days. She could feel his bones under her hands. "How about we turn it around, try to understand how it started?"

He drew in a deep breath. In that moment, she admired the hell out of him. Nothing in his life could have prepared him for what he'd just been through. He lived a life of the mind and his was sharper than most. But being kidnapped, submitted to violence, must have been such a shock.

She stole a glance at Raul. He, on the other hand, had seen violence first hand. Had seen it, had suffered it, had inflicted it. It was part of the job description. Looking at that hard face, it didn't affect him like it did Toby. Or her. She was shaken, but didn't dare show it. Toby needed her to be calm and steady.

"On the graph, it looks like things started ramping up on the 28th. Just like you said."

He nodded, looked up at her, trembling. "I don't remember putting most of this data together, Emma. It's like I'm seeing it for the first time."

Oh, Toby. Emma's heart gave a sharp pulse of pain for him. He'd lost a chunk of his life, and looked it. She tried to inject cheer into her voice.

"Well then, that just means that you're coming at the data fresh, doesn't it?" She touched his arm, and some of his trembling eased. "And there are two of us now, aren't there?"

He nodded, his head hanging.

Emma met Raul's eyes. He looked back steadily. His support was a wall she could lean against. This was her show, but he was here for her.

"Ok, then. Let's go over it again." Emma led Toby through the charts. They both pored over the data. He'd done a remarkable job of putting it together, pulling data from new and unusual sources.

"Really good job, Tobe," she said after a while.

He sketched a smile. "Thanks."

"It's telling a story, we just need to find it."

"Yeah."

He was right. Most of the short selling was emanating from

PIB, though well-hidden. The sales were from thousands of accounts, but all you had to do was check the history of the accounts to see that they were shallow, with no history. Set up that month. The first rudimentary short sales were traceable back to Whitaker Hamilton, their boss.

Emma sat back and nudged Toby. "Early sales are definitely Hamilton. And I suspect that the other sales on behalf of those other fictitious entities are his, too."

He sighed and nodded.

"But – Whitaker isn't a genius. *You're* a genius, but he isn't."

That got her a faint smile. "I'd have hidden my tracks better, that's for sure."

"Yeah. But you wouldn't have made those vast short sales."

He shook his head. "Nope. Not a dope."

"And arguably, Whitaker is. But by the same token, I don't think he'd have done something like this all on his own."

Toby turned his head to stare at her. "You think he was acting under orders?"

"Maybe." Emma shrugged. "It's one of the few things in this mess that would make sense."

"Should I hack into his email?"

She thought, then shook her head. "Even he's not *that* dumb, to leave digital dust in his emails. But maybe he saw someone? Someone who convinced him to do this? But how would we know? I mean it's not as if he has a videocam in his office."

Toby's eyes flickered.

Her eyes widened. "Toby? Tobe?"

He smiled for the very first time since they'd rescued him.

"He doesn't have a vidcam in his office, no. But there's one just outside his office that no one notices because it's right beside an air vent and almost invisible. Several years ago, city regulations required a count of the number of people circulating on each floor to determine whether ventilation was sufficient. City Hall struck down the rule but the video cam stayed, no one took it down. There's one on each floor and the one on the executive level just happens to be right outside Big Boss's door."

"Whoa. So, we'd have a record of people going into his office." Emma smiled. "If only we could hack into it."

"If only." Toby was already bent over the keyboard. "Ok. I'm in."

Colin had drifted back in from the kitchen and all four of them were huddled around the monitor. "Where should I start?" Toby asked Emma.

"Well, to be prudent, at least a week before you noticed unusual market movements."

He pressed a few keys. "Okay. The good thing about the vidcam is that it is motion sensitive and only records movement, so if the corridor is empty, it doesn't record. Saves time."

"It won't have been overwritten?"

He shook his head. "That would be against city regulations. If there's too heavy traffic for the ventilation, it wouldn't be effective if it could be overwritten. No, there's just a data dump at the end of each quarter, but the files are never destroyed."

Well, that was an enticing thought. All the drones on the lower floors speculated on what the guys – and they were all men – on the top floor did, day in day out. For a moment, she considered going back over the year and a half she'd worked for PIB but then thought – nah. They were all superbly boring men. Who cared if they stepped out of the office at 3 p.m. for a round of golf, or had the caterers bring in champagne and caviar at 10 a.m.?

"Right." Toby sat back. "I've programmed it to start on the 21st. We'll see who's been to visit our Whitaker."

Not that many people, it turned out. He was anti-social, or maybe not many people liked him. Fact was, his day was fairly routine. He'd waltz in, freshly pressed, around 9 a.m. in the morning, when the regular work day for everyone else began at 8. At 10, his secretary brought him an espresso with a little porcelain cap, God forbid it become cold in the trek from the executive club room ten feet down the hall. From the 21st to the 28th, he received, in order, the head of a German investment bank, a functionary from the SEC, and on some kind of rota system, all the vice presidents from the floor below. On the third day of the recording, a very attractive woman Colin recognized as a highly successful lawyer came out of the office an hour later with a different blouse on. Emma met Toby's eyes and shrugged. To her, Whitaker was the most sexless man on the face of the earth, but apparently Ms. Successful Lawyer didn't think so. The next day, two Japanese businessmen toting huge briefcases, then an elegant gentleman in a three-thousand-dollar Brioni suit ...

"Stop!" Raul shouted.

Everyone looked at him in surprise. He leaned down, face tight, tapped the monitor. "Toby, can you get me a close up of this guy?"

"Sure." The screen filled with the man's face. He was tall, handsome, middle-aged, with fine features and graying blond hair. Excellent haircut. Up close, it was easy to see that not only was the tie pure silk but the shirt was, too. Closely shaved, probably smelling of expensive cologne. He looked like that kind of guy. It had taken generations of careful breeding to produce him.

Raul was staring with fiery intensity at him.

"What?" It was the first time she'd seen him so tense. "Who is he?"

Raul's fist opened and closed. His index finger shot out, touched the frozen image smack in the middle of his forehead, and his thumb dropped the imaginary hammer in an imaginary kill shot.

·   ·   ·

RAUL'S HEART GAVE A SUDDEN THUMP IN HIS CHEST, HARD. LIKE it was trying to escape his chest. Jump right out and place itself next to Emma because a terrifying man had suddenly appeared next to a woman he cared a lot about.

He wasn't afraid of much, but this guy terrified him. It was a family terror he was feeling, imprinted in his DNA. Men just like the guy on the screen had changed the course of his family's history.

He stood, looked at his little audience. Toby and Colin were astonished at his outburst, as if a dog had suddenly sat up and started spouting Shakespeare. Emma just sat with her hands in her lap, waiting for him to talk. Sure that he'd make sense. Toby and Colin weren't that sure.

"Lady and gentlemen," he said, unable to keep the venom from his voice. "Meet Jorge Marin de Herrera. Otherwise known as *El Quìmico*, the chemist, because he has a PhD in chemistry from the Institute of Chemistry from the Universidad Nacional Autònoma de Mexico. One of its star pupils. A legend. He owns a pharmaceutical company known for its cheap antibiotics. But he is also known as the head of the Cabo Cartel, one of Mexico's richest drug cartels."

Emma felt her eyes round. She stared at the fixed image on Toby's screen, and felt things shifting beneath her feet. The man who looked like a distinguished businessman was a monster. It wasn't her world but she'd read enough to know that Mexican drug cartels were tearing the country apart, responsible for mass murders and misery on an industrial level.

"Fuck," Colin said. "Drug cartels? What do drugs have to do with it?"

"Nothing good," Toby answered. "Massive amounts of money, massive borderline illegal short sells and now drug cartels."

"What could go wrong?" Emma asked.

Raul's voice deserted him. His mouth had gone bone dry, as

dry as the Mojave. Up until now, he'd had a low-level buzz of worry, that rose with Toby's kidnapping. But Toby hadn't been killed, just kept away from whatever was happening. This whole thing was about money and it didn't feel violent.

That was gone, and the low-level buzz of worry surged into panic. Emma was involved in something that also involved Mexican drug cartels.

He knew all about drug cartels. He was in security and though he'd spent his professional life as a SpecOps warrior combating terrorism, anyone involved in security was painfully aware of the monsters living just south of the country's border. Not living in rat holes and caves like the terrorists halfway around the world. Nope. They lived in palatial homes and drove Mercedes-Benzes and lived like kings in the light of day because they had so much money it protected them.

But beneath it all, they were greater predators than the terrorists. And the estimated 150,000 deaths due to cartel violence, at least 30,000 people missing, made terrorists look like pikers.

They knew no mercy and they knew no law and no god beyond money and power. They were among the most ruthless men on the face of the earth and Emma was right in the middle of something that touched drug cartels.

He was terrified.

A drop of sweat rolled down his back.

"Raul?" Emma touched his hand and he grasped it, hard. Usually, he was careful with women because he had strong hands, but right now he clung to her hand because he felt like he was the only thing between her and a violent death. As long as he was holding her, close to her, she couldn't be taken away.

"Raul, are you okay?"

Raul had no idea what he looked like but he was scaring her. She tugged at her hand and he opened his. Surreptitiously she shook her hand out. He'd held her hand hard enough to hurt.

Fuck.

The last thing he wanted to do was hurt Emma. He wanted to protect her. Only the nasty surprise of a drug cartel possibly touching her life, however remotely, could have made him lose control like that.

"This is bad news," he said, throat so tight his voice came out strangled and hoarse. Colin and Toby were watching him, too. "The very worst."

Toby turned to Emma with a frown. "So, what would Whittaker be doing with a drug lord?"

She lifted her shoulders. "I don't know. I can see him with a corrupt politician or a scumbag businessman, but drugs? I just don't see it. Could it be a coincidence? I mean are we sure this guy is who you say it is, Raul?"

He didn't react to that. She couldn't know. Yes, he had every single drug lord's face, and most of their lieutenants, committed to memory, in his head through a sniper rifle's scope, in the crosshairs.

"I have every single cartel boss's face committed to memory. Sinaloa, Juarez, Jalisco, the Zetas ... all of them. El Quìmico is particularly dangerous because he is so intelligent. A drug lord killed my grandfather."

Emma's breath caught.

It was family legend, passed down from generation to generation, so strong that not one Martinez had ever taken drugs. There were some too fond of tequila and several gambled and two ate way too much, but no drugs. Ever. Any kid caught taking drugs would have over a hundred people screaming at them.

"My –" He swallowed. "My grandfather was the *alcalde*, the mayor, of a small town in Jalisco. The cartels were just starting up. The head of a cartel raped and killed a young girl and my grandfather insisted he be brought to justice. In retaliation, he was gunned down in the street, and then decapitated. His head was placed outside the door of city hall. My grandmother fled with the clothes on her back and four young children. It's the defining element of my family. I desperately wanted to join the DEA, but they said my attitude was 'too enthusiastic'. The DEA wouldn't take me. So, I joined the Navy."

He grabbed Emma's hand. "But trust me when I say I know every single head of cartel and all the lieutenants. I keep tabs on all of them. El Quìmico is not the most blood-thirsty but he is definitely the smartest. He's an unusually dangerous man."

He was panting, his heart beating fast.

Silence.

"So ... is Hamilton what? Laundering money? Does that make sense?" Emma asked.

Silence for another long minute.

"No, no it doesn't," Toby said. His voice was raw, slow. He was pale, movements sluggish.

"Money laundering isn't the kind of thing Hamilton would do." Emma drummed her fingers on Colin's sleek plexiglass desk. "It's too risky, it could come back to bite him. If a dedicated forensic economist – and the FBI has many – were to study movements they can always trace back money laundering. I don't see Whitaker being involved. Not because he'd disapprove, but because he doesn't have the street smarts, and I think he'd be too scared."

"The short selling?" Raul asked. "Does that fit his profile?"

"Definitely. Because technically it's not illegal, unless he is trading on insider knowledge, which is hard to prove. I mean I don't know why he's doing it but it's definitely something he'd be prepared to do. But – if a cartel boss is involved, that would have to be money laundering, right?"

"Would Hamilton know he was the head of a cartel?" Toby asked.

Emma opened her mouth, then closed it. She suddenly attacked her computer and after a minute, turned the monitor around. Raul bent down, unsure what he was reading.

Emma's finger touched the screen and he saw the name. Brandon Rutherford. And then a time and a date. At the top: Appointments, Whittaker Hamilton.

"Hamilton's schedule on the day," Emma said. "The guy you say is Marin is actually a man called Brandon Rutherford. There's a photo." More tapping at the keys. "Born September 10, 1971 in Napa, California. Runs some kind of import-export business. Degree in –"

"Organic chemistry," Raul said.

Emma's eyebrows rose. "Why yes."

"Can you break into the DEA and find the files on the Mexican drug cartels?"

Emma hesitated, looking at Colin. "I don't care what you hack into," he said.

She bent over her keyboard again. "Bring up Jorge Marin de Herrera and put his photo on a split screen. Together with the photo of Brandon Rutherford," Raul ordered.

In another minute, Emma had done it, and stared. They all stared.

"It's the same guy," Toby finally said. "Absolutely."

"So, when an American businessman shows up in Hamilton's office with a business proposal, he had some money behind him." Emma look at Raul.

"The Mexican drug business generates something like forty billion dollars a year," Raul said. "And a lot of it is recycled through the United States."

"Wow." Emma looked troubled. "That's a lot of illegal money. But we're not looking at an illegal laundering operation here. We're looking essentially at investments made in a way that masks the origin. So, I guess, possibly at the behest of a drug cartel?"

"Doesn't compute." Toby's words were slurred. He sat back in his chair and closed his eyes."

"That's it." Colin clapped his hands and stood up. Toby's eyes shot open. "It sounds like you guys are running around in circles. Toby's been through hell and he's running on fumes right now. And I'll bet you're tired too, Emma."

Emma started to shake her head but Raul interrupted. "Yeah. She's exhausted. How about we let the two brainiacs continue tomorrow? I think they both need to sleep on it, attack it again when their minds are fresher."

"I'm not –" Emma began.

Raul picked up her hand, carefully making sure his touch was gentle. "Yes. You are. In the Teams, we're trained to recognize when the point of exhaustion has arrived, beyond which bad decisions are made."

What he didn't say was that SEALS also trained, and trained hard, to be able to make good snap decisions or to take the shot, even well past the point of exhaustion. But it was something they were selected for and had had beaten into them after that. Emma and Toby hadn't had that training. They were both fried and weren't going to do anyone any good.

Raul's mission now was to feed Emma and make sure she rested and relaxed.

And, if the rest and relaxation part included some sex, man, he was up for that. A real bonus. But the important thing was her.

She searched his eyes, nodded. *Yes! Fuck yes!*

Raul's dick started happily rising until he realized she was saying yes to being tired, not yes to wild monkey sex, right this very minute.

So, he told his dick to stand down

Well, whether sex was in the cards or not, rest for Emma definitely was.

He put his hand under her elbow and lifted. "Come on Sherlock, time to put away that magnifying glass."

Emma sighed, tried a tired smile, gathered her things.

"Bye, sweetie." Toby buried his face in her shoulder. She closed her eyes, held him tight. You could see that they worked well together, two smart people who were unravelling a conspiracy. A conspiracy that pointed in the direction of their work place. It wasn't going to end well and they both understood that.

Toby finally let go and Emma nodded to Colin. "See you tomorrow."

"Where?" Raul asked.

They turned puzzled faces to him. In the military you repeated things twice, to make sure they were understood, like when a pilot hands off a plane. Pilot to Co-pilot: You have the plane. Co-pilot to Pilot: I have the plane.

Repeat until it sinks in.

"Where are we meeting? Can I suggest here again? Which is off everyone's radar. Colin would you be okay with that?"

"Sure. I have a lot of time off accrued. I'll call in personal time."

"You, too." Raul shot a hard look at Emma, who by the accounts of her friends was a workaholic, and coming from Felicity and Hope, that was saying something.

"But –"

"I suggest you call in sick and don't know when you'll feel better." Raul usually hated being the bad guy but he had no compunctions here. Bad juju was leaking out of the situation all over the place. Her bank seemed to be in the middle of it. Over his dead body was Emma stepping into that place.

Ever again, if he had any say over it.

Toby sighed. "He's right. At least until we can figure out what's going on."

"And why you were kidnapped and drugged and

restrained." Raul said that in a hard voice because they had to be *reminded* that bad people were serious here. "Until we figure it out, you stay away from that place."

For someone who dealt with the future all the time, she didn't seem to connect the dots.

"You know, I can't stay away forever. I mean they'd fire me."

Toby shrugged. "Do you care?"

"Well ... no. But problems have a way of following one around, right?"

"True," Toby admitted.

"So, what happens if we never figure out what's going on?"

Raul just stood there, jaws clenching. She was smart. She knew the answer. She just didn't want to acknowledge it.

Toby threw her a *get real* glance. "Girl," he said. "You and me? Together? We're not going to figure it out?"

She smiled. Apparently, in her world, she and Toby were Masters of the Universe. Capable of anything. But in Raul's world, where there were terrorists and drug cartel bosses, it didn't work like that. In Raul's world there were some seriously bad men who didn't melt away once you figured out their grift. Once they got your scent in their nose, they came after you with everything they had and they never gave up until you were dead.

And that was an image in his head he couldn't shake. Emma, dead. On the ground, that vivid red hair around a face the skim milk color of death. That color he'd seen too many times. Body slack, all that liveliness gone.

Wasn't going to happen. He wouldn't leave her side until every single goddamn string was tied up tighter than a duck's ass. Until the most serious threat in her world was too much cholesterol.

That's when the idea settled in his mind as fact and not wishful thinking. Emma was coming back with him to Portland. No question. He wasn't leaving her here, not even when the money question was solved. Because someone had kidnapped Toby and drugged him. The idea of beautiful Emma, drugged and kidnapped ... Toby might not have been to their taste but Emma sure would be.

He'd go absolutely crazy back in Portland worrying about her.

She had to come back with him. His bosses at ASI would hire her in a heartbeat. Their IT department, run by Emma's best friends, Felicity and Hope, was the heart of the company. The ASI operators couldn't imagine going on a mission without the incredible intel and super sophisticated gear Felicity and Hope provided. But Felicity was this close to popping twins and her man, Metal, wouldn't let her work more than a few hours a day. Hope picked up the slack but she was starting to be over-worked. Another computer and tech genius, and one who already meshed with Felicity and Hope, would be welcomed with open arms.

Raul wasn't leaving without her.

There were steps to be taken before then, though. First, get Emma fed and rested, second, solve whatever the fuck was going on and hide her involvement from ever reaching the ears of Marin, then getting the hell out of here.

Raul twirled his finger in the air. It was a team leader's signal to head out, part of the military's extensive sign language in the field. But after a billion movies, everyone recognized it as *let's go*.

He looked out the window at the darkening street. "Okay, let's rest up, everyone, and we'll meet back here tomorrow at ... nine?" He looked at Colin, who was feeling Toby's pulse.

"Ten," Colin said without looking up from his watch. He was frowning. Yeah. Toby'd been sedated for days. He'd held up remarkably well but he needed to rest.

"Ten it is. Emma."

She nodded, bent to kiss Toby's cheek, smiled at Colin and joined Raul at the door.

Raul held the car door open for her and watched as she sat, settled, sighed. He'd been right to insist that they call it a day. She looked tired.

It was a gorgeous evening, the kind postcards were made of. The city gleamed.

Emma turned her head to smile at him behind the wheel. "Home, Jeeves."

He pulled out. "Home it is. Is there somewhere near your house where I can pick up dinner?"

"You like Italian?"

"Who doesn't?"

"Okay, there's a place right around the corner from me. Makes great pasta all'Amatriciana, pumpkin risotto, chicken cacciatore, tiramisu to die for."

Raul narrowed his eyes at her suspiciously. "That sounded really authentic. You sure you don't speak Italian?"

She smiled. "Nope. Promise. I'm a decent mimic, though, and I've heard Raffaello pronounce those words a thousand times."

Now he frowned, making a production of it. "Raffaello, huh? Who's this Raffaello? Is he good-looking? Because the only good-looking ethnic guy you can have around you is me."

Emma laughed, as he wanted her to. "Down boy. Raffaello is authentically Italian, from near Milan, and in his way good-looking. He also weighs 300 pounds, and is very happily married to Cristina who greets customers at *Milano*, and they have three kids. His eldest works as a waiter there."

"Good enough. Here." He handed her his cell. "Put in the coordinates of the restaurant. If you know what you want, call in the order. I'll eat anything you order. Make sure you get enough food, I'm starving." He batted his eyelashes at her. "I'm a growing boy. I need sustenance."

Emma rolled her eyes, put a pin in a map of the financial district for him and called. And ordered enough food to feed an army. Great. Raul loved leftovers. As she finished the order and started to swipe the call closed, he closed his hand over hers. "Uh-uh. Not so fast, slick. They'll have your credit card number. Use mine, instead." And handed her his card.

Emma sighed, gave them his number, then swiped the phone closed. "At some point you're going to have to let me pay for something."

He made a noncommittal noise. "When it's all over, you can buy me a Maserati."

She laughed. "Not likely, especially not if I'm going to lose my job."

Raul ground his teeth together to keep himself from saying – *The job is gone. You can't go back to your job. You're coming back with me to Portland. Where you'll be safe. Where my bosses will welcome you with open arms. And Hope and Felicity will be overjoyed.*

Not the time to say that. Not yet. But soon.

13

She was exhausted. Emma felt like she had been pummeled, stomped on and then passed through a wringer. It wasn't physical, it was mental and even emotional. Seeing what had been done to Toby was like a punch to the stomach. She and Toby – all the quants actually – were used to taking risks but they were all cerebral risks. Monetary risks. Bet on this new tech, abandon that old tech. China up, Russia down. That kind of thing. It never even occurred to her that they could run old-fashioned risks, in meatspace. In the real world.

But there he was – Toby. Who'd been kidnapped, drugged, hidden. Who even knew if they'd have let him live if Raul hadn't gone in to rescue him?

This was an entirely new world, one she didn't like.

But the shock of what happened to Toby had to take a back seat to trying to discover *why* he'd been targeted. Raul had done his thing and had been incredibly smart and brave. So, she and Toby had to do their thing and figure out what had happened. But they'd fallen flat on their faces.

Something was happening on the market. There was

massive short selling but not on specific types of stocks. Most was centered around Pacific Investment Bank, but not all. Ten hours of close study of the data that tied her brain around in knots and that's all they had.

She pressed her back against the headrest and closed her eyes.

And opened them to find Raul gently shaking her. They were in her garage. And the entire vehicle smelled divine, full of Raffaello's food in containers and bags that filled the back seat.

Wow. They'd crossed town, Raul had had time to stop by Raffaello's, pick up dinner – what looked like about ten dinners – and she'd slept through it all.

Emma sighed. "I'm so sorry. I just conked out on you. I don't remember ever doing that. I'm used to working in intense stints, but I just –" she shrugged helplessly.

"No problem." Raul came around to the passenger door and helped her down. To her amazement she needed his steady hand. He opened the back door and gathered all the bags. It looked like he was moving to Australia, carrying his own food.

She reached out. "Let me give you a hand with those."

"Nope. Got it." Amazingly, he had a free elbow to offer her. She took it. It wasn't fun, feeling unsteady on her feet, but holding on to Raul meant she wasn't going to fall. In no universe, if she were holding on to Raul, would she fall.

In the elevator, they both drew in a deep breath, as the aromas of Raffaello's cooking filled the small space.

Emma didn't know if she was more hungry or tired. While she and Toby frantically went over the data, Colin had from time to time put chopped veggies and dip, a few mini sandwiches, some sliced fruit on the desk. But Emma's stomach had been closed off. Now it was yawning wide open.

Over her head, Raul held open the door and she ducked into her apartment. She loved her apartment and had decorated it with family heirlooms from her mother's side of the family. Her father had been about to throw everything away after her mother passed away, but she salvaged some nice pieces, because they'd been the only things in her life that reminded her of the past.

The result was a charming apartment that was warm and welcoming. She always breathed a sigh of relief when she came home and the door closed behind her.

It was even better now that Raul was with her. It felt like they were closing the door on big problems that couldn't be solved and the only safe haven was here.

Raul headed toward the kitchen to offload the bags of food. "I can unpack everything," he said. "If you want to take a shower or change."

As he said it, she realized she desperately wanted to wash the frustrating day off her. "Are you sure you're ok?"

He smiled. "Oh yeah. Raffaello came out and explained every single dish in detail. What to warm up, what not to warm up. How to plate everything."

She stopped. "Well, that's odd. Raffaello never comes out of the kitchen. He lets Cristina take care of customers. He'll come out to say hello to me because I'm a friend of the family, but otherwise ..."

Raul's mouth curved in a cynical smile. "Oh, I don't think he cared how I was going to plate anything. I think he wanted to take a good look at me. To see if I was good enough for you."

Emma's mouth fell open in shock. "Whoa! That's – that's not what he was ..." She couldn't even find the words. It was a foreign concept, that anyone cared who she dated. Plus, she wasn't, technically, dating Raul. They were ... well, whatever it was they were doing, it wasn't a usual dating scenario. It was more like sailors in a storm clinging to each other.

"That is definitely what he was doing, believe you me." Raul was clearly used to dealing with food. He was unpacking the bags like a boss. "I recognize it. Every guy that dated one of my sisters got the treatment. And once they'd passed muster with us, *then* they went through Mama." He gave an exaggerated shudder that made her smile.

"Well, you must have passed muster." Raul seemed to have eight arms, because the groceries were put away and he was setting the table. She leaned against the counter and watched him work.

"I did. He gave me a ten percent discount."

"Huh. That's what he gives me. You must have really impressed him."

He smiled, and waved his hand at her. "Scoot. I don't want this stuff to get cold."

Emma took a really quick shower, which made her feel better. The power of running water. She put on a green track suit, but no underwear. Because ... because.

Raul looked up when she walked into the dining room. "Ah. Just in time. Milady..." He pulled out a chair.

She sat and looked at her plate. Raul had spooned some creamy mushroom risotto, two fried polenta wedges and a tomato salad with ricotta and torn basil leaves onto her plate. On serving platters on the table were slices of tagliata, a green bean salad with parmesan shavings, a thick pasta frittata and one entire platter of sourdough bruschetta. There were still bags on the counter, full of food, and one entire bag of desserts.

"Did I order all of this?"

"I might have made a few additions."

"It all looks so good," she sighed.

Raul pointed with his fork. "So, eat."

So, she did.

THE FOOD PUT SOME COLOR BACK IN HER FACE. IT SHOULD. IT WAS spectacular. Since he'd known Emma he'd eaten some amazing food. Everything about her, except for Toby and his troubles, signaled extreme pleasure.

Now that she had color back in her face, and was worrying him a little less, there were other appetites to feed.

He put his fork and knife on his plate and pushed back.

"Raul? Do you want –"

She saw his face. "Oh."

"Yeah, oh." He stood, held out his hand. Was really happy that she put her hand in his with no hesitation at all. He led her into her bedroom, trying hard not to drag her like a caveman, though he felt like one.

In her dark bedroom, Raul turned her in his arms and kissed her and felt everything slotting into place.

She was the one.

THEY WERE AT THE BREAKFAST TABLE AND THOUGH THERE WERE mysteries to solve still, Raul was feeling *great.* He hadn't slept long but what sleep he'd got had been like a coma. Good sex would do that. It was a sunny morning and would be a beautiful day. Emma was sitting right next to him eating a cheese muffin and he was eating toast and an amazing raspberry jam she'd made. Sunlight was pouring in, turning her hair to flames and her eyes ocean blue. All was right with the world, except shadowy people were messing with the country's financial system.

The doorbell rang. Raul met Emma's startled eyes. "Are you expecting someone?"

She shook her head, frowning. "Absolutely not. I can't imagine who it could be, particularly this early in the morning. It can't be Mike, the porter. He'd call up." The bell rang again, and again, impatiently.

She moved toward the door. Raul shot out an arm. "Wait."

Her eyes rounded when she saw that he came out of the bedroom with his Glock 19 in his hand. Not taking chances.

"You have a gun?"

"Always."

"It—it might be a neighbor."

Raul nodded. "Still." He wasn't putting his weapon down until he knew who it was.

She pressed the button for the intercom. "Who is it?"

The intercom showed the face of a man outside the door. Clean-shaven, short dark hair, regular features. Mr. Nobody. Suddenly the face disappeared and a badge showed. "Inspector Ferguson, SFPD, ma'am. We have a few questions about a colleague of yours, Toby Jackson."

Emma snatched the door open before Raul could stop her. She ushered him into the living room. "Come in, Detective. Do you have any news about his –" she stopped. Behind the detective's back, Raul was shaking his head violently, mimicking a throat slash. She caught on immediately, though she was frowning. "Please, have a seat."

She led the detective to an armchair and sat on the couch. Raul sat right next to her, real close. Put his arm around her just so the detective could see that she wasn't alone.

Emma had understood that she shouldn't give anything away. So, she sat patiently and waited for the detective to say something.

He brought out a notebook and clicked a pen. He had on a sharp stylish suit and combat boots. The boots were fine, most cops wore them now. But the suit was way too expensive for a mid-level cop.

"Ms. Holland," he began, looking as the notebook, "you are probably aware that your co-worker, Toby Jackson, is missing and has been missing for –" He lifted his eyes to her.

Emma, bless her, didn't take the bait. She sat quietly. Shrugged a shoulder. "I'm not too sure. I don't think he has been in the office all week. But I'm not certain because we work in different offices. I'm just reporting what our colleagues in his office said. It's been a busy week."

He nodded, writing down something in a precise small script. "Do you remember the last time you saw him?"

She didn't answer right away. Pretended to think about it. "I think – I think Friday before last. But I couldn't swear to it in court."

He narrowed his eyes at her. "Why do you say that? Do you think it will come to a trial?"

"No, not at all." Again, she kept her cool. "It's just an expression, Detective."

"Inspector."

"Inspector."

He stared at her for a moment, then looked back down at his notebook. "Ok. So, the last time you are certain you saw Mr. Jackson was Friday before last. And not over the weekend?"

"No." She didn't elaborate.

She was doing fine, not giving anything away. Because Raul wasn't too sure about Inspector Ferguson. Something wasn't tracking.

"Do you have any idea –"

"Can I see your badge?" Raul interrupted deliberately, and not politely.

"My badge?"

"Yeah. Your badge. Didn't get a good look at it."

They exchanged hard looks. Raul was fine with locking horns. He'd locked horns with the best. And he didn't back down.

The man dug into his pocket and came out with a wallet, flipped it open and held it in the palm of his hand. Not giving it to Raul. There was a metal star and a plastic-encased card. The star was five pointed, brass. The card gave his name – Eric

Ferguson. "We don't have badges in San Francisco. We have stars."

Maybe. Maybe not.

Raul's neck was crackling.

The guy put his wallet away and turned to Emma. "Ms. Holland, has Mr. Jackson seemed worried or agitated to you lately?"

"In what sense?" she asked sweetly.

"Um. Worried. Agitated. Not himself." He frowned. "You know."

"Inspector." Emma folded her hands in her lap. "Toby and I – and all the other people in the Quantitative Analysis department—do a difficult job that has serious consequences if we make mistakes in our analyses. We're all a little agitated and worried. It's part of the job."

The Inspector blew out a breath. "More agitated than normal, then."

She cocked her head. Said nothing. Raul's admiration for her, already high, went up about a thousand points.

"Did he say anything?"

"The last time I saw him at the office, we talked about a client. The client asked us to analyze gold price volatility. So, we discussed annualized daily return volatility, returns, correlations and trading volumes."

Take that, Raul thought.

"Did he mention any plans?"

"Plans?" Emma echoed delicately.

A muscle jumped in the Inspector's jaw. "Plans. Things he wanted to do in the future."

"Oh." Emma's eyebrows drew together. "Like investment plans or personal plans?"

"Personal." This came through gritted teeth.

"No. Absolutely not. We lead separate lives. If he took off for someplace, he certainly didn't tell me about it."

Emma flicked a glance at Raul. She wasn't cooperating with a police officer on his instructions, but she wasn't happy with it.

Raul was. There was something wrong with 'Inspector' Ferguson. He was going on gut instinct and the back of his neck, and they never steered him wrong.

"Where's your partner," he asked suddenly. Ferguson turned a tense face to him. "What?"

"Your partner. Police work in twos. Why aren't you with your partner?"

"He was detained back at the station house. Which is where we'll continue with Ms. Holland." He rose. Raul rose, too.

"I think not," Raul said, smiling, showing his teeth.

"It's a formality. We've questioned the other colleagues."

"Like who?" Emma cocked her head. "Who did you question? There are twenty of us, all told. There are fourteen quants in Toby's department. So, who did you question?"

The Inspector's nostrils widened as his teeth ground. "I'm not at liberty to say. But we do need to bring Ms. Holland in for questioning."

Over my dead body, Raul thought. "Not today, no."

And then it all went to shit. Fast.

The gun appeared in an instant. Ground into the side of Emma's head. "Yes, today. Right now, in fact."

14

It happened so fast, Emma couldn't react. One minute she was dealing with a really annoying police officer that Raul didn't trust, for some reason. He'd made it clear with his body language. And it turned out he was quite right not to trust Inspector Ferguson.

The barrel of his gun ground into her temple. Something warm trickled down her face. The barrel was breaking the skin, making her bleed.

He dragged her up and away from the sofa.

The officer's arm was around her neck, choking her, pulling her. Emma reached up to pull his arm away but it was like pulling at steel.

"Uh uh," he said. She was held so close to his chest she could feel the vibrations of his voice. He was talking to Raul, who had his own gun pointed straight at the cop-not-cop. "Put that down, whoever you are. I wasn't told there'd be anyone else here, so it's going to cost them extra. Put the gun down."

Raul stood straight, unmoving, gun in a two-handed clasp.

"I said *put it down*," the man roared, "Or I'll pop her in the head. Don't think I won't. So drop it."

Emma wheezed, trying to find her voice. Raul couldn't drop his gun! It was clear to her what would happen next. This creep would shoot Raul the instant he was unarmed, then drag her wherever it was he wanted her to go. He had to keep his gun!

Raul dropped the gun, and it clattered onto her tile floor. It didn't even have the good taste to go off and hit the guy in the leg. Though it would hit her in the leg first. Raul stood there, facing them, hands open and low, palms out. Totally vulnerable.

If he had another weapon she didn't see where it could be.

It hit her like a blow. She understood what Raul was doing. Raul was preparing to sacrifice himself for her. He understood, too, that the fake cop was going to shoot him and make off with her. He was willing to put his life on the line to buy her some time. Because the guy holding her was clearly serious. He wasn't trembling, he wasn't sweating, his voice was firm. He wanted to kidnap her, like Toby was kidnapped. And he wouldn't mind getting Raul out of the way while he did it.

No. No. A thousand times no.

She knew suddenly, without a second's doubt, that if she didn't have a gun to her head, Raul would have fought to his last breath. Would never have given up his weapon. Would never have stood like that, straight, hands open and weaponless, waiting for the fatal bullet.

He was not willing to risk her life, at the cost of his own.

No. No. *A thousand times no!*

Something switched on inside her. Up until now she'd held her heart a little out of whatever it was that was happening with Raul. He was ... almost too much. Too handsome, too charming. He was even good friends with her best friends. Something too good to be true. In her experience, things that were too good to be true were just that. Not true.

She'd had bad luck with men, so often that being on her

own felt like her natural state of being. Better to hold her heart safe because it would be broken, sooner or later.

But ... fuck that, as Felicity would say.

Right before her was a man of substance, a brave wonderful man, who was preparing to lay down his life for her. He could take down this fake cop, of course he could. He'd taken down two professional bodyguards with ridiculous ease. But the fake cop had a gun to her head, so he deliberately gave up his weapon. Making himself a target. All for her.

This was a man to cherish and no fake cop was going to take him away from her.

What to do? Well, Raul was brave but she was tricky.

The cop was dragging her backwards toward the door, one arm around her shoulders, one hand holding the gun to her temple. They were moving slowly, but moving. In a moment they would be in the hallway. She could work with the hallway.

They were in the hallway.

Emma suddenly slumped, making herself a deadweight. She could feel the surprise as the guy tightened his hold on her. She loosened her ankles, not holding herself upright. He was bearing her entire weight.

"Hey!" he shouted angrily.

Emma let out a long high keening cry. An animal cry of pain, loud and wrenching. "Oh God, I'm going to die! I don't want to die! Please God I don't want to die!" She was trembling from head to toe, shaking in terror. Her voice was waterlogged with tears as she babbled and wept. "Don't do this, let me go! I don't want to die!"

She shook and panted and wailed and trembled.

But her eyes were dry.

Raul was watching her carefully. She wailed and flailed, shaking wildly. Then, looking him straight in the eyes, writhing and crying out, she slowly winked. He didn't change expression in any way but she saw him put more of his weight on the balls of his feet.

"Fuck this!" The guy shouted. "Settle the fuck down!"

She'd turned slippery as an eel, her head bobbing up and down, making it hard for him to keep the muzzle against her temple. His arm around her neck tightened.

Just what she needed. An anchor.

Right in the middle of a wild keening cry, trembling with spasms, Emma burst into action. It had been years since she'd trained as a gymnast, but the muscle memory was there, and she didn't have to be perfect. She just had to create an opening for Raul.

She looked him straight in the eye, still sobbing loudly, and suddenly did a parkour move, a wall run, stepping straight up the wall, anchoring herself against the arm around her shoulders. As she did so, she pulled back, something really dangerous if she were alone. But she wasn't alone. She was pulling back with Fake Cop, who was completely unprepared and fell straight on his back with her on top, his head meeting Raul's knee on the way down.

On his way down, he shot his gun. The bullet simply punched a hole in her ceiling, but the gun had discharged not far from her right ear. It hurt!

She fell harmlessly right on top of him and scrambled to get out of the way, because Raul kicked away Fake Cop's gun and kneeled and punched him in the face then put him in a choke-hold. The man's eyes opened wide in panic. Raul was like a statue, unmoving.

But above all, Raul looked ... scary. His face was drawn, eyes narrowed, the muscles in his forearms ropy with effort. Even when fake cop slumped in his arms, unconscious, he continued holding him in the chokehold.

A few seconds went by, but he wasn't loosening his hold.

Emma had gone deaf, so it was like watching a tableau from hell, with the sound turned off.

Fake Cop was turning blue and Raul showed no intention of letting up.

Emma leaped to him, pulling at his arms. It was like trying to move steel pipe. "Raul! Let go! You're going to kill him!"

She couldn't hear herself and apparently, he couldn't, either.

"Raul!" she screamed at the top of her voice, though she could barely hear herself. All she could hear was a high-pitched ringing noise. He could finally hear, though. His eyes had lost their focus and now re-focused on her. He suddenly let the man drop and pulled her into his arms, holding her so tightly she could barely breathe.

Raul's head dropped to her left shoulder, near the undamaged ear. She could hear snippets through the whine. "—thought I'd lose you. I can't believe --- where did you --?"

He was breathing heavily. Something she couldn't hear but could feel as his chest bellowed in and out. Could it be he was trembling?

She patted his back, pet his hair. He was doing the same to her, checking for wounds. She reassured him. "It's ok. I'm okay."

He pulled back. He'd lost that frightening blank taut look, cupped her head. "You're yelling."

"What?" She couldn't hear him over the whine in her ear, though it was rapidly dissipating

He pursed his lips, exaggerating the words. "You're. Yelling."

"*What?*"

He bent to her good ear. "You're yelling!"

Oh. She lowered her voice to a point where she could barely hear herself. Looking down, she said, "What are we going to do about him?"

Raul got down on his haunches and frisked the man, who didn't move.

"Is he – is he dead?"

"No," he answered, looking up so she could read his lips. Luckily, her hearing was coming back. "Just out."

Emma didn't know what she felt about that. Glad he wasn't dead because Raul might have legal problems, but still angry at the son of a bitch who'd held a gun to her head and was definitely planning on shooting Raul while kidnapping her. This was a scumbag. No doubt part of the crew of scumbags who had kidnapped Toby.

She hauled her foot back and gave Fake Cop a huge kick in the side. The son of a bitch wanted to kidnap her? Kill Raul? *Take that!* She was wearing boots and it was very satisfying.

Raul looked up at her questioningly.

She shrugged. "He hurt himself falling down."

He nodded and stood up. "Guy's clean, except for the badge, which is clearly a fake, and an ID with a company logo."

"Don't tell me. In the name of Sierra Security Services."

His jaws bunched. "Bingo. So, before we do anything else, we immobilize him." He turned his head and looked at her, narrow-eyed. "I can't believe you did that. Not only that you had the courage to do it but that you *could* do it. You're not secretly a special forces operator, are you?"

The ringing in her ears had almost died down.

"What? No! Are you joking?" She stared at him. He was having trouble keeping a straight face. "You *are* joking. Good grief! I wouldn't know which end of a gun to hold."

"And yet ... Fuck, that was one crazy move. Have no idea how you pulled that off. It was crazy dangerous. I nearly lost ten years of my life."

He didn't even mention that it was *his* life that had been in danger. Fake Cop had wanted to kidnap her, not kill her. But he would have killed Raul or at least shot him.

He looked up at her. "What was that? That walking up the wall thing?"

"It's an element of parkour. I anchored myself to the man's arm and did what is called a wall run. I'm not particularly good at parkour but I was a gymnast when I was in high school." She ran a hand down in a *look at me* gesture. "I've always been built close to the ground."

He narrowed his eyes. "You weren't training for the Olympics or anything, were you?"

Emma laughed. Her first genuine laugh in what felt like forever. "No. Not even close. I was bad at tennis, soccer and softball. But decent at gymnastics. And I was lucky that the guy was taken by surprise."

"Yeah." Raul closed his eyes, blew out a breath, stood up and hooked an arm around her neck, pulling her close to him. "He could have –"

"I know," Emma said quietly. He could have pulled the trigger when it was against her head. So instead of having her ear ringing, she could be lying dead, with her brains splattered all over the dove-gray walls of the entryway. But she was not going to be kidnapped like Toby had been. No way. She was not going to be drugged and tied to a bed. The risk she took to avoid it had been worth it.

She was held closely to him. "So, what do we do now?" she asked into his shoulder.

Emma felt more than heard the big sigh. "First, I'm going to put this asshole in restraints, then I'm going to call someone to cart him away and then we're getting out of here and I'm taking you to Portland, where I can keep you safe."

Emma pulled away, looked up at that drawn, handsome face. He wasn't in charming mode, he was in worried warrior mode, nostrils pinched, deep brackets around his mouth, pale under the olive skin.

The idea of being whisked away to Portland was really

enticing. Felicity and Hope were there, with lots of security guys who were good at what they did, she'd be super protected. She'd be *away* from all of this, whatever the hell it was.

But ... Toby. She simply couldn't leave Toby, abandon him like this.

"Raul." Emma put her hand on his arm. "I'd love to wait this out in Portland, but I can't. I can't just turn my back on Toby. He needs a hand in figuring this out. I'm now up to date on his data and he can't pull anyone else into this because there isn't anyone else."

Raul's eyes had widened, the whites showing like a spooked pony's. "Wait, *what*? You want to stay in San Francisco? That's insane! You have to get out of Dodge, Emma. You can't stay here. They already sent one guy, and they'll keep sending guys until they get you. I'll be by your side, but I can't guarantee they won't take me down first. The only way I can guarantee your safety is if you're in Portland and I have my team. A plane could be here in a couple of hours."

He made sense. But she just couldn't abandon Toby. "Maybe Toby could come, too?"

Raul thought about it, head cocked to one side. "Mm. But I think Toby would want Colin and I don't think Colin could just take an indefinite leave of absence without losing his job and jeopardizing his career. Wait. Maybe Black Inc can help."

He pulled out his cell and called someone. She understood from the context that it was someone from Black Inc. "Hey. Raul Martinez here from ASI. I need some assistance." He explained the situation and listened carefully before closing the connection.

He turned to her, holding her hands. "Okay, this is a compromise but I want it understood that this whole thing is against my wishes, Okay? If you're wrong and I'm right, and you get hurt, I am going to be very angry and I am definitely going to say *I told you so*. We clear on that?"

Emma didn't smile because the guy on the floor, still out, was a living example of the seriousness of the situation, but she wanted to. Raul was so earnest, threatening to say an 'I told you so' as if it were a nuclear deterrent.

"Yes, we're clear. What's the plan?"

"A team of Black Inc guys are coming with two vehicles. The team will take out the trash –" he nudged the Fake Cop's body with his boot toe, "and leave a new vehicle for us, so if someone is watching the garage exit, they won't know it's us."

"The special film," she murmured.

"That, yeah, and it'll be a different vehicle from the one I drove here. On the GPS system will be the address of a safe house, and Black Inc's safe houses are pretty good. We hole up there and you and Toby keep working, either separately, or Toby comes to you, to us."

Emma nodded. "Yes. This whole thing is coming to a head, I can feel it. It won't be forever. In fact, if you need to get back to your job, I'm sure I can—"

"What the –" Raul reared back, shock on his face. "And *leave you*? With violent men after you? No way. Don't even think about it. For the moment, this is my job. Keeping you safe. I would even if my company objected. But the fact is, for ASI, keeping a friend of Felicity and Hope safe is a prime objective."

Emma tried not to slump in relief. She'd made the offer but the fact was, she was scared and really happy that Raul was staying with her.

"But –"

Raul's cell pinged. He checked it and went to the door. "The Black Inc operators are here. I suggest you pack a small bag. Anything you need that we don't have we can get."

There was a soft knock at the door and he opened. Two men stood there. They didn't look like Raul but they had his look. Well-built, competent-looking, athletic. One sandy-haired, one brown-haired. Raul knew the sandy-haired one.

"Hey man, good to see you." He gave one of those manly thumps on the back and held his hand out to the second man.

"Emma, the cavalry is here." He indicated the sandy-haired man. "This is Eddie 'Eagle' Forest. We went through Hell Week together. Fun times. And this is –"

The brown-haired man held his hand out. It was massive and calloused and nicked. And so huge it was scary. In her work she basically used her brains and her hands for keyboarding. But he held her hand gently for a couple of seconds and let it go. "Declan O'Rourke, ma'am. Most people call me 'Irish'." He looked down at the ground, at Fake Cop, still out, nudged him with his foot. "What do we have here?" Both men looked at Raul.

"Emma and I are in the middle of something nasty, potentially very nasty. This joker came to the door with a fake SFPD ID, asked her to come downtown to the station house. When I objected, he grabbed Emma and put a gun to her head. But Emma is a super hero and walked up a wall and took him down."

As one, the two men turned to her, eyes wide.

She blushed. "Um. No. It wasn't quite like that. I did a parkour run at the wall to break his grip. Raul grabbed him immediately once he was off balance. He was the one who took him down."

The two men turned back to Raul.

"Nope," Raul said. "Not even close. She took that fucker down like a boss. She's a real badass."

Emma didn't know how to reply to that. She didn't feel like a badass at all. Luckily, a noise distracted them all. The man at her feet stirred and Raul kicked him in the head and he subsided.

They were back to business.

"Okay," said Eddie. "I understand this asshole belongs to SSS, right?"

"Yeah," Raul said. "I found this together with his fake badge." He held out a piece of plastic. Emma saw a company ID, with SSS across the top. The same one that had been in the pockets of the two guards where Toby had been held.

"Okay." Eddie pulled out a plastic restraint from his back pocket. "You got his hands but we'll need to get his feet. So, we'll take care of this joker, and dump him on SSS's doorstep. I'm assuming you don't want law enforcement involved."

Emma looked at Raul and shook her head. She didn't want to have to explain things and would undoubtedly mess everything up and involve Toby. And the police didn't have any tools that would help. Raul nodded to her and turned to the two Black Inc guys.

"Nope."

"Okay," Eddie said again. He didn't look like he cared that much about calling in law enforcement. Emma imagined that these were men used to looking after things themselves. "So, like we agreed, we each came in a separate vehicle, here are the keys to one of them with the address of a Black Inc safe house in the GPS." He tossed a fob at Raul, who caught it one-handed. He also tossed a set of keys. "And the keys to the safe house. I'll text you the alarm code. There's food in the freezer and a list of local takeout places. Jacob Black said to use it for as long as you need."

"Not long, I hope." Raul said and sent her A Look. He wasn't happy staying here and not going back to Portland with her. Emma wasn't happy either, but it was what it was. She couldn't abandon Toby and leave him to deal with this mess all alone. "Emma, why don't you pack some stuff?"

She looked at him and the two operators. "I'm going to disable all the cameras in the building and in the garage, and in the vicinity of the garage exit. For how long should I disable them?"

The two men looked at each other. "That would be really useful. For maybe forty minutes. You can do that?" Eddie asked.

Raul nodded. "She could turn off the lights in Beijing if she wanted to."

They turned again in unison to her, eyes wide.

She shrugged. "Maybe not *all* of Beijing. Just a few districts. So, I'll turn off the cameras for forty minutes. You might want to tell security downstairs."

Raul nodded. "He's one of your guys. BHS."

Eddie pulled out a cell and talked quietly in it.

Raul was talking quietly to Declan as he restrained Fake Cop's ankles. Nothing for her to do here. She walked into the bedroom to pack. For how long, she had no idea.

She packed as if she were going on a business trip for a week, plus a light non-work wardrobe. She looked around her room. She loved her room. She loved her whole house.

For the foreseeable future, her pretty little apartment was going to be off limits and she had no clue when she could come back. Or even if she could ever come back.

15

Raul clenched his teeth as he drove to Black Inc's safe house, keeping back all the words he wanted to say, but wouldn't. Everything about this situation made him angry with nowhere to put his anger.

He was mad at the world because Emma was going to be staying in San Francisco instead of Portland, where she'd be safe, he was mad at Toby for involving her in this, he was mad at whoever the fuckheads were who were doing whatever the fuck they were doing.

It enraged him.

He welcomed the rage because it hid what was lurking underneath – sheer terror.

He'd been in battle and knew how to push fear way down, so it didn't affect him. His teammates, too, were unaffected by it. He knew they could handle fear. They'd been trained for it, had been taught how to deal with it. Had had fear pounded out of them, or at least knew how to ignore it.

So, nothing prepared him for the sheer terror he'd felt when that SSS fuckhead had grabbed Emma and screwed the muzzle of a gun against her temple so hard it broke the skin. Watched the blood trickle down her face.

Raul had had no idea how stable the man was. Whether this was a ploy to grab her or whether he got off on seeing brains splatter. His former commander had been one of those. He enjoyed planting bullets in human heads. Considered it almost an art form.

Raul had seen a lot of bullets plow their way through a lot of heads. What was left was pitiful. A human dropped where he stood like a puppet whose strings had been cut. What made them human – their brains – were reduced to gray matter mixed with blood and skull fragments, in a puzzle that could never be put back together again.

And that could happen to Emma.

The thought nearly brought him to his knees.

All SEALs knew that going into battle, they could lose teammates. Raul had lost two teammates – good, brave men who were mourned. But also men who knew the risks they were taking and had the tools and the training to fight back.

Not small, delicate Emma. Not beautiful, smart, lively Emma, who vibrated with life and intelligence. He'd been falling for her since he first set eyes on her, but right then, with a gun to her beautiful head, he realized he wasn't falling, he'd fallen.

This was the one. He'd never felt like this before. Never been so fascinated, never been so attracted. Never felt so excited and relaxed at the same time. She was everything he wanted without knowing she existed. A miracle of smarts and humor and kindness. Easy to be with, fun to be with, but also serious and dependable.

It was like some giant algorithm in the sky, some celestial Tinder, had reached inside his head and pulled out the formula for the ideal woman.

Emma.

The thought that any second that miracle woman could drop dead at his feet, a pink mist clouding the air, drove all tactical and strategic thoughts from his head. He was reduced to jelly, sweat breaking out all over his body.

All he could think about, over the drumbeat of his heart, was Emma's lifeless body lying boneless on the ground. All that liveliness, all that spirit and beauty – gone.

Gone before he could explore her – this fascinating woman who spoke languages but would not speak of her family.

He'd half planned it already in his head – Emma in Portland, reunited with her best friends, creating magic for the ASI operators. He'd already planned on introducing her to his abuela, who'd love her. True, the Martinez clan were a rowdy lot, but she didn't seem like the kind of woman who scared easily.

All this was already in his head, when all of a sudden Emma had a gun at her temple, and the bottom dropped out of his world. The man holding her was an operator. His gun was rock steady. When he ordered Raul to drop his weapon or he'd pull the trigger and annihilate Emma, Raul didn't know if he meant it or not. It was possible the man was bluffing. That he needed Emma alive. It was also possible he wasn't bluffing and had orders to bring her or drop her.

When Raul tossed his gun, he was well aware that he was sacrificing himself. That it was almost impossible that he was going to walk away from this alive. But he had no choice.

It broke his heart to hear Emma wail with terror. To see her tremble in panic and fear. To hear her weep with fear.

Only – no tears. And her crying and shuddering had the effect of making her slippery. Slowing the fake cop's progress toward the door. He was finding it hard to hold onto her.

And then – she winked! Raul's heart soared when he saw that. She wasn't panicking and out of control with fear. She had a plan. He had no idea what the plan was but he trusted Emma and whatever the plan was, he would do his damnedest to help.

It was a ploy. She hadn't given up. He couldn't either. So, while she trembled and writhed in fuckhead's grasp, making it hard for him to hold her and keep the gun at her head, Raul had started pulling in air. Preparing himself for God knows what, but whatever it was, he was going to follow Emma's lead.

He wasn't expecting her to fucking run up a wall.

But when she did, he was ready. Fucker's head encountered Raul's knee on his way down to the floor. Hard. And now Fucker was hog-tied and on his way to being dumped on SSS's doorstep, the third man that had happened to.

Raul checked constantly on Emma as he drove. He needed to reassure himself that she was okay. She sure seemed okay. She wasn't dissolved in hysterics, as she had every right to be, considering someone had threatened her life not too long ago.

She was a little paler than usual, but composed. Looking out the window but not seeing anything. Her eyes weren't tracking what was outside, but what was inside. He was used to this. Felicity and Hope would disappear inside themselves like this, in a fugue state it wasn't smart to interrupt, because it meant they were working something out.

He hoped she was figuring out what the hell was going on, because in twenty-four hours he was tempted to channel his inner caveman and drag her with him to Portland, whether she wanted to go or not.

He didn't want to bully her. Normally he wouldn't even contemplate making her do something she didn't want to do. But her life was at risk and no one knew the direction the risk was coming from. Raul was willing to compromise but he wasn't happy with this compromise – staying in the city where there was danger to her.

He turned into a leafy road in the suburbs, carefully

reading the street numbers through massive foliage, and there it was. The Black Inc safe house.

Black Inc did things right. It looked upscale and comfortable, on a quiet street. It looked like a normal upper middle-class home, the kind that had a lawyer dad and professor mom, 2.5 kids designed in a lab to be doctors and lawyers, with maybe an allergen-free dog.

But Raul knew it was a fortress. Black Inc would have made it nearly impregnable. On the console between seats was a remote control and he had all the codes. For the gates, for the garage, for the front door. It would have carefully disguised security cams all around, IR sensors, motion sensors, even sensors that could distinguish, by weight, animals from people. The walls would be coated with a substance that was impervious to radar and infrared. The windows would be treated and bullet resistant and the shutters bullet proof. Most Black Inc safe houses nowadays had door handles embedded with HD video cameras and smart locks equipped with biometric fingerprint scanners.

Raul had no doubt that Black Inc had retrieved his fingerprints and Emma's and programmed them into the security features.

Emma was going to be safe here. And while she was here, he was not going to be more than a hand's span from her. Nothing was going to happen to her.

The codes worked, as did his handprint, and soon they were inside.

Raul dropped his bag and both Emma's bags – she insisted on carrying her own electronics – and looked around. Some safe houses, particularly those which weren't used much – looked like abandoned morgues. Dead flies, pizza cartons stacked in corners, musty smells. This wasn't anything like that. It was a perfectly pleasant space, nicely decorated without any personal touches. Like a four star hotel suite. It still smelled of lemon polish. It wasn't going to be a hardship staying here.

He stood in the foyer, bags at his feet, almost quivering with ... something. Some strong emotion he couldn't figure out. The neutral colors and soft armchairs didn't help. He couldn't square what he was seeing with what he was feeling – restless and anxious. Raul didn't do restless and anxious. What the fuck?

"Raul?"

He whipped his head around to Emma, who was dressed in a green cotton sweater, tan cotton pants and loafers. The perfect outfit for whatever it was they were going to face.

She put her hand on his chest. "Are you okay?"

It was as if her hand burned through his clothes to his skin. Was she sensing something wrong with him by touch?

He put his hand over hers.

"No," he said starkly. "I'm not okay."

She just looked up at him and said nothing.

"You could have died back there." His voice came out scratchy and deep, rough. As if he hadn't spoken in years.

"I know," she said softly. "I was terrified I'd end up like Toby – drugged and tied to a bed."

He closed his eyes in pain. "I kept seeing your brains splattered over the wall."

"Yeah," she answered. "Management would have been so angry. It takes forever to get blood out."

He spluttered out a laugh, though it wasn't a laughing matter. He opened his arms just as she walked into them, both having the exact same thought at the exact same time. To be as close together as possible.

Raul held Emma tightly, hoping he wasn't crushing her but his arms simply wouldn't loosen up. He'd been especially frightened that he'd be dead and they could do what they wanted with Emma. What brutal men could do to women didn't bear thinking about, but Raul had seen it. He tightened his grip around her.

She wriggled in his arms. "Raul? I need to breathe."

He looked down at her, at that lovely, intelligent face that in a short span of time had become so important to him.

"Breathe through me," he ordered, and kissed her.

She kissed him back, oh yeah. It was many things, heat and desire, but for both of them it was a celebration of life. They were alive, both of them, when they could have been dead. The Martinez clan would claim his body and bury him in the family crypt in San Diego. His parents, his siblings, his abuela—they would all weep bitter tears at his loss.

Who would weep for Emma? Hope and Felicity and Riley, for sure. Her father? Just the mention of him made her face close up. Maybe he wouldn't mourn the loss of his wonderful daughter.

He and Emma would have had no chance to see where this wild attraction would take them. They'd be dead bones in the cold ground.

The drumbeat of urgency thrummed in his veins. It was as if he'd never made love before. Everything was new and so exciting he could barely breathe. Her mouth, soft, still tasting faintly of coffee, tongue tangling with his. Her skin. Oh god, the softest thing in the universe, like warm silk. Her clothes were in the way of touching all that skin and he impatiently undressed, stopping just short of ripping everything off her because it felt obscene to have cloth between his hands and lips and her skin.

Pulling off her sweater made her hair lift in waves that crackled with static electricity. Red locks tumbled over her shoulders, one perfect lock curling around her nipple, like an offering.

Well, it *was* an offering, her breast, made for his mouth. He licked her cherry red nipple and heard her gasp, then started suckling hard. Her back arched to offer herself even more to his mouth. He lightly nipped his way across the soft skin of her chest and latched onto her other breast. Oh god the *taste*. Like salty ice cream with a salty cherry on top. One arm was around her back, the other was busy opening her pants, pushing everything down so that ... ah! There she was, warm and wet, soft folds just waiting for him to enter her. He started with a finger, reaching inside her heat.

Every moment was a moment that took them further away from that point in time in which they could have been both dead. Every moment was a celebration of life.

"God, Emma," Raul gasped. "I can't go slow. Just can't. Sorry."

In answer, she pushed herself onto his finger, writhing around it. He felt her contract once, twice.

She was coming.

He had to be with her. Had to.

Two steps away was a couch. He had no idea how, but in a second, he'd stripped them both and was kissing her mouth and entering her sex with one sharp thrust. She moaned into his mouth, then gave a sharp cry, holding him tightly as she came. Heat filled his body, shot down his spine and came out through his dick as he came, too, pounding into her until every single drop of liquid in his body had emptied itself into her.

Raul slumped onto her, completely wiped out, muscles like rubber.

It took a while for his breathing to slow and for him to realize where they were. He'd fucked her like a wild wolverine. This was Emma. Emma!

Regret filled him.

He was better than this.

Was she still talking to him?

Only one way to find out.

"You, ah, you okay?" he ventured.

He felt her wriggle fingers and toes. "I think so. Hard to tell. I think I died and came back."

"You're not mad at me?"

"For giving me the best orgasm of my life? What am I, stupid?"

He grinned. "No, you're not stupid." *Nail it down,* he thought. "So – you're not mad at me?"

Emma lifted her head an inch then let it fall back. She wriggled her butt. He was still inside her and they smelled of her perfume and sex. "But I think we just left a wet spot on this very expensive couch."

16

There was loud music coming from somewhere. Familiar music. The Star Trek theme. What...?

Emma opened an eye. She was not in her bedroom but it was a nice one. Heat against her back. Raul.

"Ignore it," he mumbled and tightened his arms around her.

It all came rushing back – the attack, the move to the safe house. The wild sex. A massive meal from a local Thai restaurant. Ready to go back to bed when Colin called and said that Toby had passed out from fatigue.

So, Emma had felt duty bound to continue Toby's research. He'd uploaded everything to a super secure site in the darkweb and she downloaded and continued analyzing his data until 3 a.m., when she fell asleep with her cheek on the keyboard. It was 3:30 by the time she slid into bed. Raul was fast asleep, but turned over and held her. It felt so good she fell instantly into sleep and hoped to sleep at least until nine am.

It wasn't nine, it was ... she cranked open an eyelid. There was a clock that projected the time onto the ceiling. Six a.m.! She'd barely slept two and a half hours!

But the Star Trek theme kept playing.

"Don't answer that," Raul said again.

She checked her cell. "It's Toby."

That woke him all the way up. He sat up straight in bed, black hair tousled, a dark shadow of stubble darkening his jaw. He looked so incredibly sexy she nearly forgot to breathe.

Raul moved to sit next to her. Her glance fell to his lap where, amazingly, he was starting an erection. He shrugged and pulled the covers over his lap. "Don't pay him any attention. Put Toby on speakerphone."

She fumbled for a moment, still sleep-ridden and distracted by Raul.

"Tobe?"

"Emma!" Toby voice came amplified out of the speaker. His hair was tousled and he had huge dark circles under his eyes. He sounded excited and scared. Both. And looked worried. "Listen, sorry I conked out on you. But I was just now going over the data again and I think I have pinpointed at least the date."

"The date?" she echoed stupidly. It felt like her head was on a time relay. "What date?"

"The date of whatever event is supposed to trigger the short selling."

She sat up straighter, wide awake now. "Do you know what the event is?"

"No." Emma could hear the disappointment in Toby's voice. He looked away for a moment, as if ashamed. "But like I said, I know when it is. It's the moment that the short selling begins to take effect. And there will be a cascade effect for at least three days."

"So when?"

"10:30 a.m. today, June 10. And I have a horrible suspicion we're going to see markets completely wiped out. Not to mention that the event might be something awful."

Yes, she thought. To place huge bets on short sales, whatever it was would be something awful. Maybe worse than 9/11?

She shuddered, threw back the covers and fumbled with her feet for her slippers. The drumbeat of anxiety beat in her chest, but she didn't know what to do with her anxiety. Something bad was going to happen very soon, but ... what?

Earthquakes and tsunamis couldn't be predicted months in advance, so it had to be man-made. And the head of a drug cartel was involved, so it couldn't be good.

"Toby – the date and the time ... are you sure?"

On her cell screen Toby looked determined and worried. "Almost. I'd say yes but there's always Heisenberg."

Raul was at her shoulder, staring at the cell monitor. Emma edged the cell in such a way that the camera didn't broadcast the fact that he was naked. Though they were together in a bedroom at six a.m. She sighed. Toby wouldn't care. If anything, he complained that she didn't date enough.

Raul bumped her shoulder with his. "Who is this Heisenberg?"

"It's an uncertainty principle."

"A what?"

"It's a lower bound on the product of uncertainties of a pair of conjugate variables. Usually, it takes the position and momentum to be the conjugate variable."

Raul sat back, sorry he'd asked.

"Man, I wish someone else could look at this stuff. Maybe we're too close to the data," Toby said.

"Nobody at PIB," Emma said, alarmed.

"No. God no." Toby scrubbed his face. "Anyway, what I have right now is that something will happen that will earn someone or a consortium of someones at least a trillion dollars and the data shows that that something will happen in a few hours. Today. That's my best analysis."

Emma's heart had taken up a desperate drumbeat. "Wait. Stay on the line."

She kept the connection open but closed the video function. She was hastily dressing and Raul took his clue from her and was pulling up a pair of jeans. Looking at Raul, she said, "I'm going to call Felicity and Hope in on this."

"Good thinking," he said. "But just have Hope come in to the office, not Felicity. She can do her thinking at home. She's pretty close to her time and Metal would kill me if she has to go into the office."

"She won't have to. We can loop her in from home."

Emma told Toby to continue waiting, went into the spacious living room and connected her call to the maxi flat screen up on the wall. Toby's worried face filled the screen. "Hey, Tobe. I think we might be both maxed out. I'm calling in some friends in Portland to analyze this stuff."

"Your old friends from the NSA?"

"Yeah. And Hope worked in a bank for a while so she has some financial background. I think we might be missing something because we've looked at the data for too long."

Emma could tell Toby's leg was shaking, which was a trait of his when he was under stress. "We don't have much time if I'm right about the timeline."

"Yeah. Can you condense the data that led you to today so they don't waste time wading through extraneous data?"

"Okay." Toby disappeared from the screen.

Emma called Hope. She didn't wake her up, she was in her kitchen, drinking coffee with her fiancé, Luke Reynolds, Raul's friend. He waved.

"Emma." Hope spoke into her cell, her face projected up on the wall. She smiled. "Good morning. You're up early. Making another billion for that bank of yours?"

Emma didn't smile back. "Hm. I might have quit my job. Maybe."

"You *might* have quit your job? Isn't that an either/or proposition?"

Raul leaned forward so the camera could catch him. "She hasn't been to work in two days, and will never go back."

Emma rolled her eyes. Hope blinked. "Huh. Okay. So, Emma, you were right that something bad is happening there?"

Emma swallowed. "Yeah. We don't know quite what. In fact –"

"Whoa!" Hope interrupted excitedly. "If you're not working for that bank, that means you are out of a job. Come here and work with us! Oh God, it would be perfect! My bosses would hire you in a heartbeat. Give you a huge signing bonus. Felicity and I can barely cope with the workload and Felicity, bless her, is about to pop. Twice. She would probably continue working while delivering her twins, but Metal is putting down his size thirteen boot pretty heavily."

Emma leaned forward. "We can talk about the future later. Right now, I'm uploading data. A lot of it is from the darknet."

Hope's dark eyebrows flew upward. "Financial data from the darknet? Someone's being very naughty."

"Someone's short selling something like several billion dollars, betting that something bad is going to happen. And we just discovered that the due date is today. As of 10:30, which is when the first batch of shorts comes due. If there is a catastrophe bad enough, someone will make over a trillion dollars."

Hope's pretty face turned shocked. "Sounds like 9/11 all over again."

"Only not concentrated on airline shares." Emma blew out a breath. "Well, whatever it is, most of the short selling is coming from my institution, the Pacific Investment Bank."

"What?"

"I suspect the CEO has used company funds for a huge number of shorts. The people directly over him have no clue how to read the data and if he has bet correctly, he will make

PIB a ton of money. The people under him wouldn't dare question the investments."

Hope shook her head. "Get out of there, honey."

"Don't worry." Raul pushed his face toward the monitor. "She's not stepping foot in there again." He slanted his eyes toward her, daring her. "Ever."

She wasn't arguing. However ...

Nope. Not going there. She wasn't going to get into a pissing contest with Raul. He was tougher than her and probably meaner. Plus, she had a creepy feeling about the place, now. She didn't want to go back and she didn't have to. She didn't even have any personal belongings there. The computer belonged to the bank and the data she generated belonged to the bank, too. In her desk drawer was a Chanel lipstick, a cheap pen and cheaper notebook for the few times she jotted things down, a comb and the business card of a Vietnamese takeout place.

Her only real friend there was Toby, who was never going back, either.

There was nothing there for her. For them. Not anymore.

"No," she agreed. "Not going back. And maybe I might come up and give you a hand, at least for a while." She ignored Raul's gusty sigh of relief. "But right now, I just have this horrible feeling. A feeling that something terrible is going to happen very soon and that someone or several someones is going to make a ton of money off it."

"More than a ton," Hope said earnestly. "A ton of $100 bills would be a little over 90 million dollars. Many tons."

Emma slid her eyes to Raul and saw him smile a little. She smiled back.

"Plus, your feelings are pretty good indicators. Remember that feeling you had about ISIS members meeting in Rome when we were at the NSA?"

That wiped out her smile. Alarmed, Emma turned to Raul.

"What's your clearance level?"

"Probably not as high as yours," he replied. "We didn't analyze, we just kicked down doors. But I'm not talking, so don't worry. Worry about what might be happening today."

He was right. She got back to business.

"Hope, I'm looping in Toby Jackson, my colleague at PIB."

"*Former* colleague," he said tartly, coming online. "Current friend."

Hope waved. "Hi, Toby."

"Hey, Hope." Toby lifted his hand. "Heard a lot about you from Emma."

"Gang." Raul leaned forward. "Let's get back on track. What do you want Hope to do, Emma?"

"Well, Toby and I are going to keep refining the data and we'll go over it together when it's been consolidated. There's a lot of noise to signal. We should talk when it's signal only."

"Right. So, what do you want me to do?" Hope asked.

Emma glanced at Toby. "Do you think you could do a deep, deep dive on this man?" She put up the photo of Brandon Rutherford entering Whittaker Hamilton's office. "I'll be sending more photos and what we were able to dig up." Raul opened his mouth and she lay a finger across it. "Raul tells me that somehow he is also the head of a drug cartel in Baja, known for its production of fentanyl. He has perfected a variation known as santalucia. In both incarnations, he has a degree in chemistry and in Mexico is known as El Quìmico. His name is also Jorge Marin de Herrera. There's not much on him. Can you do a deep NSA dive on him?"

She knew what she was asking. A 'deep NSA' dive meant hacking and cracking illegally into databases.

"Sure," Hope said, as if it were no big deal. As if she wouldn't be tried as a cyber-criminal if she were caught. She'd also have to make sure nothing came back to ASI. "You'll have to mask ..." Emma began.

"On it," Hope answered. "And in a few minutes, I'll loop Felicity in. Hoping I won't have to run interference with Metal."

Felicity was the Atom Bomb of hacking and cracking.

Well, Emma had two of the finest minds in the business on this. She'd have called in Riley, but Riley had gone offline diving deep into some esoteric NRO project. The clock was running ...

A cup of coffee magically appeared at her elbow. Together with a flaky croissant. She looked at Raul with gratitude.

"Nothing else I can do for you," he said grimly. "Not at this stage."

Well, considering he'd saved her life ...

She and Toby turned back to the data.

6:30 a.m. on a day in which something bad was going to happen at 10:30.

On the screen, Toby was looking grim and exhausted. He'd been held captive and drugged, of course he was exhausted. But he was doing his very best. She had to, too.

They had to figure out the pattern of the short selling. It didn't seem to be linked in any way to a specific sector of the economy. Which was nuts, because whatever it was that was supposed to trigger a swift downturn of the economy, it had to be linked to something. To airline crashes or mass poisoning or *something*. But the stocks were bought in every single sector. Insurance, manufacturing, computers, hotel chains, vehicles. She and Toby tried to find any commonalities, any local threads running through them, but they couldn't. They ran algos Toby created on the spot to find underlying links, but there were none. The only commonality was that the investments were huge.

Whatever it was, it was going to be big. And bad.

7:30. Emma stopped for a moment when the figures started blurring, hanging her head. A strong hand rubbed her sore neck muscles and shoulder muscles. God, that felt good.

7:32. She bent back over the keyboard when Hope's face appeared on the monitor. She was in her office. Her boyfriend Luke hovered in the background, looking grim. A third person appeared on the big wall monitor and Emma did a double take. He looked like the husband of a friend of Hope's and of Felicity, Lauren Jackman. Emma had seen photos of her husband. Jacko Jackman, a frightening looking man everyone said was a genuine hardass except around his wife, Lauren, and daughter, Alice. And around Felicity and Hope. Everyone else had to watch out.

The man on the monitor looked exactly like Jacko Jackman except thirty years older and with a full head of steel gray hair where Jacko shaved his head.

Hope appeared at the man's side, talking fast. "Emma, this is the father of one of the operatives here at ASI, Jacko Jackman. Lauren's husband. His name is Dante Jimenez." Huh. He didn't share a name with his son. Well, Emma was not one to question the way families worked. Her own was strange enough.

"How do you do," she said politely.

Raul bent to the camera. "Dante, we are in a time crunch here..."

"I think I know what's about to go down." Dante's deep voice was stark.

Everyone snapped to attention.

Raul leaned forward. "Talk. We don't have much time."

Hope made room for Jimenez in front of her computer monitor. Both their heads showed, Luke pacing in the background.

"Today there is a meeting, in a mansion that has been emptied, of all the heads of the security apparatus of the United States. It's being held about twenty miles from San Francisco. Almost a thousand people, the men and women responsible for the safety of the country. It's absolutely Top Secret. Apparently there'd been chatter of a biological attack, and a decision was made to address it and to use the meeting to coordinate the various agencies. I'm ex-DEA and I was asked to submit a report on the drug trade. But I'm retired and my granddaughter, Alice, is starting summer day camp. I want to be there."

Silence.

Raul drummed his fingers once on the desktop. "All the agencies?"

"Every single one," Jimenez answered grimly. "The principals alone are 300 strong. Each principal will bring at least two deputies. We're talking the top tier of the entire intelligence and law enforcement community. All the three letter agencies and some five letter ones."

"Haven't heard anything about it," Raul murmured.

"Me, either," Luke said.

"No, you wouldn't. A meeting like this has never been held before. The intel has been tightly compartmented. The mid-level officials of the agencies wouldn't even know. They'd only know that their boss and his deputies were gone for the day."

Emma was thinking furiously. "How – how much damage would there be if something happened at this meeting? Suppose an attack were to kill all the members at the meeting. What would happen? I mean all the agencies have plenty of personnel, right? Life would continue, right?"

The muscles of Jimenez's jaw worked. "No, it wouldn't. It would be devastating beyond words. The first thing would be to assume that it was an attack by one of our enemies, an act of war. Either by Russia or China or some second-tier state that had a stroke of luck and cut off the heads of our intelligence community. It would take some time to figure out whether this was an act of terrorism or of war. The country would come to a grinding halt."

"How so?" Emma asked. A grinding halt. Perfect for a storm of short sales.

"Would it be as bad as after 9/11?"

"It would be worse. Much worse. All transportation would be stopped, immediately. All planes in the air rerouted to the nearest airport, no planes allowed to take off, no trains, no road transport. All banks would shut down immediately. Schools and shops closed and everyone sent home. Economic activity would cease. The National Guard would be called out and would patrol the streets. Posse Comitatus would be suspended. There would probably be a strict curfew. The military would definitely go to DEFCON 3, known as Round House. Air Force ready to mobilize in 15 minutes. They could go up to DEFCON 1 – known as Cocked Pistol."

Emma sat back, mind whirling. "If there was no follow up, how long would the emergency last?"

"You mean if there was no further attack?"

She nodded her head, throat tight.

"A week."

"Tobe," she murmured.

"Yeah." The screen adjusted to include his tired face. "The shorts last about a week. And a lot of money will have been made and a lot of money will have been lost."

"Oh," Jimenez said. "The effects will last much, much longer than a week. Things will never go back to the way they were. When the military goes to DEFCON I – which it never has, by the way, but an assassination of the entirety of its intelligence community would qualify – it takes time to de-deploy. Not to mention the fact that if some lower-level grunts think one of our enemies is responsible, we might launch a few nuclear missiles and there is no coming back from that."

"Worse than 9/11," Hope whispered.

"It would make 9/11 look like a Sunday walk in the park."

"When does the conference start?" Raul asked.

Jimenez turned his face and it looked as if he were addressing Raul directly. "It started an hour ago."

17

It took a lot to scare Raul and now he was terrified. What Jacko's dad was talking about was essentially the end of the United States for a generation, maybe more. Knocking it far back, maybe to depression-era status.

Lives would be lost, lots of them. The mayhem Jimenez described came with riots which would have to be ruthlessly repressed. Hospitals which wouldn't function for weeks, maybe months. Maybe even years. Kids losing school years, maybe forever. There were four hundred million guns in private hands and they would come out, real fast.

He checked his watch. 8:58.

Anything he and his teammates could do, anything at all, to stop this, they'd do. There was still time.

"Do we know anyone there?" he asked Jimenez.

"Sure." Dante nodded his head. "I know the representatives of the DEA, the FBI and some Homeland Security people. But overall security is overseen by Jacob Black and his people. We should contact him."

Raul had Jacob Black on speed dial. Everyone at ASI did. ASI and Black Inc worked together often.

Black answered on the second ring. "Raul. Talk to me." There was the low buzz of voices in the background, mostly male, some female.

Jacob Black showed up on the huge wall monitor. Black was dressed in a sharply cut suit, which Raul knew Black hated. He was a field guy and usually dressed in jeans and a flannel shirt and combat boots.

"Can you go somewhere private, Jacob? It's important."

If what Dante said was true, Jacob was providing security for one of the most important security meetings in a generation, but he didn't betray any emotion or exasperation. "Can it keep?" he said. "I'm in the middle of something."

"I know. I have urgent intel about your meeting."

"Give me a minute." The video and sound cut off and then a moment later Jacob Black came back online in a darker room and with no background noise. "So, what's up?"

Raul looked to the side. Maybe Emma was better suited to explain the background. "I'm going to let Emma Holland explain. She was with Felicity, Hope and Riley at NSA. She knows what she's doing."

Black's craggy face lit up. "Are you a friend of those genius women at ASI?"

Emma sketched a faint smile. "Yessir, I am."

"Well, before you go any further, let me offer you a job. I envy ASI those women and I'd like one of you for Black, Inc. We'd treat you well."

Emma looked taken aback. She was probably flattered. It was actually extremely flattering that such a powerful man wanted her to join his company, which was one of the premier security firms in the world. He'd offer her a great salary with great benefits.

But ... no.

Raul slung an arm around her shoulders. "She's coming up to Portland. Joining the old gang, at ASI."

Emma slanted him a glance but said nothing.

Black gave a frosty smile. "Understood." Raul was sure he understood it all. "So, Ms. Holland, what is this about? I'm sorry to say that my time is limited."

"Mr. Black, I understand that you are at a secret summit of America's intelligence and security community." Black opened his mouth but Emma held up a finger.

And Black's mouth shut.

Emma had somehow morphed from a very pretty young woman to a figure of authority that could shut even Jacob Black up.

"It doesn't really matter how we know—"

"I might have an idea how this happened," a deep voice interrupted.

The screen opened a new field and Dante Jimenez appeared in the top right-hand corner. "Black," he said, nodding.

"Jimenez," Black answered, nodding back.

"About three months ago a DEA agent went missing. He was operating in Baja and had links to informants there connected to the Baja Cartel. We haven't had word from him since early March. There were rumors that a US agent was tortured to death but we haven't had corroboration and believe me when I say that we have been conducting scorched earth investigations. We don't take lightly attacks on our agents. The Baja Cartel is headed by Jorge Marin de Herrera. Marin is a gifted chemist and is known to be able to extract any kind of info pharmaceutically, coupled with torture when necessary. If our agent was tortured, he knew about the meeting. Marin is a new generation of jefe—smart, tech savvy, using violence surgically."

Emma picked up the story. "Marin, in the guise of an American businessman, visited the CEO of my company, Pacific Investment Bank, about two months ago. I am an analyst at PIB and a colleague of mine, Toby Jackson, a very gifted quant, started picking up odd movements in the financial markets."

"Odd?"

"Yes, investments that made no real sense. And they picked up in force and size until it became a torrent. Billions of dollars in short sales, much of the money invested in dark pools. Toby, do you want to continue?"

Onscreen, Toby shook his head and rolled his index finger forward. He looked wiped out.

"Okay," Emma continued. "Dark pools are private exchanges for trading securities that are not accessible by the investing public. They are essentially a way to make huge investments without people knowing and without distorting the market. They allow institutions to hide big trades from speculators and coat-tail investors. Selling short is a way to bet against something, if you think that market will tank. So, Toby traced massive short sales, many of them back to our employer, PIB. And all of them starting to come due as of today. As of 10:30 this morning, in fact, and continuing on for the next week."

Silence.

"Obviously, these massive investments, these huge short sales, presuppose knowing that something bad is going to happen today, at around 10:30. In about an hour. The short sales are spread across various sectors. We are assuming that wiping out the US security and intelligence community would be a disaster of vast proportions.

"If our suspicions are correct, there will be an attempt made on the lives of the people at that summit and someone will walk away the world's first trillionaire."

Black listened to this with a sober look on his face. "Security is very tight here. Very tight. No one will get within ten miles of this place. We have cordons. We have drones flying in the sky. Every person in the building has been vetted by the

FBI. My company was given the contract to be backup to the Homeland Security agents and we have gone over every single contingency. My company has been working on this for a month. I don't doubt what you're saying, but I just don't see how terrorists could attack us here."

"They wouldn't be terrorists, not in the sense you mean. It's not a political act but a financial one."

Raul chimed in. "We're talking a lot of money, Black. Almost unimaginable amounts of money. Lotta people do a lot worse for a lot less."

Black's face creased with thought.

"Are there no issues there? None at all?" Raul pushed. "Nothing even slightly out of place?"

If they were mistaken, if something else entirely were to happen, they were wasting time. It would be too late to do anything about it.

"Everything is fine, unless ..."

Raul's neck crackled wildly. He felt something all down his spine. "Unless?"

"Well, it's ridiculous. But the toilets aren't working and we can't get water. But we've set up Portajohns everywhere and we have thousands of water bottles. It won't really affect the meeting."

At his side, Emma had been furiously typing on her laptop.

She lifted her head. "Ah, Mr. Black. Just before leaving the NSA, we had a briefing on new threats. There's a new type of explosive which is liquid. A slurry."

Black's eyes narrowed. "True. But we've had sniffer dogs all over the place and the compound has been cleared."

"In my briefing, there was mention of a new type of liquid explosive that had only been seen once. It had a low percentage of ammonium nitrate and was very hard for sniffer dogs to smell. Plus, they could actually be in the water pipes which act as insulation."

"Well, we'll go over the place once again, but we've had surveillance drones on oversight for a month now and there hasn't been any disturbance. How would they infiltrate the place?"

"You've gone over the footage?"

"Not personally, no. There's over 740 hours of footage. But we've run it through our computers, in an excess of caution. Nothing."

"Not nothing, no," Emma interrupted. She turned her laptop around so Black and Toby and Hope and Dante could see it. It was a video that had been stopped. Everyone leaned forward. Raul had the best view. It was the conference venue from on high. The resolution was extraordinary, far beyond what a drone could give. The image was taken in step-optic pairs, side by side images taken at slightly different angles, giving a 3-D view.

Emma pressed a key and the scene sprang to life.

There were two vans, with *Sloane Plumbing* painted on the sides, and seven men in overalls were hauling out material from the back.

The date was given in the top right-hand corner. May 28. Twelve days earlier.

Jacob Black's face was taut and expressionless as he sat back. "That's twelve days ago."

"Yessir," Emma said.

"Where'd you get those images?"

"I – ahem – borrowed them from the National Imaging and Mapping Agency. And they got them from a Keyhole satellite." She stopped the video, leaving only a still shot. "The video only lasts five minutes. As you know, Keyhole satellites are not stationary overhead."

Silence.

Keyholes were among the nation's top secret lines of defense. No photograph taken by a Keyhole satellite had ever been published. Hacking into NIMA and grabbing KH images was breaking about twenty different laws. Emma would be very aware of all of this. She would also be aware that if she were in the military, she could be court-martialed and sent to Leavenworth for the rest of her life. As a civilian, she could be tried in a court with no jury, closed to the public and sentenced to several decades in prison.

Raul bristled. This magnificent woman was *not* going to jail because she was doing her very best to stop an attack on US soil that could bring down the nation's intelligence and security apparatus.

And then wreck the economy.

He stared hard at the monitor, as if he could stare right into Jacob Black's eyes. Black was the wild card. He was the only outsider who knew. There wasn't anyone else who could blame Emma for hacking into NIMA. "Emma was with the NSA and had the clearance to do what she just did. Which was on our order. She is not to be held –"

Black held up a big hand. "Can it, Raul. Nobody is looking to do anything but thank Emma for a very big break. Tell her to stay on the line because we'll probably need her again. Tell her to send me that video with all the metadata scrubbed."

Emma immediately bent to her laptop

He left, but the square where his face was remained empty.

It was 9:15.

"Sending scrubbed photos," Emma said, to the air. But she continued working frantically.

"Got them," Black said, a disembodied voice off-screen. "Thanks." He kept the video function on and Raul could follow him through endless halls, with gleaming parquet floors, huge flower arrangements. An enormous coffee and tea station piled high with pastries, cakes, fruit. What looked like a thousand people milling around in the security and intelligence community in a form of Brownian motion.

An awful lot of people would die if they were right and didn't stop this in time.

For a moment, Raul wished they were wrong. That some other calamity was about to hit somewhere else, far far away. On the other side of the country, far away from the brave men and women he saw through Black's feed. Men and women who worked constantly to keep the country safe.

But logic and the crackling on the back of his neck was very clear that the danger was right here and right now.

Black was conferring with some serious looking dudes. Even the four women in the circle were dudes.

9:30.

"Black," he interrupted. "I think you guys are going to have to start thinking of evacuation plans, even if you haven't had time to look at the water pipes. It's going to take a while to evacuate all these –"

"Wait!" Emma looked up from her computer monitor. Raul put a hand on her shoulder. That was panic he heard in her voice. She trembled under his hand. "How many security drones does the conference have operating at the moment?"

Black didn't even have to think about it. "Ten over the compound, another fifteen around the perimeter. Why?"

"I'm getting the feed of twenty over the compound and twenty-five up to two miles out." She was white down to her lips. "They're watching you. If you start the evacuation, they could make the place blow at any moment. They might not wait."

Black held up a long finger. "Bringing in the big guns. Wait a minute."

He cut off the video again.

Raul and Emma waited. Toby was still pounding his keyboard, Raul had no idea why. They were past the discovery stage and were now trying to stave off disaster, both financial and physical. He didn't care that much about financial disaster.

What frightened him was the head of his country's security and intelligence apparatus being lopped off. He couldn't even think of the consequences, though SEALs were trained to evaluate worst-case scenarios. This one didn't bear thinking about. His country would be fully open to its enemies for a while. He was running through his mind all the possible consequences when the big wall monitor sprang to life.

Black was flanked by Bob Bender, Director of the FBI, Martin De Martino, the head of Homeland Security and Anne-Marie Ingels, Director of the CIA.

Black introduced them to Emma, though Raul was certain she was already aware of who they were. "I briefed Bob, Martin and Anne-Marie already. We're aware we're short on time, and –"

He glitched and the next sentence was lost. When he came back online, he was looking seriously annoyed. "Sorry – we had –"

Emma bent forward. "That was me, sir. I'm experimenting with degrading the signal. Whoever is behind this is watching from the drones, you can be sure of that. I think I can degrade the signal in a way that looks natural, and not suspect. It would take them about half an hour to find out that the signal is being suppressed and they will send in more drones. In the next half-hour you're going to have to send in EOD and evacuate the delegates. Whoever is watching cannot have a clue. I'm splicing together footage from the past few days, making sure it's with the sun in the same position. You guys should evacuate as quietly as you can. I really hope they don't have observers."

"Everyone here is super vetted," the Director of the FBI, Bob Bender, said. "If there are observers, they are remote, and it looks like you're taking care of that. We sent bomb experts who are on site to check the water mains and –" He touched his ear, held a finger up – *just a minute* – and turned away. When he turned back his face was taut and stressed. "You were right."

This was the country's top security experts, so there were no expressions of outrage or fear. Except everyone's faces were now taut and stressed.

"Mr. Black, your associates –"

"Raul Martinez, Emma Holland and Toby Jackson."

Bender nodded. "They were correct. I sent two explosives experts from our office and two Army Intelligence experts to check out the water mains. They are indeed filled with a slurry explosive. And they found the detonator right under the main conference Hall. They are defusing it now."

"Tell them to be careful!" Emma said, panicked. "It is very likely that there will be more than one detonator. And that they have a line back to the perpetrator's headquarters, with a trip-wire telling them if the bombs have been defused! I have no idea what frequency they could be using."

Bender touched his ear again and smiled. It wasn't a nice smile. "Found another one. And we've identified the tripwires and will defuse without alerting them. We've started evacuation. Vans are arriving and will take the delegates to the Moscone center. It will no longer be a secret meeting. It is now obvious how badly we need to have a Security and Intelligence Summit." He turned directly to the camera monitor. "I have no words to express our gratitude to you, Ms. Holland. This would have been an attack on our country like no other. Much worse than Pearl Harbor, striking at the very heart of government. The meeting will start at 3 p.m. when everyone has been delivered to the Moscone Center, and we'd like to thank you publicly."

"No!" Raul shouted. Not only did his neck crackle but every cell in his body went wild. "You can give them citizen citations, write a nice letter, which they will put in a safe deposit box, but no one must ever know what part they played." Particularly Emma. She thwarted a drug cartel, probably cost it a lot of money. They would find inventive ways of torturing her, keeping her alive for days, before allowing her to die. He couldn't even stay in the same space with the thought. "Emma, Toby, I'm so sorry. You've done amazing things but no one must ever know what you've done. These are people who never forget."

He saw the surprise in their faces. They were totally intent on the problem itself, and hadn't thought through the consequences. Raul had. No one could ever associate the name of Emma Holland or Toby Jackson with anything to do with the Cabo Cartel and the thwarted attack. At the thought, his balls shriveled and tried to climb their way up inside his body.

"You'll get letters of recommendation up the wazoo, you can go anywhere you want afterward but no one must ever know what happened here."

Toby could go anywhere he wanted to go. Some power-house bank in New York or Singapore or London. He'd be compensated for this, maybe he could buy Colin a hospital he could run in the Bahamas. But Emma – Emma was staying with him.

Bender nodded. "Understood. We can easily say we had a confidential informant and then cover it up as a matter of national security, top secret. As a matter of fact, besides myself, the Homeland Security Secretary and Jacob Black, no one else knows of your involvement. But rest assured Ms. Holland, Mr. Jackson and Mr. Martinez, we know we owe you a debt of gratitude that can never be repaid."

He disappeared and Jacob Black's tough, dark face reappeared. "Well, I guess Bender said it all. Gotta go, because we're going to have to corral almost a thousand people and transport them down to the city center, but my company and I owe you a lot. Our lives, for starters. One of the EOD guys told me there was enough explosive to blast us to the moon. Someone wanted to ... make a statement. So, from now to the end of time, consider Black Inc at your disposal. Ms. Holland, you sure you don't want to reconsider my offer of a job?"

Emma was white, but his words put a rosy glow in her cheeks. "Thanks, but I think I already have a job." She looked at him, as if unsure of what she was saying. Raul kissed her on the forehead. Oh yeah. She had a job, a boyfriend and later a fiancé if she wanted.

Because he wanted it all.

Cabo San Lucas
   2 p.m.

So, Marin thought as he sipped his aged tequila, it didn't work. He had men stationed a couple of miles out, watching for a massive explosion which didn't come. It wasn't a technical error, he'd used only the best experts. So, they must have somehow found out. As of 9:30, the signal of his drones started degrading and he had his doubts right then.

It had been a good plan – an excellent plan –carried out perfectly, but subject to some random error and hadn't worked.

Pity.

He'd been looking forward to retiring from the trade but it looked like he was stuck for a few more years, since he'd lost almost a billion dollars in one morning.

But money was like an irresistible river, flowing downhill. It could be dammed up, but not stopped.

Marin also had a few new experimental drugs that he'd been testing and which looked extremely promising. And profitable. El Quìmico would not be held back. And he would be staying on this side of the border for a good long while. He'd been extremely cautious but who knew if he'd left some bread crumbs somewhere?

He was a king here, and respected. Even a minute chance of exchanging his life of luxury here for a cell in San Quentin ... he shuddered.

He wondered vaguely what happened to that banker. He'd used the banker's greed against him. If fate had tipped one way the banker would have become one of the richest men in the world. But alas, fate had tipped the other way.

Too bad.

PACIFIC INVESTMENT BANK
   San Francisco

WHITTAKER HAMILTON IV STARED AT THE PRINTOUTS IN FRONT of him. The first of his short sales were coming due, a first tranche of fifty million dollars. The second tranche would come in two hours, another would come due at the end of the business day, another tomorrow morning. In all, over the next days, ten tranches would come due for a total loss of almost a billion dollars of PIB's money.

He'd spent the morning glued to the news, certain that any minute some catastrophe would be announced and he could start counting the money. It never came. The deadline came and went and thereafter he was frozen at his desk, with four financial news sites open, two big flat screen TVs tuned into two business programs, and plugged into a few places in the dark web that dealt with money. They would be the first to know.

Around noon, his secretary called to know if he wanted to order lunch or make a reservation at La Valois, the latest expensive French restaurant. He could barely get the words out that he didn't want anything, then vomited breakfast into his wastepaper basket. The acrid smell of bile filled his office.

He'd sweated through his Armani shirt and Hugo Boss

jacket. The view from his office, usually so pleasing, was now nauseating, as it showed the ant people scurrying to and fro. Only, those ants were not in the deepest hole in hell that he was.

He watched on the screen as his short sales started coming in for payment. The money was rushing out like a river in spate. Soon a colleague would notice. Then he or she would talk to someone else and by end of day there would be a delegation here.

He'd lost the bank so much money. Of course, a hundred times that was supposed to come flowing in, if things had gone according to plan.

He himself had personally cashed in all his assets and taken out loans and now had nothing except the clothes he stood in.

He had no money at all to pay the expensive lawyers he would soon need.

His colleagues would be here, clamoring for blood, by the end of the business day.

It didn't bear thinking about. The bank fuckheads barely paid attention when he made vast amounts of money for them. They watched the profits pile up

and had no idea how he'd done it and they didn't care. All they cared about was the little green bar showing profits.

But they noticed immediately the slightest loss. And this wasn't a slight loss. It was a hemorrhage, a lake of red.

In an hour, another tranche would be bought. Several of the stocks were more expensive than when he'd done the short sales.

This was shaping up to be the single biggest loss in the history of PIB. In a period of market stability, so he had no excuse. Nothing to say to them. All the money he'd earned for the bank would be as nothing. Nobody would remember that, they would only remember this day, June 10, as the day Hamilton had bet big and lost bigger.

It was entirely possible that he would bring PIB down, single handedly.

He'd be fired by end of day but that wouldn't be the end of the disgrace. He had a fiduciary duty which he'd betrayed. There would be a law suit that would last decades. They would impound everything he owned, which was nothing. He would spend the rest of his life not only poor, but reviled.

His second wife, Charlotte, was suing him for divorce. She hated him and would latch on to this like a bloodsucker, terrified that she wouldn't get her pound of flesh before he lost it all.

He could hear her screams in his head.

He'd lose his memberships and, it went without saying, all his friendships. He'd be a pariah, an object of scorn and shame.

He'd be ... poor.

Like all the little people he saw walking to and fro on the sidewalks, tiny insects.

He didn't know how to be poor. Had no idea.

Poor.

God.

He leaned his hands and forehead against the sparkling glass, looking out across the Bay. There wasn't anywhere within a hundred miles of here where he could afford to live. Maybe he'd become homeless.

It was unthinkable.

He peeled his forehead away from the wall of glass, leaving drops of sweat.

The window couldn't open. He couldn't lean out into the open air and fling himself out, flying for a few moments before hurtling to the ground.

But there was another way out. It was in a locked drawer. A relic of a period several years ago when there'd been some muggings in the area. He'd bought himself a Glock19 and had taken lessons. The gun felt good in his hand. He felt good knowing he had it. But he didn't finish the course and always forgot to carry it with him when he left the office.

Still, it was there.

He unlocked the drawer and looked at it. Dark gray, a precision instrument, finely machined, perfectly suitable for the task.

He reached out with a finger then pulled the finger back, as if the metal were hot. It wasn't. It felt cool to the touch. Like a laptop, or an iPhone. Or a fine bottle of whiskey.

He checked the market and winced. Already, PIB was suffering its worst losses ever and it was barely noon.

Soon alarmed accountants would be calling, then lower management then upper management. By the end of the day, he would be a man brought so low he would never recover in this lifetime.

Poor.

Poor, poor, poor. Forever.

He remembered how to insert the magazine, which was fully loaded. He remembered that all you had to do was pull the trigger. Four pounds of pressure. And the pain would be gone.

Wherever he was going, surely he wouldn't be poor?

He put the muzzle in his mouth and exerted the four pounds of pressure just as his phone bank lit up.

ASI

Portland, Oregon
Two months later

"HEY, YOU UP FOR LUNCH AT THAT NEW VIETNAMESE PLACE?" Raul shivered as he entered ASI's IT center. Damn it was cold.

Emma had been staring at her screens with that cute little

scrunched up frown between her eyebrows that she got when she was concentrating. She shook her head, blinked, and smiled up at him.

His heart gave a huge thump in his chest. It did that often when he was around her. He'd been hoping that seeing a lot of her would dial that right down, but it hadn't. He was hooked. It was nice that she was hooked, too. She was fiercely focused at work, but her face softened when she saw him. He wasn't alone in this.

They made an effort to be professional at work, but he simply couldn't help stroking a finger down her soft cheek. So amazingly soft. Outside work, they didn't have to rein themselves in. He slept most nights at the little studio apartment ASI gave new recruits, but he was working up the nerve to ask her to move in with him.

His abuela, who'd met her two weeks ago when the entire clan came up in a convoy to Portland to meet her, called him every other day to find out how things stood. Everyone understood that this was important to him, though he'd tried to play it cool. But there was no playing it cool around Emma.

His whole family adored her and far from being uncomfortable at being the center of attention of curious and nosy Martinez family members, she loved it. She grew all rosy when they were around. His sisters loved her and his brothers and male cousins were jealous as hell.

Damn right. Emma was a real catch. And he'd caught her and wasn't letting her go.

"So – Vietnamese? Can you leave what you're doing?"

Emma had arrived just in time. There was a ton of work, and Felicity was in the last few weeks of her pregnancy and confined to her home. Metal made sure she rested. He was a real hard ass about that.

Hope couldn't keep up and was really happy Emma joined them. They both thrived at ASI. They did excellent work and were super appreciated, treated like goddesses. Though Luke and he made sure the operators were all hands off. Two beautiful, smart women – it was catnip to the testosterone-fuelled operators. They mostly behaved, though.

Emma was talking to Pierce, on one of the wall screens. He was in Washington, DC, negotiating a contract for the company. Raul suspected he'd insisted on travelling to DC because he was working up the courage to ask Emma and Hope's friend, Riley, out to dinner. Tough badass SEAL, scared of a beautiful computer scientist.

"Not doing anything urgent," Emma said. "I'm following the China crisis. It's scary."

It was. If Raul and his teammates had been in the Teams, they'd be gearing up to be deployed. Chinese commandos had attacked a group of American surveyors and geologists in Congo and tensions were high and ratcheting higher. A Chinese destroyer had shot across the bow of the USS Ronald Reagan in the Taiwan Strait and the president had sent four elements of the Seventh Fleet to China's southern coast.

The situation was heating up fast.

Pierce was frowning down from his screen. "Word here is that the People's Liberation Army has just received orders to mobilize."

"What?" Emma switched screens and read quickly. "Oh my God. The president will put us on a war footing, too."

There was a peculiar noise and then the monstrous Goblin King appeared, shouting *"Bring up the Bonebreaker!"* The HER room. Three members of the HER room were in Portland, so it could only be Riley. Up on the wall screen, Pierce put down his tablet and leaned on his fists.

"You guys use the HER room only for emergencies, right, Emma?"

She nodded. "Riley must be in trouble."

The Goblin King dissolved and Riley Robinson's pretty face

appeared. She was walking fast, disheveled, glancing behind her. "Emma, I need help."

Emma leaned forward. "Tell me what's wrong?"

Pierce leaned forward, too. She'd see him on her screen. "Riley, I'm a friend of Emma's. Name's Pierce. What's the matter? Are you in trouble?"

She ducked into an empty corridor, panting. "Are you guys following the news? Out of China?"

"Yeah."

"It – it wasn't the Chinese who attacked. I have proof. But someone wants war with China and is after me. I escaped one kidnapping attempt but I don't know what to do now. Help me, please!"

Pierce looked at Emma and Raul. "I'm going after her."

THE END

ALSO BY LISA MARIE RICE

Men Of Midnight Series

Midnight Man

Midnight Run

Midnight Angel

Midnight Quest

Midnight Vengeance

Midnight Promises

Midnight Secrets

Midnight Fire

Midnight Fever

Midnight Renegade

Midnight Kiss

Midnight Embrace

Midnight Caress

Midnight Shadows

Her Billionaire Series

Charade

Masquerade

Escapade

Dangerous Passions

Reckless

Hot Secrets

The Christmas Angel

Murphy's Law

Woman On The Run

Fatal Heat

A Fine Specimen

The Italian

Don't Think Twice

Port Of Paradise

ABOUT THE AUTHOR

Lisa Marie Rice is eternally 30 years old and will never age. She is tall and willowy and beautiful. Men drop at her feet like ripe pears. She has won every major book prize in the world. She is a black belt with advanced degrees in archaeology, nuclear physics, and Tibetan literature. She is a concert pianist. Did I mention her Nobel Prize?

Of course, Lisa Marie Rice is a virtual woman and exists only at the keyboard when writing romance. She disappears when the monitor winks off.

9 781648 393549